"Another woman was murdered last night."

"Where wa̶̶̶̶̶̶̶̶̶̶̶̶̶̶̶̶̶̶̶̶̶̶̶̶̶̶̶̶̶̶ rembled.

"Outside of ̶̶̶̶̶̶̶̶̶̶̶̶̶̶̶̶̶̶̶̶̶̶̶̶̶̶̶̶̶̶ vered.
His eyes se̶̶̶̶̶̶̶̶̶̶̶̶̶̶̶̶̶̶̶̶̶̶̶̶ lling me?"

"I grew up i̶̶̶̶̶̶̶̶̶̶̶̶̶̶̶̶̶̶

"Tough place for a kid."

"That neighborhood is a tough place for anyone.
I hated it so much."

"You've certainly moved up in the world. Do a lot of
people know you grew up there?"

"No. I've tried very hard to keep my past behind me."

"Why? We all have a past. Good or bad, it's what
shapes us into who we are."

"Spoken like someone with nothing but sunshine and
rainbows in their rearview mirror."

"That's about as far from the truth as you could get.
But that's a story for another time. Right now I need
to know why the killer left a body in Melrose. Maybe
it was a way of telling us they know a lot more about
you than we thought."

"What was the name of the nail salon?"

"Polish Me Pretty."

"My brother was killed outside of that nail salon fifteen
years ago."

* * *

**If you're on Twitter, tell us what you
think of Harlequin Romantic Suspense!
#harlequinromsuspense**

Dear Reader,

Writing romance has always been a passion of mine. Writing romance for Harlequin has been a dream I was never sure would come true. I am thrilled that *Matched with Murder* is my very first Harlequin Romantic Suspense book, and that you have taken a leap of faith in this book and me. Words can't describe how much that means!

When I started writing *Matched with Murder*, not only did I want to dive into the dark side of something that scared me—trusting people on the other side of my computer screen—but I didn't want to write about a billionaire bachelor. I wanted to bring to life a billionaire bachelorette. I wanted a strong heroine who'd worked hard for everything she had. Someone my own daughter could look up to. Samantha Gates is strong, smart and knows her value in life. She needed a strong man who wasn't intimidated by her beauty and brains. Enter Max Green, homicide detective for the NYPD. These two might bump heads at first, but it doesn't take long for respect and admiration to blossom—on both sides—and attraction to turn into so much more.

I hope you have as much fun reading this fast-paced thrill ride as I had writing it! Thank you again for supporting my dream.

With all my love,

Danielle M. Haas

MATCHED WITH MURDER

Danielle M. Haas

HARLEQUIN

ROMANTIC
SUSPENSE

Recycling programs for this product may not exist in your area.

ISBN-13: 978-1-335-75952-8

Matched with Murder

Copyright © 2021 by Danielle M. Haas

All rights reserved. No part of this book may be used or reproduced in any manner whatsoever without written permission except in the case of brief quotations embodied in critical articles and reviews.

This is a work of fiction. Names, characters, places and incidents are either the product of the author's imagination or are used fictitiously. Any resemblance to actual persons, living or dead, businesses, companies, events or locales is entirely coincidental.

This edition published by arrangement with Harlequin Books S.A.

For questions and comments about the quality of this book, please contact us at CustomerService@Harlequin.com.

Harlequin Enterprises ULC
22 Adelaide St. West, 40th Floor
Toronto, Ontario M5H 4E3, Canada
www.Harlequin.com

Printed in U.S.A.

Danielle M. Haas resides in Ohio with her husband and two children. She earned a BA in political science many moons ago from Bowling Green State University, but thought staying home with her two children and writing romance novels would be more fun than pursuing a career in politics. She spends her days chasing her kids around, loving up her dog and trying to find a spare minute to write about her favorite thing: love.

Books by Danielle M. Haas

Harlequin Romantic Suspense

Matched with Murder

Visit the Author Profile page at Harlequin.com for more titles.

To everyone who's walked alongside me, lifting me up as I followed the long road to achieving my dreams. To my husband and children for always encouraging me. To my amazing critique partners and friends, Samantha and Julie, for helping polish my work and always being a text away for whatever crisis I encounter. To my editor, Megan Broderick, thank you for giving me and my book a chance. To all my readers, you will never know how much I cherish each and every one of you. Your trust in me is the reason I get to wake up and do what I love. Many thanks and love to all of you.

Chapter 1

No, no, no.

I can't handle another dead body haunting my dreams.

Not today.

Samantha Gates took one step in retreat. She sucked in a sharp breath and the freezing air burned her lungs. The dead body lay only a short distance away, separated by yellow crime-scene tape and a cluster of spectators. Dark hair spread around the frozen face like a halo, dark eyes staring lifelessly into the early-morning sky.

Samantha yanked the earbuds from her ears, vision tunneling, as she took another step away. Her heel crushed brittle blades of grass along the concrete path of the Jacqueline Kennedy Onassis Reservoir. Her heart hammered, and her breath appeared on the frigid air in short spiraling puffs. Instinct told her to turn and run.

Heavy footsteps crunched on loose gravel behind her. More runners came to a stop beside her to gawk at death. Whispered comments circled around her and pressure built in her chest. The voices morphed and warbled as Samantha's ears began to ring.

"I think it's a woman."

"It's hard to tell, but she looks pretty young."

"I wonder what happened? Anyone with half a brain knows to stay away from here at night."

A hard knot of anger formed in Samantha's gut. Why did people do that? Why did they place blame on the victim? The circumstances of this tragedy were unknown to the idiots gawking at her like vultures who waited for their next meal. She hadn't asked to have a knife jammed into her heart.

Another blast of February wind slashed across Samantha's face, drawing goose bumps over her already crawling skin. Tearing her gaze away from the body, she focused on the two officers studying the victim. A flurry of activity wasn't buzzing around the scene yet. The victim must not have been found too long ago. If Samantha had left for her morning run at her usual time, she could have been the one to stumble upon the body.

If she hadn't received the letter from the Department of Justice this morning.

If the man who'd ruined her life hadn't been released from prison.

Bile slid up her throat, and she pressed the back of her hand to her mouth to keep it from seeping through her lips. She needed to get the hell out of there.

She turned on the balls of her feet and ran into a man nearly twice as broad as her and several inches taller. The impact pushed her backward and knocked her off-balance. Two strong, steady hands braced against her biceps and kept her on her feet. Samantha gripped his arms to steady herself until both feet were planted firmly on the pavement. Her gaze traveled from the fitted leather jacket sculpted to a broad chest, up to a square jaw covered in few days' worth of dark stubble, and into hardened aquamarine eyes.

His gaze flickered over her face before turning to the crime scene. She licked her lips. God, had he recognized her? Usually her unkempt, early-morning runs allowed her to escape the lingering gazes of the public, but the brief flash of surprise in his eyes left no doubt that he knew who she was. Everyone in the city knew her face—made up with cosmetic products or not— because of all the stupid ads with her picture plastered everywhere. She hated the fishbowl she lived in just because she'd created a successful dating app.

His hands dropped from her biceps, and her skin blazed beneath the fabric of her running shirt. Her fingers tightened for an instant around the supple black leather covering his arms before she let go and took a step back.

"You okay?" he asked, already moving toward the crime scene. His words came out in a rush.

"I'm fine," she croaked, forcing the words through her tight throat.

"Good." His voice trailed behind him as he continued forward. Gathering her courage, she turned and let her gaze follow him. His dark boots beat against the frozen ground and his gray slacks hugged the curve of his backside.

She watched one second more before turning to run home. Her presence wouldn't help the poor soul lying in freezing water. She needed to go home and let the police do their job.

The impact of the concrete slapping against her feet vibrated throughout her body. The assault of honking cars and the chatting of throngs of people clogging the sidewalk set her on edge. She'd grown up with these noises, but for once, she yearned for silence. She reached her town house and took the stairs of her front stoop two at a time, hurling herself into the foyer of her Upper East Side building. She slammed the door closed behind her. Turning to press her back against the hard wood, she slowed her breath and evened her rapid heart rate. She was home, and she was safe. Away from the nightmare she'd stumbled upon.

She'd already lived through one nightmare. She didn't need to find herself in another.

Detective Max Green drew the cold air in through his nose and out his mouth to calm his jagged nerves. The call that had gotten his tired ass out of bed this morning echoed around his brain. If Jack hadn't given him a heads-up, the jerks from the Nineteenth Precinct would have tried to take his case. He might not work this part of the city, but one look at the dead woman with a knife in her heart and a red rose in her hand was all he needed to know she was connected to the murder of Emily Steele at Columbia University last week.

The murder he still needed to solve.

"What are you doing here, Green?" The faint hint of amusement in Detective Sal Caspano's voice made the hackles in Max's neck raise. "You can't stay away from the Upper East Side, can you? Having breakfast with the folks this morning and thought you'd go for a stroll?"

Ignoring the passive-aggressive dipshit's comment about his parents, Max crouched beside the woman on the ground. He forced all the pity and sadness far from his mind. Even after serving on the front lines in Afghanistan, then coming home to work on the force, staring at death never got easier. But someone needed to serve justice, and he'd taken an oath to help those who could no longer help themselves. "This is my case, Caspano. Thanks for taping off the scene and calling it in, but I can handle it from here."

"Like hell it is." Detective Caspano hefted his considerable weight and marched toward him. "I got the call. This is my turf. There's no reason for you to be here."

"Call your lieutenant, and you'll learn otherwise. I already cleared it with my boss."

The crunch of snow under Caspano's boots drifted away, but not far enough for Max's liking. Good. The prick could take his attitude to someone else. Max continued to study the body. Damn, not only were the rose and the knife wound identical to his case, but so were the dark hair and dark brown eyes. The woman in front of him could have been Emily Steele's sister. The eyes, the hair, the build were exactly the same.

He glanced at the other officer on scene. He recognized the rosy-cheeked rookie but couldn't recall his name. Max stood and lifted his chin in the younger man's direction. "Do you have an ID yet?"

"Not yet. No wallet or purse found."

Max walked a wide semicircle around the jean-clad legs and booted feet. The woman's gray peacoat weighed down her body and her blue blouse was buttoned with no rips or tears marring the silky material, aside from the singular fatal wound.

Her coat was splayed out like angel wings and exposed her fatal injury. A two-inch slit sliced through the fabric to the left of the breastbone. The black handle of a large butcher knife protruded from the hole and dried blood turned the dark blue of the shirt around the knife an inky black. Blue jeans covered slim thighs and appeared untouched. The medical examiner would do an autopsy, but just like with Emily Steele, he likely wouldn't find any sign of sexual assault.

"Have you called the ME? Is CSI on the way?"

The rookie snapped to attention. "Everyone's on the way. Should be here any minute. Caspano and I didn't get a chance to do much before you showed up." The rookie's words didn't hold any contempt, just stating the facts.

"I'll talk to them when they get here. I've already got a team working a similar case. I want them in on this one, as well. The two are connected, and I don't need anything slipping through the cracks."

Caspano stalked toward him, his thin lips pulled down in a bulldog frown. "This is ridiculous."

"You mean that a young woman was murdered and left to freeze in a public park?" Max raised his brows and let his disdain for Caspano fuel the anger in his veins. To hell with a clear head, anger always helped to urge him forward in an investigation.

"No, I mean that you're the lead on a case on my turf." He crushed the toe of his boot against the frozen ground as if putting out a cigarette.

"I already have a leg up on this. I've been working another murder case with a similar knife wound, the same kind of rose left at the scene. Hell, it looks like the same damn woman. You trying to wave your dick in the air about this will just slow everything down." He let his gaze wander back to the woman on the ground. "She deserves better."

Caspano used the palm of his hand to wipe the frown, and God knows what else, from his round face. "Here. This will help." He held out his phone.

Max took the phone and glanced at the screen. "Who's this?"

"Linda Hoyt. Missing person's report filed after she didn't come home last night. Looks like we found the identity of our victim." Caspano dipped his chin in the direction of the young woman on the ground.

Max studied the picture on the screen, and he tightened his grip around Caspano's phone. Linda Hoyt was a ringer for Emily Steele. There had to be a connection between the two women besides their murders. "What was in the report? Have you run any information on her?"

"Her roommate called the police. Linda had a date last night and never came home. Said it was unlike her to stay out all night, especially with a guy she'd just met."

A shiver ran down Max's spine that had nothing to do with the plummeting temperature. He swiped his finger across the screen and searched for any other information he might need. "Did the roommate mention where Linda knew this guy?"

"Some online dating site."

Max thrust the phone back to Caspano and turned in the opposite direction. "Thanks. I need to make a call."

He pulled out his phone and numbness crept into the pads of his fingers. He blew hot breath into his cupped hand, and then swiftly pressed the contact information for Jack. It paid to have a best friend who worked cybercrimes—even if he worked in a different precinct.

"Hey, man. Are you at the crime scene? Is it connected to the Columbia murder?" Jack must have been waiting for his call. Despite the early hour, Jack's voice didn't hold one hint of fatigue.

"I'm here. Caspano gave me a name I need you to run. Specifically look at dating sites. Name's Linda Hoyt. Had a date last night and never came home."

A low whistle vibrated in his ear. "Can't be a coincidence. Give me a second."

The sound of computer keys rattling came through the speaker, and Max turned to survey the area while he waited. Uniformed officers walked under the yellow tape threaded between the trees, and the siren of an ambulance pierced the somber sky.

"Bingo." Jack's voice brought Max's focus back to the call.

"What'd you find?"

"I need to dig a little deeper, but I already found what you want. Linda Hoyt subscribed to *EternalMatch*."

If murder weren't staring him in the face, he'd raise a fist in the air. Another connection. He thanked Jack and clicked off the line. Max lengthened his strides toward the hub of activity buzzing around Linda's body. He needed to dig a little deeper, too. And part of the digging would be around Samantha Gates. *What was she doing here this morning?*

An image of her in her tight black running pants and a formfitting shirt flashed in his mind. Her doe-like eyes had been filled with horror and a desperate need for escape. A far cry from the formal pantsuits and composure she usually wore. This morning had been his first encounter with the billionaire with the heart-shaped face and pouty mouth. But after the dating app she'd created had been connected to a second murder, he'd see her again soon. She could have the answers he needed. Answers that could lead him to a killer.

Chapter 2

The city whirled through her numb brain even as the town car moved along the crowded streets at a snail's pace. Normally she'd never have her driver take her the three blocks to her mom's apartment, but she didn't trust her legs to carry her there this morning. She raked her nails over the soft leather of the seat beneath her and kept her gaze fixed out the window. Hundreds of people clogged the sidewalks, going about their usual morning routines.

People whose pasts weren't coming back to taunt them.

People who hadn't just seen their second dead body.

Gooseflesh prickled her arms despite the heat pouring from the vent above her. The eerily peaceful face of the poor woman from this morning floated into her mind. How sad to have a life cut short so young.

"Ms. Gates?" The deep voice of her driver penetrated her thoughts and forced her gaze to his. She met his kind green eyes in the rearview mirror. "We're here, Miss. Would you like help out?"

Samantha took a deep breath and fixed a relaxed smile on her face. Years of practice had taught her how to keep her emotions hidden behind a mask of easy confidence and happiness. All it would take was one picture, one glimpse of her with a piss-poor expression or tension in her shoulders for the expertly crafted world she'd built to crash down around her. No one wanted to join a dating site run by a tense shrew.

"I'm good, James, but thank you. I don't know how long I'll be, so you can take off. I'll walk to the office from here."

A deep line ran the length of James's weathered forehead. "Are you sure? It's awfully cold today."

"I'm sure."

"Then take these." James removed black gloves from his hands and dangled them behind his shoulder, his gaze never leaving hers. "If you'd brought yours, you'd be wearing them."

She glanced down at her hands. The birthstone ring she always wore sparkled up at her, but he was right, no gloves. She took the gloves and a spark of warmth chased a bit of gloom from the black cloud over her head. "Thanks. I'll call you later if I need you."

She pushed the back door open. Resolve straightened her spine. Her thin heels clicked on the sidewalk, and she pushed herself to her feet. She turned and gave James a little wave before stepping under the green awning stretched above the front door of the building. She gave a nod of greeting toward the doorman…Peter?

Paul?…as a gust of wind whipped around the building and slapped her exposed cheek. Hunching her shoulders, she hurried inside and made a beeline for the elevator. She rode up the ten floors to her mother's apartment in solitude and used her key to let herself inside.

"Hello?" a calm, quiet voice called out seconds before her mother's caretaker, Mrs. Walsh, poked her head around the corner. A broad smile ignited a ripple of wrinkles across the face Samantha had loved for most of her life. Her short gray hair curled around her face in the same style every woman over the age of seventy must be required to have. She stepped toward Samantha with a dish towel in one hand, her other stretched out to give her shoulder a squeeze. "What are you doing here this morning? We didn't expect you."

"Hi, Mrs. Walsh. How is she today?" Samantha kicked the lingering bits of snow from her sleek black leather boots against the cheerful mat by the front door.

Mrs. Walsh helped her out of her cashmere coat and hung it on the rack beside the door. "She's all right. Had a rough night last night, so that always messes with her the next day."

Samantha nodded and took in the sights of the apartment her mother shared with their old neighbor from the Bronx. Mrs. Walsh might be an odd choice for her mother's caretaker since she was a few years older than her mother, but her mom hated change. And with her fragile state of mind, having a familiar face around was the best medicine Samantha could provide.

Her gaze landed on the opened letter on the oak table behind the sofa, and her heart rate kicked up. The bold print on the front boasted the address of the Department of Justice. "Did she read the letter?" Her toothpick heels clicked against the parquet floors much like the ones she'd grown up with. She snatched the letter from the table and tried to decipher Mrs. Walsh's sorrowful expression.

"Not yet." Mrs. Walsh's thin lips dipped down at the corners.

Samantha tightened her grip around the paper and crushed it in her palm. "Where is she?" She tried to keep the quiver of emotion from her voice, but it didn't work. The relief that her mom hadn't read the notice of release yet was short-lived. Now she'd have to tell her.

Didn't she?

Mrs. Walsh crossed the small gap between them and forced the letter from her hand, tearing the corner in the process. "In the kitchen. She's finishing her breakfast. Samantha, dear, there's no reason for her to know about this." She gave the letter a little shake before folding it and slipping it into the pocket of the white apron she always wore when she worked in the kitchen.

Indecision weighed back and forth in Samantha's brain like a teeter-totter. Her mother had a right to know the man who'd murdered her son had been released from prison. But would she even understand? Samantha was very careful never to mention her mother, or their past, when she spoke with the media. If Samantha didn't tell her about the letter, no one else would dare to, if anyone was even aware of it.

She sagged against the tall sofa table, gaze fixed on the lacy outline of the apron pocket where Mrs. Walsh had tucked the letter. "What if she finds out from someone else?"

"Who else would know? You've never been connected to your brother's murder. Not after you changed your name."

A slice of guilt shimmied through her, tightening her chest and turning her stomach. She'd distanced herself from the girl she once was out of necessity. Having the press connect her to her brother's brutal death or her sick mother would be detrimental to them all. But sometimes the nasty edges of betrayal had her doubting her decisions.

"Sylvia? Where'd you go? Is someone here?" her mom's clear voice called from the kitchen. The voice of her childhood, of a strong woman who'd raised two children on her own. Not the weak, unstable voice she'd grown accustomed to hearing.

Samantha locked eyes with Mrs. Walsh and raised her brows. "I'm here, Mama." She dropped her hands to her sides and stepped around the corner to the kitchen.

She wished like hell her mom would let her buy her a bigger place, or move her into the town house, but any kind of change sent Maria into a tailspin. Going from a single-bedroom apartment in the South Bronx to the lap of luxury on the Upper East Side was too much. It'd been hard enough to get her mom to move to the nice apartment building just east of Central Park.

The tiny table tucked in the corner came into view and Maria's entire body lifted in delight. Pins secured her long, dark hair in a tight bun at the back of her neck and light pink lipstick accented her full lips. "What a nice surprise. Is your brother with you?"

And just like that, the teeter-totter of indecision crashed down on one side. She wouldn't tell her mom about the letter. What was the point? Sometimes ignorance was bliss.

* * *

The sound of the ticking clock bounced around the exposed brick of the uptown headquarters. Max studied the massive space. *EternalMatch*'s corporate office was nothing like he'd expected. He'd anticipated the top floor of a fancy high-rise with clean lines, pretentious paintings and glassed-in offices with minions running amuck trying to please their queen bee. Not warm colors and homelike touches in a large open space. Desks sat scattered about the room, no walls or cubicles to block them off. People worked quietly at their stations, or stood around tables studying who the hell knew what.

But only one person held his interest right now. The good-looking blonde acting as guard to Samantha Gates's office. From what he could tell, this was the only private space in the whole damn area. He held his badge in the air for her inspection. "I need to speak with Ms. Gates."

"Ms. Gates has a very busy schedule today." The secretary pinched her features together and stared him down.

He pressed the heel of his boot against the wide-planked floor and suppressed a rude response about how justice waits for no one. "I'm sure she does, but it's important I speak with her now."

Two perfectly groomed eyebrows arched. "If you'd tell me what this is regarding, I could ask her to squeeze you in."

Christ, enough was enough. He pressed his badge on the desk directly below the pretty blonde's nose. "I'll speak with her now."

He rounded the side of the antique desk and strode toward the closed door. The chair behind him squeaked against the floor and heels clicked at him like an attack of squawking birds. "You can't barge in there. She's very busy." The secretary's stern voice belied her anger at being ignored but that didn't stop him from swinging the door open and marching into the office.

"Samantha Gates?" Annoyance made his voice hard, but he didn't give a damn. He had important things to discuss and he wouldn't be put off by anyone. Not even by one of the wealthiest women in the city. Her time wasn't more important than finding a killer. He hated the world of wealth and privilege and the idea that someone was better because of the size of their bank account.

That's why he'd left it.

The only doors that world opened for him were the ones his father had paid to gain admittance, as long as dear old Dad approved—something Max hadn't known until years afterward and it pissed the living hell out of him. He'd worked damn hard, and for what? His father had used money to bribe people to move Max's life along the path his father wanted while Max was none the wiser, forever tainting every accomplishment he'd ever worked for. Since then he'd fought to get where he was, which made his position as a homicide detective even more important to him.

A woman with calm brown eyes and perfectly straight hair that barely managed to brush the tops of her shoulders stared at him with interest. A far cry from the frantic woman who'd run into him that morning. He preferred the makeup-free beauty over the picture-perfect woman in front of him—the type of woman his parents preferred he'd end up with. The type of woman who'd use the resources he'd been born with to advance her own position. Her head tilted to the side a fraction of an inch, but the rest of her body remained locked in the same position he'd walked in on.

"Hello. Can I help you?"

The secretary skidded to a stop behind him. "I'm so sorry. I tried to stop him, but he insisted on speaking with you. He's with the NYPD."

Full lips curved up, and she spared a quick glance over his shoulder. "It's all right, Laurie. I have time to speak to him."

He swallowed a snort. She sure as hell *did* have time, and no choice in the matter. But he'd keep his opinion to himself. No use letting his jaded views skew his interview. The door closed behind him. Samantha returned her gaze to him and gestured toward the chairs in front of her. Taking a seat, he pulled out a notepad and pen.

The heat from her laser focus stood in stark contrast to her cool demeanor and passive expression. Her lips formed a straight line with just a hint of lift at the corners. No lines marred the smooth olive skin. No wrinkles gave away even the tiniest inkling of what ran through her mind. She gave no hint of remembering their run-in.

"I'm Detective Max Green and I have a few questions for you. I'll try not to take too much of your time."

She dipped her head and tapped the tip of her index finger against the edge of her desk. "Is this about the young woman in the park this morning?"

She remembered him. He cleared his throat and collected his thoughts.

"Yes. I'm investigating the murder of that young woman, as well as a woman murdered last week."

She furrowed her brow. "All right. I don't know how I can help you. The police had already found the body when I arrived this morning, and I don't know anything about a murder last week."

"Did you know Emily Steele or Linda Hoyt?" The likelihood of Ms. Gates being personally connected to either woman was a long shot, but he still needed to ask the question.

She shook her head and the highlights in her dark hair shimmered from the sun streaming in through the glass wall of her corner office. Here was the view he'd expected. "No. I've never heard either of those names."

"How involved are you with the *EternalMatch* app?"

A tiny tick tapped above her eye, but the rest of her expression remained the same. "I created the concept, developed the app and run the entire operation. I'm not just a figurehead who's brought out at Christmas parties. My finger is on the pulse of everything that happens here."

He fought to keep his admiration from showing. Maybe he'd let his past cloud his judgment as far as Samantha Gates was concerned. Not all women were like his conniving ex, who'd left him once she knew he wasn't on the path that led to his family's fortune. He cleared his throat to drive off his wayward thoughts. "So you'd be able to dive into the accounts of these women and the men they were supposed to meet on the nights they were murdered?"

The tiny tick turned thunderous and her shoulders tightened. "I'm unable to give private information regarding our clients to anyone without a warrant."

"But you said you're involved with everything." He scooted to the edge of his seat and leaned his elbows on his knees. "Finding information about these men could be key in stopping a murderer. Do you want the life of an innocent victim on your head? It will be, if I have to waste time securing a warrant and someone else is killed."

Fire shot from her eyes, singeing the chocolate brown to burnt lava. "The only way I'd be responsible for someone's murder is if I'm the one who pulled the trigger. I will not jeopardize this company's integrity— or reputation—by handing out personal information to any person who asks for it."

He leaned back against his chair and matched her glare with one of his own. "I'm sure the women who Richard Pike stalked last year would have been more than happy for you to divulge personal information to the authorities. It sure as hell would have spared them from the nightmare they'd found themselves in."

"And the woman in the park's life would have been spared if you'd already found her killer." Samantha's finger finally stopped tapping and she rose to her feet, fists anchored on her desk. "I have nothing more to say to you until you bring me a warrant. Better yet, take it to my lawyer."

Anger—and a little bit of guilt—burned in Max's gut. He shot to his feet as a tentative knock sounded on the door. The secretary walked in carrying two loose long-stem roses. Brown ribbon tied them together and looped through white card stock that hung on the side. "Someone sent you flowers."

The hard glint in Samantha's eyes must have scared the perky receptionist. She dropped her gaze to the floor, hurried to hand the delivery to her boss and skirted out the door. Samantha's slender fingers curled around the stems and her eyes moved along with the words on the card. A sharp gasp rang from her open mouth and the flowers fell to her desk. A shiny sheen of perspiration beaded along her now-ashen forehead and she sank down into her chair.

What the hell? He crossed the short distance to her desk and picked up the flowers. He turned the card around and read:

Roses are red. Violets are blue. Two women down, but I'm far from through.

He dropped the card as if it were on fire and whipped his gaze up to study Samantha. Blood pounded in his ears. Fury sank its nasty fangs into his sternum. "What aren't you telling me?"

Chapter 3

Max regretted his harsh tone the second the words came out of his mouth. But dammit, she was hiding something. He'd assumed *EternalMatch* was the key to finding the person who'd murdered Emily Steele and Linda Hoyt, but now he had a different perspective. The key was Samantha Gates.

She shook her head back and forth and her gaze stayed locked on the card now lying faceup on her neat-as-a-pin desk. "I don't… Who would… I can't." Her breathy voice hitched higher and higher with each word she spoke, spiraling toward panic.

Max rubbed his jaw and forced the blood zipping through his veins to calm down. She was going into shock, and who the hell could blame her? In one day she'd stumbled upon a dead body and been sent a threatening note. Not exactly an everyday occurrence.

At least he hoped not.

"Okay, calm down. I need you to focus." It took all his effort to keep his voice calm when his insides were screaming for answers only she could give. He reached toward the corner of the desk for a box of tissues, and was surprised when he turned toward her and found no tears clouding her eyes.

She waved him away, sucked three deep breaths through her nose, and straightened in her chair. She met his gaze, but this time fear dilated her pupils. He preferred the fire.

"I'm fine."

"Good. Any idea who sent you those flowers?" He settled back into the seat across from her.

"No." Her too-quick response had alarm bells blaring in his brain.

"Have you ever received a threat before?" He studied every line in her face, every movement of her body.

She choked on a laugh and tried to cover the sound with a cough. "I run a billion-dollar company. I've seen my share of threats."

He raised his brows. "Anything as blatant as this?"

Her sexy red lips dipped down and she dropped her gaze to the bold black letters on the white card stock. "Are we sure this is a threat?"

"Are you kidding me?" Frustration forced him to his feet.

"That's twice you've raised your voice at me. I won't tolerate it again." Her words slapped out at him like a cracked whip—fast and hard and with unrelenting firmness.

He raised his palms and reigned in his temper. "How in the hell could you see this any other way?

Two women are dead, and now you get this?" He gestured to the flowers in front of her.

She shrugged. "It's a big city, Detective Green. The chances of the cases you're working on being connected to me, *EternalMatch*, or whatever lame excuse of a joke this delivery was, are low. I meant what I said about you talking to my lawyer. There's nothing else for us to discuss." She picked up a pen and dove back to whatever it was she was working on before he'd arrived.

She couldn't be serious. He curled his hands into tight fists so he wouldn't lean across the desk and shake some sense into her. "The intent of that message is crystal clear."

The crown of her head stared up at him. "Only because you want it to be. Have a nice day."

Dismissed like a schoolboy from the principal's office, Max chewed into his cheek as heat flooded his face. He refused to let her treat him like an annoying gnat she could swat away.

"You're willing to bet your life on that message being a random coincidence?"

On a heavy sigh, she lifted her gaze to glance up at him through heavy lashes. How could someone so infuriating be so damn sexy? "If I reacted every time someone sent me a letter that could be construed as a threat, I'd never get any work done. People don't like a strong woman in a powerful position, Detective Green, and they don't mind letting me know."

Her firm words spoke of a woman who didn't let threats, empty or otherwise, chip through her armor. But her reaction when she'd read the card spoke differently. She was hiding something and he'd get the answers one way or another.

He shrugged and aimed for casual indifference. "Fine. If you aren't worried, neither am I. But I'm taking the card with me as evidence."

The tiniest of wrinkles marred her smooth forehead. "Why do you want it?"

Tucking his pen and notepad back into the back pocket of his pants he said, "Might as well try to get prints. If you're right and this is just some weird coincidence, no harm done. If I'm right and this is connected to two murders, it might help me find the killer and stop a third."

Her throat rose on a swallow, and she tapped her finger against the desk again. "Fine, take it."

"Thank you." The gratitude tasted bitter on his tongue. He grabbed a tissue and used it to shield his prints from the card as he detached the card from the flowers and picked it up between his thumb and forefinger. He turned to leave, but something nagged at his gut. With his free hand, he reached into his pocket, pulled out a business card and tossed it on the corner of her desk. "If you need anything, call me."

"Thanks." She nodded toward a glass dish filled with cards. "Take one. Let me know if you find anything from the card."

Reaching for the business card, he stopped and held her gaze. "I'll be calling regarding the men who met Linda Hoyt and Emily Steele. A warrant won't take long to secure. Why don't you just answer my questions now?" He was pushing his luck, but it was worth one more shot.

Samantha bit into the corner of her lip, but the smallest hint of a smile poked through. "No."

He grabbed the card and a smile of his own cracked

through the tense muscles of his face as he walked away. Samantha Gates was a woman who was used to getting her way, but she'd never encountered him before. He'd stop at nothing to get the answers she was hiding, starting with running fingerprints on the card and finding out where those flowers came from. If he was lucky, the answers would lead him to the killer.

Making a pit stop beside the lovely Laurie, he rapped his knuckles against the top of her desk to gain her attention.

She finished stapling a stack of papers and glanced up at him with a pronounced pout of her lips and pissed-off squint of her eyes. "Yes?"

"Who brought up the flowers for Ms. Gates?"

Puzzlement furrowed her brow. "The courier, Bill. Any deliveries brought to the reception downstairs get brought up by him."

"Where can I find him?"

She lifted her slim shoulders. "You'd have to ask downstairs. He runs errands all over the building."

"Have any other suspicious deliveries come through recently?"

Her eyes widened. "The flowers were suspicious?"

"Possibly."

She shook her head and blond strands of hair fell in front of her ear. "Not that I know of."

He pulled out another card and handed it to her. "If anything strikes you as out of the ordinary, call me."

He left before she could reply. Eyes followed him as he made his way to the elevator, the heat of their stares burning through his jacket. He kept his shoulders straight and his focus locked on the opening doors of the elevator. A small horde of people came out, leaving the space empty. *Thank God.* He pressed the bottom button for the lobby and leaned back against the reflective wall with the card tucked between the tissue in his palm.

Names, places and everything in between bounced around his brain. Tension formed a hard ball in the pit of his stomach. Time was running out and he had so much information to wade through he didn't know which way to turn. He needed help. He'd call his lieutenant about requesting uniforms for assistance with some of the digging, but he needed more. He needed someone who had an understanding about what went down on the Upper East Side. The people who worked here, the stores tucked into the quiet corners, hell, the little blue-haired ladies who walked their damn poodles every day.

Lord help him, he needed Caspano.

A bell dinged as the elevator reached the bottom floor and the doors slid open. He stepped onto the marble floor and pulled out his phone. His fingers protested with every number he punched, but dammit he had to put his pride aside this one time.

The line clicked on after the second ring. "Caspano here."

"Hey, Sal. It's Max. I need your help."

Shit. What were the odds of the police being in Samantha's office when the roses were sent? Seeing the look of terror on her face when she stepped out of her office was a long shot, but no way her panic would be as intense after talking to a cop about it. He probably comforted her and made all her worries go away.

She should be very worried.

She had everything. She didn't care that she'd taken

everything away from others. That other people suffered because of her selfishness. She'd pay.

But it'd have to be sooner than planned, which was a real pain in the ass. The thrill of the chase, the fear-provoking hunting was more fun than expected. To give that up now would be tough. But it had to be done. The cop showing up at *EternalMatch*'s office today wasn't just a wrench in the plans, it was a big wake-up call to get things over with.

They had figured out the connection already. Who knew what else they'd figured out. It was too risky not to take care of business sooner rather than later. Samantha had no idea what was coming for her.

Ping.

A text alert from her phone had Samantha halting at the door with one hand already turning the knob. She'd put in two hours of work this morning at home, and energy bounced around her body and begged to be released. She hadn't gone for an early run this morning. Too much had happened and she needed some distance from the horror she'd stumbled upon in the park. But she couldn't put it off forever, and she couldn't be chased away from the only place—the only thing—that gave her overworked mind a break. She'd look at the text when she got back. Right now, she needed to run. Needed to escape the constant questions centered around who'd sent her flowers. She wanted to believe the note and the flowers were a coincidence, but she wasn't stupid. Sleep had evaded her as she'd tossed and turned, wondering who could have sent them and why.

She stepped outside and the still air nipped at the exposed skin on her face. At least there was no wind howling through the concrete columns around her. She could handle the cold, but a windy day in February always made her miserable.

Raising her arms high above her head, she reached the tips of her well-manicured fingers toward the morning sun and stretched her tight, sleepy muscles. Her muscles may be sleepy, but her mind buzzed like a college kid's after three Red Bulls. Her daily therapy beckoned her forward and anticipation surged to the tips of her toes.

Her run was the one time of day when peace settled over her frantic mind—the one time she unplugged from the world and left all connections to work at home. She craved losing herself in the gentle pulling of muscles and the quickening of her heartbeat. She loved starting her day with a clear head, but when the sun didn't rise until after 7:00 a.m., she had to start her day answering emails and checking stock reports. She refused to run on a treadmill, and after stumbling along a dead body in Central Park, she'd wait until after daybreak to head back to her normal running route. Even if images of Linda Hoyt were still fresh in her brain.

Pushing the bad memories of yesterday from her mind, she turned away from her Upper East Side town house and filled her lungs with the crisp air. She kept her stride slow as she took off toward the park. Not many people clogged the sidewalk at this time of morning…especially this time of year. Early February wasn't a huge month for tourism. The ball at Times Square had been dropped, the tree at Rockefeller Center was long gone, and the city she loved could finally slow down.

A tiny chuckle tickled the back of her throat and

her lips curved up into a smile. New York City slowing down was like a fish deciding not to swim. It simply didn't happen. But at least this morning, with a schedule jammed with meetings and conference calls, she could get to the park without a gaggle of tourists ogling the opulent homes nestled together across from Central Park.

Samantha came to the stoplight in front of the park entrance and readjusted her wireless headphones that allowed her the freedom to leave the phone at home. Music vibrated through the speakers and she jogged in place while she waited for the light to change. A tingly sensation built in the pit of her stomach, and she glanced around. Was someone watching her? Cabs, town cars and buses sped by and the constant chatter of the city encased her. A familiar car stood out, its dark blue paint and tinted windows one that scratched at her memory, bur she couldn't put her finger on why. The light changed and she charged into the street ahead of the handful of people waiting for the pedestrian light at the curb.

An engine revved to life, its roar cutting through the rock song playing in her ears. Tires screeched, the sound shocking Samantha's system and freezing her in place. Her heart raced and she whipped her head to the side as a flash of blue barreled toward her. Instinct took over and she raised her arms in a pathetic attempt to shield her body.

"Watch out!"

The words broke into her panicked mind and she lunged to the side just as the front of the vehicle clipped her side. The impact had her careening onto the hood and tumbling to the unrelenting asphalt. Pain exploded inside her like a bomb. Asphalt scraped against the palms of her hands, and her wrist screamed in agony as a sickening crack vibrated her bones. Muffled screams barely penetrated her thoughts and darkness clouded her vision until her whole world went black.

Chapter 4

Frustration rippled through Max. He'd gotten the results back from the lab and the only prints found on the card belonged to him and Samantha. Not that he was surprised. Anybody smart enough to get away with two murders wouldn't be stupid enough to leave prints on anything. He could already imagine Samantha's I-told-you-so look when he called to tell her.

Damn, the woman was infuriating. How could someone be so oblivious to their own safety? It didn't help that he'd spent hours digging into her history, only to find jack shit. She was clean as a whistle, except the bad press she received last year when Richard Pike terrorized several women he'd found and stalked on her app. But even that wasn't enough to dim the shine of respect that crept over him for her hard work and philanthropic contributions.

That didn't stop every ounce of his being from dreading calling her this morning to tell her he hadn't found anything. She'd take it as a sign she had been right, and her not taking him seriously was dangerous.

Grabbing his phone in one hand, he held up Samantha's business card in the other and punched down on the numbers on the screen, As he waited for someone to answer the other line, he plunged his free hand into his pocket to protect it from the cold and marched up the street. The man who'd taken the order for the flowers sent to Samantha's office would be in first thing this morning, and he had more questions to ask.

"Hello, Samantha Gates's office. Can I help you?"

Annoyance flared at being directed to Samantha's receptionist. "I need to talk to Ms. Gates. This is Detective Green."

"She's not in yet, but can I take a message?"

The perky voice only added to his irritation and he tightened his grip on the phone. "No way she's not in. I'm tired of you people giving me the runaround. Put her on the phone."

Silence hung on the line, then a feminine cough sounded in his ear. "She's really not here. She never comes in before her run. I'll let her know you called." The line went dead.

Max ground his teeth together and thrust his phone back in his pocket. He'd deal with her later; first he needed to talk to the florist. Rounding the corner, he walked in front of the store and swore. No lights shone from the windows and a closed sign dangled from the glass door. *What the hell?* The store was supposed to open twenty minutes ago. He shot his foot out and the tip of his toe connected to the door. He didn't have time for this.

Spinning in a circle, he took in the section of the city he usually avoided and the bare trees of Central Park two blocks away grabbed his attention. He checked his watch. If Samantha ran before work every day, chances were she ran the same path. The crime scene where Linda Hoyt was found wasn't far from here. If he got lucky, he might find her and get this conversation over with.

If he was really lucky, she might be so surprised to see him that she gave him more information than she had before. Then he could swing back around to the florist after they spoke. Burying his hands in the pockets of his coat, he hunched his shoulders to block out the cold and took off toward the park.

A scream split the air, chasing the chill from his bones. People gathered in a clump in the street and Max lengthened his stride to a run. Cars blasted their angry horns, put off by whatever the hell was keeping them stuck in gridlock. Max's long legs ate up the sidewalk; he was pushing people from his path as he went. He reached the edge of the sidewalk across from the park and spotted a trail of blood among the pedestrians trying to help. Beyond the street, food carts lay overturned and injured people lay scattered on the ground. None of them was as badly injured as the woman on the road.

Grabbing his badge, he held it in the air and shoved people out of his way. "NYPD. Move to the side. Get the hell out of my way."

A woman lay in a ball in the middle of the street. Dark hair tangled around her face, dirt and blood matted through it. He pulled out his phone and called 911 as he crouched down beside her.

"911, what's your emergency?"

"I've found a woman near the entrance to Central Park on Ninety-Sixth and Fifth. Looks like a hit-and-run. Get an ambulance here now." He lifted his chin and glanced around at the chaos. "Make that several squads. Looks like the asshole fled the scene by driving on the sidewalk. Not sure how many injuries, but the woman in the street is by far the most serious."

Max clicked off the line and glanced at the crumpled body in front of him. An invisible fist squeezed the air from his lungs. Gently, he reached out a finger and pushed the hair from the woman's face. He sucked in a breath.

Shit, shit, shit.

Samantha's eyes remained closed and blood trickled from an open cut on her forehead. Tattered bits of clothing showed nasty contusions on multiple parts of her body and her right wrist tilted at an awkward angle. Guilt slid down his throat. He should have been more forceful with her, made her take the threat she'd received more seriously. He'd let his need to rise to her challenge cloud his judgment, and someone had tried to kill her.

Hell, if help didn't come soon, he might be looking at murder number three.

A small groan rumbled from her throat and his pulse leaped in his ears. He dropped to his knees and moisture from the sludge-covered street seeped into his pants as he hovered over her, but he didn't care. He kept his gaze fixed on her face, willing her to open her eyes. "Samantha? Can you hear me?"

The groan turned louder and her eyelashes fluttered. The crowd pressed in around him for a closer look. Cries for help and answers turned to gasps of recognition. He glanced behind his shoulder. People held cell phones high above their heads, trying to snap a picture of Samantha as she lay in the street and fought for her life.

A low growl gurgled in the back of his throat and he leaped to his feet like a coiled panther ready to attack. "For God's sake, put your damn phones away. This is a crime scene, not a circus."

Slowly, hands lowered and phones disappeared. He sank back down beside Samantha and blocked her body from the lowlifes watching her. Using the pad of his thumb, he wiped a bit of dirt from her cheek and cradled her face in his hand. "Everything's going to be okay, Samantha. It's Max. I'm here with you. Help's on the way."

Her eyes remained sealed shut but she leaned into his touch just enough to let him know his words had penetrated the pain and the fog and whatever else kept her unmoving on the cold street. This was how she'd looked yesterday when he's seen her in the park; this was the real her, no designer suits and expensive makeup, just a woman going for a run. Something inside him understood; she was more than her world as he had been more than his. Maybe he'd been too quick to judge—God knows he'd been judged unfairly for most of his life. Maybe she was more than she seemed. What he wouldn't give to see that fire light her eyes right now.

"Fight, dammit," he whispered in her ear.

Sirens blared from a distance, their warning call growing louder the closer they came. The crowd parted, but didn't scatter. Max couldn't worry about it now, couldn't manage to move away from Samantha or this strange connection he felt for a woman he'd disliked at first sight. Tires screeched to a halt a few feet away and heavy footsteps pounded toward him. A second ambulance skirted around them to tend to the lesser injured on the sidewalk. Two men ran toward him and he tore his gaze from Samantha's bruised face to speak to them.

"You need to step away so we can assess her injuries and get her in the back of the ambulance." The bigger of the two men brushed him aside before he could respond. He didn't want to leave her, but he couldn't do a damn thing to help her. He'd be more useful trying to find the person who'd mowed her down.

"Green!" For once, the deep baritone voice of Caspano didn't piss him off. He turned to face him as he pushed his way through the crowd. "What the hell's going on?"

Max rubbed his jawline and the metallic scent of blood filled his nostrils. He twisted his wrist so the back of his hand came into his line of vision and winced at the blood trickling down his finger.

Samantha's blood.

He wiped his hand off on the side of his pants and cleared his throat. "I don't know. I showed up after she was hit. Didn't see a damn thing."

Caspano nodded past Max's shoulder toward the entrance of the park. "My boy's checking out the wreckage on the sidewalk. They found a stolen car abandoned in an alley across the street. We need to comb through it."

"I want to talk to the crowd. Find out if anyone saw something. I'll meet up with you when I'm done." Then he needed to call his lieutenant. If someone wanted Samantha Gates dead, the NYPD would have to take special steps to deal with such a high-profile case.

Caspano grunted his agreement and took off in the opposite direction. Max's gaze followed the detective and stopped when he caught sight of Samantha being loaded into the back of the ambulance. He had work to do, but lead weighed down his feet as he watched the ambulance scream off down the clogged street.

Dear God, please let her live.

A steady *beep, beep, beep* pounded against Samantha's temple and forced her to open her eyes. A bright light pierced her pupils, driving her to shut them again. Stars exploded behind her eyelids. Tension froze her muscles, and she strained against the invisible force keeping her still.

The beeping echoed around wherever the hell she was. She grew frantic and her heart hammered against her chest. Her breath sputtered from her pressed-together lips. A light touch skimmed over her hand and her heart rate slowed to normal. A large, rough hand encased hers and the heat chased away the chill from her fingers. She lifted her gaze and met the cool blue eyes of the detective from her office.

Her mind spun and she tried to remember his name. Dammit, she couldn't wade through the fog in her brain to remember his last name. "Max?" His name felt weird on her tongue, as if she spoke around a mouth full of cotton.

He scooted on the edge of the chair, moved it closer to her bedside. His grip tightened on her hand and she winced. "Sorry."

"Max?" an unfamiliar voice repeated with a hint of

amusement from across the room. Max glared at someone on the other side of her.

Heat flooded her cheeks and if she could have pulled her hand from Max's, she would have. Pain and drugs clouded her mind, or she'd never have been so informal with him. Hell, she'd only spoken with the man once. Clearing her throat, she asked, "What happened?"

Max settled his gaze on her again. "You were hit by a car. Do you remember anything?"

She tried to shake her head but the movement caused a hammer to beat against her skull. "No. The last thing I remember is going for a run."

"You don't remember the car that hit you? What the driver looked like? Anything?" The deep voice on her other side asked her questions, but she couldn't find the energy to turn toward him.

"Blue. I remember a blue streak racing toward me." She closed her eyes and tried to bring back the memory of what had landed her in the hospital. "I was crossing the street and someone screamed. Tires screeched and I tried to dive out of the way. Then everything went black. But the car. It was familiar. Like I've seen it before, but I can't remember when."

"Great."

Max dropped her palm and ran a hand through his tousled dark hair. If fire could have shot from his eyes, it would have singed the man she'd yet to meet. "Enough, Caspano."

"Is that your partner?"

"Hell no," Max said on a snort. "We work in different precincts. I'm investigating the homicides I believe you're somehow connected to. Detective Caspano was called in to investigate the hit-and-run. He's used to working the Upper East Side, so we're unofficially helping each other."

Hard soles slapped against linoleum and a bulky man with a full head of slicked-back brown hair and a face with cheeks the consistency of putty rounded the end of her hospital bed. "Ms. Gates, it's nice to meet you, even under these circumstances. I'm going to do everything I can to find the person who did this to you." He dipped the end of his pointed chin toward her broken body.

Her injured body screamed at her like a group of pre-schoolers demanding attention. Every nerve ending in her body sparked to life, alerting her brain to the over-whelming pain surging through her. "Thank you," she said through gritted teeth.

"Caspano can come back later and ask more questions." Max turned his glare on the other man and Samantha wanted to kiss his feet in gratitude. "Is there anyone we should call? You underwent minor surgery for your broken wrist, and I'm not sure when you'll get out of here."

She didn't have her phone with her. "I left my phone at home while I ran. I'm ashamed to say I don't have a single number memorized from my contact list." Not like she'd have anyone to call anyway. Her mother would be a mess if she found out she'd been hit by a car, and she didn't want to worry Mrs. Walsh. Her pathetic personal life lacked a lot of close relationships. The demands of her very public life made that next to impossible. Maybe that was why she felt so thankful for the man at her bedside. She knew it was his job, but waking to someone who cared—even if it was only for his case—felt really nice for a change.

Concern furrowed Max's brow. "You shouldn't be

alone. Do you want me to have an officer stop by your place and get your phone? Maybe some other personal items? We have a couple guys stationed outside your door. I can send one of them."

The idea of strangers combing through her house, no matter how trustworthy, made hives hover beneath her skin.

"I really would like my phone. I can make calls to get whatever else I need after I talk to the doctor and find out how long I'm stuck here." She cut her stare to the closed door and then back to Max. "I don't want someone I don't know walking around my house."

His furrow deepened. "What do you want me to do?"

She tucked her bottom lip between her teeth and weighed her options. It didn't take long since she didn't have many. "Can you do it?"

Max's eyes widened and he leaned back in his seat as if she'd shoved him. "Me?"

"Please. I can't think of another option, and I'd feel better if it were you." She realized with a start it was true. He didn't seem to like her, but he'd come and waited for her to wake up, and there was something honest in his eyes. Maybe it was the drugs or her emotional state, but she wanted to trust him. Believed that she could.

He scratched his head and scrunched his face into a scowl. "I've got work to do. I'm glad I was here when you woke up, but…" His voice trailed off as he searched for an excuse.

Nonsensical rejection pinched her already achy chest. This was what she got for being vulnerable. As usual, she'd have to bribe or trade to get what she wanted. People were so disappointingly predictable. "If you do this for me, I'll tell you everything you need to know about the men on *EternalMatch*." She wasn't stupid. No way the murder in the park and the creepy flower delivery weren't somehow related to her being plowed over by a runaway car. She had to give him whatever information he needed to find out who was behind the attacks, and if she could get something out of it, even better.

The side of his mouth hitched up in a smirk. "I've got a warrant."

She raised her brows and matched his smirk with one of her own. "What about information regarding Richard Pike?"

Max straightened and a full smile curved his lips. "You've got yourself a deal."

Chapter 5

"I'll be back as soon as I can. One of the officers at the door can help you if anything comes up while I'm gone."

"Is that really necessary?" Weariness took some of the annoyance from Samantha's tone.

"Someone tried to kill you this morning. They followed you and then ran over you with a car. Yes, protection for your safety is necessary." Max ran his hand through his hair and shook his head as if her desire for privacy—even from the trusted men in blue—was a ridiculous notion.

"How do you know it was intentional? Hit-and-runs aren't exactly uncommon in this city. I probably walked when I shouldn't have. Drivers here are insane." Her mind desperately yearned to buy into the bullshit she spewed, but a tickle at the base of her spine sang a different song.

A harsh laugh came from Detective Caspano's wide mouth, and Max's jaw dropped.

Max closed the gap between them and crouched down, invading her personal space. "Are you kidding me? You're a smart woman, Samantha. Look at the facts. First you were sent a threatening note and then you were almost killed by a runaway car that even you said you've seen before. Those things don't just happen."

She rounded her eyes and pressed the back of her head against her pillow. The minty smell of his breath mixed with the antiseptic smell every hospital room possessed. "But maybe—"

"But nothing." His words came out clipped, as if it pained him to speak. "Someone is after you and we need to figure out who."

A light knock on the door stole Samantha's attention. The door opened just enough for a doctor to shimmy through the narrow slit before she closed it behind her. A warm smile lifted her lips and she glanced at the tablet in her hands. "Hello, Ms. Gates. I'm Dr. Wilson. I need to go over everything with you. Would you like for the officers to step out?"

Max stood and nodded toward the doctor. "We were just leaving."

Samantha reached down for the key she kept in the slit of her running pants and heat flooded her face. She wasn't wearing pants. Of course she'd be in a hospital gown, and vanity had her wishing she could fix her face. But what did it matter? Max Green was the last man she needed to impress…except for maybe the grumpy officer standing beside him.

She shifted her attention to Max. "Do you know where my stuff is? My house key was in my pants."

Max glanced around the room while rubbing the back of his neck. "Umm, I don't know where your pants are."

Oh my God, was he blushing? She coughed to hide a chuckle.

"Your belongings were placed in a plastic bag and should be in the closet in the corner." The doctor nodded toward a built-in closet behind Max.

Whirling around, Max opened the closet and pulled out the bag. He stretched his long arm toward her and she shook her head, the motion causing pain to shoot through her skull. She sucked in a deep breath, which sent a tidal wave of agony rippling through her entire body. Closing her eyes, she leaned back against the pillow and waited for it to pass.

She opened her eyes and grimaced. "You get it." The words came out on a breath of discomfort.

Max's jaw tightened and he ripped the bag open, rummaging around until he pulled out a key. "What's your address?"

"Give me your phone and I'll plug it in." The doctor and the other detective certainly weren't threats, but she didn't want her address being passed around. Better to write it down where only Max could see it. She tried to lift her hand to take his phone and a heaviness kept it glued to her side. She glanced down and grimaced.

"You have a broken wrist," the doctor said.

Samantha heaved a heavy sigh. "Great. I'm sure a broken right wrist won't be an inconvenience at all. I can't even sign my name like this."

Max laughed and she glared at him. "Just tell me and I'll write it down."

Samantha's gaze darted around the room before landing back on Max. "I'd rather do it myself."

"Here. I'll hold my phone while you type in the address." He lifted the screen in front of her.

Kindness cracked through his rough exterior, warming her, and she fought to keep her gaze from studying the softened lines around the corners of his eyes. She struggled with each press of her finger. Even the smallest movement sent stabs of pain to her side.

"A broken wrist is a pain in the ass, but it could have been a lot worse," Max said in a low voice that brushed over her skin like the delicate stroke of a feather.

She shifted her gaze to meet his and the intensity in his clear blue eyes sucked all the air from her lungs. Heat rushed into her neck and beads of moisture clung to her palm. She cleared her throat and fought against the reaction he stirred in her. "My phone is on the table in the foyer. Should be pretty easy to find."

"All right, if you got what you need, let's go." Caspano's no-nonsense tone broke into the moment.

Max dropped his gaze to his worn black boots. "I'll be back soon."

The doctor waited until the men left the room to speak. "How are you feeling?" Dr. Wilson rounded the end of the bed to stand beside her.

"To be frank, like hell." Samantha attempted to shimmy up, but she didn't have the energy and stayed at an awkward half-sitting, half-lying position on the bed. The rough cotton of the blanket scratched against her exposed skin.

Dr. Wilson checked the tablet in her hands, and then

glanced up at the noisy-as-hell machine beeping beside her. "I'll have the nurse increase your pain medication if you'd like."

Gritting her teeth and pushing the pain into the furthest corner of her mind—not that it helped—she said, "No thank you. Just tell me how badly I'm hurt." Pain or not, she needed to be in control.

"As you already know, you suffered from a broken wrist. You underwent minor surgery, and the cast needs to stay on for four to six weeks. You also have some bruising on your ribs and some nasty contusions. We detected an irregular heartbeat during your initial evaluation, so we're going to monitor your heart while you're here. Detective Green was right—this could have been so much worse."

Samantha forced herself into a sitting position and numbness cascaded down her body. She'd never even had stitches before, and now she was lying in a hospital bed with a whole litany of injuries. "How long do I have to stay here?"

"You'll be able to go home tomorrow if everything continues to look good. You'll have to take it easy. You'll be a little weak and sore for a few days, especially your ribs."

"Okay." Her mind spun with everything she had to do. She couldn't take time off work. She had too much on her plate.

"I do have one more thing to tell you."

Samantha held her breath and a stabbing pain pierced her ribs. What more could there be?

"A lot of people saw you get hit, and unfortunately there has been some footage leaked. We are taking the risk to your safety, and your privacy, very seriously here. We have ordered all reporters off the premises, and the officers at your door have strict orders not to let anyone but the medical staff and police into your room."

An invisible fist squeezed her heart and Max's words came back to her. Someone wanted her dead. She tried to focus on the doctor. "Is the footage online?"

Dr. Wilson pressed her thin lips together and regret darkened her green eyes. "Online and on television. I'm sure it won't be long before it's in print."

Dammit. Did people not have anything better to do than gawk at her in her most vulnerable moment, and then try to make a buck off it? Hell, most of the idiots she'd encountered tried to capitalize on her fame simply for a little notoriety. Now she needed to worry about if her mom had already seen whatever the hell was being plastered all over the media.

"What about other information? Does the public know I'm okay? Or did they just want the money shot of me hurt in the street?" She couldn't keep the edge of resentment from her voice. She'd never understand people's fascination with her. She worked hard to build a successful business just like a million other people out there. Just because her business earned her a ton of money, that didn't make her any different than anyone else.

"I believe I saw an update saying you were stable."

"Thank you for the heads-up. When I leave tomorrow, we'll have to come up with a way to get me out without drawing a lot of attention. I really don't want any more pictures out there."

"We will. Don't worry. Are you sure you don't want a nurse to up your meds?" Concern made the doctor's eyebrows dip down.

"I'm sure." Like hell she was, but she didn't want to rely on drugs. Better to take the minimum amount to function.

Dr. Wilson nodded. "Okay. You should rest now. Push the button beside your bed if you need anything."

"Thank you."

The doctor left the room and Samantha caught the profile of one of the officers standing outside her door. A chill swept over her and she used her good hand to pull the stiff blanket over her shoulders. Policemen had to be stationed outside her door to protect her. Not from paparazzi or arrogant spectators who acted as though her life was a public show, but from the person who'd tried to kill her.

Dark sludge coated the sidewalk. The snow had stopped, but the freezing temperatures kept it clinging to the ground. The pure white powder had turned to a mess of wet gray slush, and if the upcoming weather forecast was right, the disgusting mix would stay for a while. God, he hated February.

Max kept on high alert as he walked toward Samantha's town house. Not an apartment, not even a penthouse like his parents had, but a freaking town house. He couldn't imagine looking out his window and seeing a lake of trees like Samantha did. Hell, screw the trees. He wouldn't live in New York City if nature was high on his priority list. But it would be nice if the streets outside his Brooklyn apartment smelled of the street food served across the street instead of the greasy Chinese food from the restaurant below him.

Turning to the stoop of the house number he'd been given, Max took in the area around the house as he walked up the steps. Luxury vehicles and town cars lined the street and took up the limited parking. An idling black car caught his attention. The car was parked four spaces in front of Samantha's residence and a middle-aged man with salt-and-pepper hair sat in the driver's seat. Even from a distance, the tension in the man's shoulders was evident. Max took two steps toward the car before it slid onto the empty street and drove away.

Grabbing the key from his pocket, he memorized the license plate. If someone ran Samantha down during her regular jog, chances were they were familiar with her routine. Which would mean someone had been following her and knew where she lived. He'd run the plate number as soon as he got a chance. Right now, he needed to get inside, grab what he came for and hurry back to the hospital.

Max turned the key in the knob and swung open the heavy front door. He took one step inside and whistled through his teeth. Her foyer had to be half the size of his entire apartment. A curved staircase to his left led upstairs and a giant chandelier hung from the tray ceiling. Gleaming hardwood floors sprawled across the entryway and led to a pair of pocket doors on the far side of the room. Mirrors filled the wall opposite the staircase and a distressed table nestled against it.

A blast of wind blew in through the open door and up the back of his neck. He closed the door and walked farther into the house. His heavy boots *thunked* against the floor. He spun a slow circle, taking in the small glimpse of the house he could see. Money and material things meant little to him, but damn, he wished he could see the rest of the place. Even his parents would be awestruck. A trail of drool would be left behind his idiot brother. Both because of the house and the beautiful woman who lived here.

He returned his focus to the table. Her phone lay right where she'd said it'd be. He retrieved it and studied the rest of the contents beside it. Just like the desk at her office, the table in her foyer was neat as a pin. He ran the pad of his finger along the smooth wood and wasn't a bit surprised not one speck of dust clung to his skin. Two lamps flanked each end of the table, a stack of magazines sat neatly in the center and a few framed pictures rested in perfectly angled positions.

Leaning closer, he studied the pictures. One picture was Samantha when she was younger—fifteen? Sixteen? A younger boy with short brown hair and a goofy grin stood beside her. Another picture had to be Samantha's mother. She sat on a park bench with her upturned face basked in the sunlight. Warmth virtually emanated through the frame. The last picture was of Samantha at her college graduation. Her broad smile beamed on her face and she held a diploma in front of her chest for all to see. He picked up the frame and held it closer to his face.

I'll be damned. Columbia University. How did I miss that?

He dropped the frame as if flames had burst from the silver edging and scalded his skin, but his eyes stayed glued to the photo. An image of Linda Hoyt and Emily Steele entered his brain. How had he not seen it before? Samantha had the same warm brown eyes, the same full lips and pouty mouth, the same olive skin. All three women had straight dark hair that fell to their shoulders. Add to that, Emily Steele was found where Samantha had gone to school and Linda Hoyt on the route of her morning jog. Someone didn't just want Samantha dead, but they'd gone to great lengths to learn everything about her.

They'd stalked her.

He had to get back to the hospital. He had to find out everything he could about Richard Pike and anyone else who could be after Samantha. He spun on his heel and opened the door, bracing himself for the damn blast of wind that would come.

"Put your hands in the air where I can see them and step back inside." The man with the salt-and-pepper hair stood in the doorway with a gun pointed at Max's chest.

Max swallowed past the lump in his throat. His gaze darted over the man's shoulder and he searched the deserted street for a sign of someone he could alert.

Where the hell was everyone? Someone was always around in New York. But not on the quiet streets of the Upper East Side on a cold, gloomy day.

The man thrust his arm forward and the hard metal of the barrel of the gun wedged against Max's leather jacket. "I said back up. Now."

Max reached forward and grabbed the barrel of the gun, twisting it away from his chest. The man stumbled forward and Max thrust his elbow toward the asshole's nose, but the man ducked out of the way. The smooth metal of the gun slipped from Max's palm. The man yanked it free from his grasp, raised it in the air and brought the hard butt of the gun down on his temple.

Stars exploded and his vision blurred. He stumbled backward, but fought to stay on his feet.

"I said put your hands in the air."

Max held his palms in the air and took a step back in retreat. His gun was tucked under his coat. No way he could get to it before this jerk put a hole in his chest. His mind spun as he tried to come up with a plan.

The man followed him into the elegant foyer and slammed the door shut with his foot. "I think you and I need to have a little chat."

Chapter 6

"Are you aware you're holding a member of the NYPD at gunpoint?" Max had to get the man talking. If he was talking then he wasn't shooting.

"I don't give a rat's ass who you are. What are you doing in Ms. Gates's home?" The hard edge in the man's voice was sharper than the butt of the gun that had slammed against his skull.

Ms. Gates? What the hell was going on? Max squinted his eyes and studied the older man's face. Fog crept into his vision and a hammer pounded against the inside of his head. "Who are you?"

"I'm the one asking the questions. How do I know you're a cop? And even if you are, why are you inside Ms. Gates's home without her?"

"My badge is clipped to my belt and my ID is right beside it. You can see it clear as day if you let me unzip my jacket." Max's palms itched to make a grab for the gun threatening his impending death, but the man had obviously had training. He might not have shot him the last time he tried to take it, but that didn't mean he wouldn't if he failed to disarm him again.

Not to mention his reference to Ms. Gates and the way his eyes didn't flip around the opulent room. The man had been here before, or awe would have darkened the pupils in his hazel eyes. That didn't mean he wasn't Samantha's stalker, but it did ease Max's suspicions a fraction of an inch.

"Leave one hand in the air while the other slowly unzips the coat. If you try anything, I won't hesitate to shoot you. As far as I'm concerned, you're trespassing on private property."

Max hooked one eyebrow up. "And what are you doing?"

The man tightened his jaw. "Protecting Ms. Gates. Now show me your ID."

His response piqued Max's interest enough that he did exactly as he was told. Not like he had much choice. When the zipper was down, Max shifted to the side and gave the man a glimpse at the badge on his hip. His ID was clipped on the belt loop in front of the badge.

"Give them to me."

Max kept his gaze locked on the man's eyes. His fingertips brushed against the hard badge. He unclipped it and tossed it to the man. Next, he found the metal clip holding his ID in place, yanked it off his belt loop and flipped it through the air.

Keeping the gun trained on him with one hand, the man used his free hand to catch both pieces of evidence of Max's profession. He lifted them to eye level and then slowly lowered the gun to his side. He threw them back across the room and Max let them fall to the ground. The man used his free hand to scratch the back of his neck. "Sorry about that, Detective Green," he said, even as his finger stayed next to the trigger. His tone stayed firm and spoke much louder than his words.

"Now it's your turn. Who are you and why did you point a gun at me?"

"My name's James, and I work for Ms. Gates."

James might have lowered his gun, but the adrenaline pumping through Max's veins still kept him on the balls of his feet, ready to pounce. "How do I know you're not lying?"

A sneer twisted James's plump lips and made his thin mustache quiver. "You're not in a position to question me, are you?"

"Still threatening me, huh? I could arrest you for assaulting an officer, as well as for pointing a gun at me. Maybe drop the attitude and fill me in a little?"

James lifted his broad shoulders and kept his face passive. He had a good twenty years on Max, but the man stayed in shape. No extra weight wiggled beneath his black sweater or spilled over the waist of his slacks. Hell, even his full head of hair cried out in defiance against his climbing age. "You still need to tell me what the hell you're doing here. I've never seen you before, and Ms. Gates hates strangers in her personal space. How did you get in?"

"With a key," Max said through clenched teeth. He didn't have time for this bullshit. He shot back with a question of his own. "How do I know you work for Samantha?"

"Don't you think I would have shot you already if I didn't?"

Max shrugged and dropped his gaze to the gun still dangling at James's side. "You still might."

James's mouth shifted from side to side as if he chewed on the lining of his lips. "Fine. I'll put the gun down." He bent his knees to crouch to the ground while keeping his eyes on Max and placed the gun on the floor at his feet.

Tension pulsed through the air. James stood and Max held his breath. His heart pounded in his chest and his head throbbed. James lifted his palms in the same position Max's hands had been in moments before.

Ring, ring, ring.

The shrill sound of Max's phone sliced through the air. He reached into his pocket and James took a step forward. Max hurried and pulled out his phone and showed it to James before answering. "Green here."

"Hey, Max." Jack's deep voice came through the speaker. Should he tell him he was in the room with some psycho who'd pulled a gun on him? Or did he follow his gut and trust the stranger in front of him?

"What's up? I'm kind of in the middle of something." He hoped the weariness in his voice didn't tip Jack off.

"I heard about the hit-and-run. Caspano's in-house making calls. Sounds like it's another connection to the murders."

Max kept his gaze fixed on James's weathered face as he spoke. "Definitely, but I need to convince her of it. Samantha's laid up in the hospital and she still—"

"What?" The word exploded from James's mouth. He took another step forward and the tip of his shoe collided with the gun at his feet. The gun slid across the smooth wood floor and Max bent to pick it up. The familiar weight of the Glock made him feel safer.

"I'll call you back, Jack." He straightened and put his phone back in his pocket. He trained the gun on James. "Looks like it's my turn to ask the questions."

All the color had drained from the older man's face and a glassiness shone from his eyes. "I'll tell you anything you want to know. But tell me what happened to Ms. Gates. Why is she in the hospital? Dammit, I should have known something was wrong when she didn't come back from her run. I waited so I could take her to work." He tunneled his hand through his thick hair.

Either James was a damn good actor, or he had nothing to do with Samantha's hit-and-run. "How do I know you work for her?"

James's gaze darted around the room as if he'd find the answer written on the cream-colored walls. "Call her. She'll tell you. I'm her driver and I look out for her like a daughter. She's a real nice lady and doesn't have too many people in her corner. She'll tell you everything… if she's able. Is she hurt? Can she even talk?" His voice cracked on the question.

"She'll be fine, but she doesn't have her phone and I can't waste time looking up the hospital's phone number. I came here to get her phone."

The lines on James's face lifted. "Let me call her. My name will pop up. That's gotta prove something."

James grabbed his phone and Max fought a laugh. The guy had a flip phone. Samantha's phone rang and he took it from his pocket and read the screen.

The name James Buckley popped up along with a picture of the man in front of him. "Okay. Your name's in her phone, but that doesn't mean I trust you. Someone who knows an awful lot about your boss is out to get her. Who better to know her every move than the man who drives her around?"

A deep crimson stained James's face. "I'd never hurt her. She'll tell you that."

"She better tell me something, because I'm still considering arresting you for assaulting an officer."

"I'll do whatever I can to help you and protect her. And then I'll kill whoever the hell is after her."

Max's gaze traveled from the heated look in his eyes, to the tight set of his mouth, to the fists clenched at his sides. James might be telling the truth, but he'd have to get through Max first. He wouldn't kill whoever was responsible, but he would make sure justice was served.

Hushed whispers echoed around Samantha's hospital room and penetrated the haze of sleep keeping her eyes glued shut. A man's low growl alerted her to the tension in the room.

Max? No, his voice held a more gravelly tone.

"I couldn't stop you from following me here, but I can stop you from going into her room."

No, that was Max's voice. Why was he always so pissed off?

"Like hell you can. I need to make sure she's all right."

The smooth, rich voice had her lifting the corners of her mouth and opening her eyes. She blinked against the bright lights pouring down on her and tried to focus on the commotion by the door. "James?"

"Ms. Gates. How are you?" James pushed past Max. The rough edge that had been in his voice moments ago disappeared and he approached the bed. He clasped his hands in front of him and dipped his chin.

"I'm okay. I can go home tomorrow. What are you doing here?" Her gaze flicked to Max. "What happened to your head?"

Max touched his fingertips to his temple and his entire body flinched. "Nothing. Just a little accident."

James huffed beside her. "We had a misunderstanding."

She turned her head too quickly to study him and a wave of nausea rolled inside her.

"So this guy works for you?" Max asked.

"Yes. He's been my driver for over five years."

"Are you aware he carries a firearm?" The annoyance in his voice had her narrowing her eyes at James, who only shrugged.

Her smile widened. "James takes his responsibilities seriously. I spend a lot of time with him, and I need to know he can protect me if the situation arises."

"He's definitely up for the challenge, if he's actually around."

James pivoted and sent poison-dipped arrows with his eyes in Max's direction and then returned his kind-eyed concern to her. "I'm so sorry I wasn't there. I waited for you to come home, and assumed you'd either taken a long jog or had gotten caught up in something."

"It's not your job to watch over me twenty-four hours a day," she said.

Max snorted. "Maybe it should be. Someone wants you dead and it's time you take that seriously."

The force of Max's words hit her in the middle of her forehead and she closed her eyes against the impact. Her mind had raced all morning like a long-distance runner speeding along a track—constantly traveling in a circle only to end up where it had started. No one would want her dead, would they?

Except Jose. He'd want revenge.

No. He couldn't have found out so much about her while he'd been in jail. She'd changed her name and did everything she could to keep the details of her life private. He'd only been out of prison for a few days. No way he could have done this.

Taking a breath, she lifted her eyelids and glanced at Max. "Did you find my phone?"

He nodded and grabbed it from his pocket.

"James, can you call Mrs. Walsh and let her know I'm all right? I didn't want to worry her, but I've been informed my accident's all over the news. She needs to be prepared to shield my mom from anything she may overhear."

"I can take care of that. Do you need anything else?"

"I'll need to speak with you about getting me home tomorrow, but first I need to talk to Detective Green. Can you step outside?"

A quick flash of hurt dilated his eyes and then faded away. James was a close part of her inner circle, but she didn't want him to know the details of everything she had to tell the detective. Especially in regard to Richard Pike.

"Of course. I'll be in the waiting room when you need me."

James grabbed her phone from Max's hand and stepped out of her room.

"You have one very protective driver," Max said and his fingers floated to the wound on his head.

"Good. Looks like I need it." A hard knot formed

in the pit of her stomach. She'd never pictured herself in this position. Hell, did anyone ever see themselves as prey? A trickle of apprehension slid down her spine and caused gooseflesh to erupt on her back.

"I'm glad you've finally opened your eyes to the threat on your life." Max sat in the chair beside the bed and grabbed a notepad from inside his jacket. "When did you graduate from Columbia? And why didn't that information come up when I looked into your background?"

"Wait. What? I thought you wanted to talk about Richard Pike?" Confusion clouded her drug-muddled mind.

"We'll get to that." He leaned back in his chair and hooked his ankle overtop his knee. "I told you a woman was found murdered at Columbia University and you didn't even bat an eyelash. Why didn't you tell me that's where you attended school?"

"I didn't know it was relevant. Why does it matter where I went to college?" A hint of defensiveness crept into her voice and she wished for a robe or at least an adequate pair of pajamas to hide her vulnerability in the damn bed. Hide the hideous hospital gown she'd yet to get out of.

"It matters when two murders were found in two different spots related to you." Max's long finger scratched the spot on his jaw just above his chin. "I find it odd this never came up when I ran a quick background check. Now that I think about it, not a whole lot of information did come up. I mean, I only skimmed through it because I didn't realize how vital the information was, but I'm certain that would have jumped out at me."

Beads of perspiration clung to the curling hair

around the nape of her neck and she licked her chapped lips. She'd gone to a lot of trouble to keep her past buried. She couldn't throw it all away because of this. Her life might be in danger, but she needed to protect her mother. She had to figure out a way to tell Detective Green what he needed to know to keep her safe and keep her past buried along with the dead.

Buried along with her brother.

Chapter 7

A whoosh of air squeezed from Samantha's lungs. Max sat with those blue eyes trained on her, as if he could read every single thought in her mind. God, she hated this. Hated not being in control. Hated having to answer to someone else, even if it was to find whoever had put her in this damn hospital bed. She couldn't back down just because she lay here broken and bruised. Now was when she needed to be strong, to be smart. Hers wasn't the only life on the line.

Pushing away her fears and insecurities, she pulled the mask of strength she adorned herself with every single day back on. Lips pressed together with a small curve on the corners, eyes sharp and focused, brow smooth. "All you had to do was ask and I would have told you what you wanted to know."

Max snorted. "Because you were so helpful when I stopped by your office?"

She clamped her teeth together to keep her nostrils from flaring. "What you asked me to do was invade the privacy of the people who've trusted *EternalMatch* with their information. Not only is that unethical, but it's illegal."

"What I asked you to do was help me stop a killer." He pointed the end of his pen at her like Oprah pointed out guests in her audience for prizes. Except he didn't have a brand-new car for her. Only suspicion and lots of questions. Questions she needed to find a way to answer without giving too much away.

"You got a warrant so I don't see why this is an issue." She measured her words, the pace at which she spoke, every damn detail.

Max lowered the pen and tapped it against the bottom of his shoe. "Okay. What about Columbia? Why didn't that come up during my search?"

Keep eye contact. Don't fidget. Don't let him see you sweat. Stay calm or the stupid beeping of the machine might give you away.

"I use a different name now than when I attended Columbia. My life is a bit of a circus and there are people I wish to protect. People who didn't sign up to have their pictures taken every time they step out of the house or gawkers following them when they're in the grocery store."

Max dropped his raised leg to the ground and sat up straight. "You've been followed? Recently?"

Samantha shrugged and the stiff-as-sandpaper blanket dropped from her shoulder, exposing the thin hospital gown. She refused to lift it back over her chest, but every ounce of her was aware of her heavy, bra-free breasts pressed against the material. Color crept underneath the dark stubble on Max's jaw, but thank God he kept his eyes fixed on her face.

"People always follow me. At the store, in a restaurant, everywhere really. They all want to see a glimpse of megarich Samantha Gates." This time, she couldn't help but let a little bit of resentment slip into her tone.

"I think it's more than that. I don't know for how long, but someone has been following you everywhere. They knew you'd be jogging this morning. I talked to witnesses after the ambulance brought you to the hospital. That car shot forward long after the light turned red."

She swallowed past a ball of fear lodged in her throat. "And you think this same person killed those women you told me about? The one I saw in the park and the one at Columbia?" Dammit, the quiver in her voice spoke of weakness. She couldn't be weak. Not now. Not ever.

Max arched his back and slipped his hand into the front pocket of his trousers. He grabbed his phone and spent a few seconds messing with the screen. He leaned forward and turned the screen toward her face. "This is Emily Steele. The first woman who was murdered and her body found at Columbia University. Does she look familiar?"

Samantha shook her head. "No. I told you I've never heard her name before."

Max's thumb swiped across the screen and another picture filled the screen. "What about Linda Hoyt?"

She studied the photo. "I don't know her, but she resembles the other woman."

"Who else does she resemble?" For once, Max's

words were soft and the gentle timbre of his voice skimmed over her skin.

Pressing closer, she let her gaze take in every inch of the face that had haunted her dreams last night. Without the frozen fear of death etched on her face, Linda Hoyt had exuded joy with her wide smile and dark eyes. Her rich brown hair blew behind her petite face in the picture, as if she were caught in a windstorm. The white summer dress she wore showed off her naturally bronze skin and… Samantha's breath caught in her throat and the beeping next to her raced wildly along with her rapidly beating heart.

Her gaze flew up and she locked eyes with Max. "Oh my God."

A grim set of his mouth showed off Max's strong jawline and the truth darkened his blue eyes. "They both look like you."

The door opened and a nurse hurried into the room. She hustled to the machine and checked the vital signs screaming their alarm. "Your heart rate is very high. You need to take a few deep breaths for me and try to slow it down." She glanced at Samantha as she spoke in a calm but do-as-I-say voice, and then focused on the number on the machine again.

Samantha tried, but her breaths caught on that damn ball of fear that had tripled in size in the last two minutes. Short huffs of air wheezed from her open mouth and burned her throat. Her lungs shrank and pressure squeezed her chest.

Max covered her cast-free hand with his and squeezed. The heat from his palm warmed her down to her toes and she clung to his fingers like her life depended on it. "Listen to the nurse, Sam. Take a deep breath and try to calm down."

The tone of his voice coupled with the familiarity of his touch felt like something she'd experienced a thousand times instead of only a few, and the nickname… Her heart thundered for new reasons now. Her heart rate slowed and her fear slipped away, but the tightness in her chest remained. She lifted one corner of her mouth and moisture clouded her eyes. But it didn't matter. That name had transported her to another time and place. "No one's called me Sam in a very long time. Not since Robbie's been gone."

The contrast between the tough-as-nails woman and the one now in front of him with tears in her eyes shook his core. Gone was the pigheaded woman who showed no sign of weakness, as well as the woman caught up in the panic of fear. In a matter of seconds, a softness had taken over the normally severe lines of her face and had his heart aching at her vulnerability. Dammit, the woman was intoxicating. The combination was unlike any he'd ever experienced and drew him to her like a moth to a flame. He didn't only want to know what secrets she kept from him, but what made her tick. A connection like this hadn't happened in years, and he yearned to explore it.

Shaking his head, he cleared his throat as well as the ridiculous thoughts running rampant in his head. What he needed was a little more sleep—not complications from a female like a Samantha Gates. Complications that could not only ruin him personally, but professionally. And he'd worked too damn hard for too long to risk everything he'd earned.

He needed to get information from this person and nothing more so he could catch a killer and move on to the next case. "Who's Robbie?"

Even though he kept his voice low, it was enough to snap her back to the moment. Samantha blinked in rapid succession and the tears hovering over the rim of her dark lashes evaporated. The hard edges came back to her face and she pulled her hand from his grasp. The lack of warmth from her small hand left a void in the pit of his stomach.

Clearing his throat, he wiped his palm on the thigh of his pants and asked, "Are you all right?"

"Your vitals are back to normal," the nurse answered for her. Damn, he'd forgotten for a second she was here. "You need to rest. Maybe he can come back later?"

Samantha shook her head and her tangled dark chestnut hair danced around her bruised face. Matted strands stuck to her cheek. "No. I'm fine and we need to finish this conversation."

The nurse squeezed her lips together and raised her overgrown eyebrows. "Fine. But if you have another episode, he'll have to leave."

A heavy silence hung in the room like thick clouds on a rainy day. The nurse gave them each one last look before she stepped out the door and closed it behind her.

Max couldn't tear his eyes from Samantha. The air of professionalism she always carried came back in full force. The haunted shadow that had darkened her eyes when he'd called her Sam was long gone, but his need to understand the change in her clung to him like a burr.

"Who's Robbie?"

"My brother." She pushed the hair from her face, but it rebelled at the movement and fell right back on her cheek when she moved her hand. "No one calls me Sam. It caught me off guard."

That was an understatement. She'd transformed into a whole new woman. The two different sides of her stood in stark contrast to each other, and dammit if he didn't want to know them both. "Does he not call you Sam anymore?"

"No." The word came out small.

He waited for more, but she didn't offer any more information. "Okay. Well, what can you tell me about Richard Pike? Did he ever threaten you?"

"Not in any way that ever made me feel unsafe. He made the common vague threats against the company and anyone associated with it. We were at fault. We provided him a place to find women to stalk. He took no responsibility for his actions. Showed no remorse."

"What about the victims? I can't see any common thread between them. Did he ever mention what drew him to the women he stalked?"

Something flashed across her face. Regret? Annoyance?

"Last year we played around with some new ideas to improve our services. When I first created *Eternal-Match* there were no other dating apps out there. Now they're a dime a dozen and each one is pressing into new territory to make a name for itself. We were about to go forward with our initial public offering, and the pressure was on to come up with something new and exciting to make sure our stock remained valuable."

"What does that have to do with the women victimized by Richard Pike?"

Samantha's gaze darted around the room and landed anywhere but on him. "I had the idea of creating chat rooms dedicated to specialized fantasies. Things people might be too embarrassed to put on their dating profile, or even bring up once they agreed to meet someone. If someone signed up for one of these chat rooms, they had the option of remaining anonymous until they were more comfortable or found someone into the same things as them."

The muscles in Max's stomach clenched. He'd read the file detailing the ways Richard Pike terrorized these women. He hadn't assumed the women's sexual preferences were the common denominator, or that the bastard had used that information for his own sick pleasure.

"Did he befriend them? None of the women mentioned knowing him, not even through a dating app."

Samantha took a deep breath and then doubled over and grabbed her side. "Dammit."

He jumped to his feet and his notepad and pen fell to the ground. He closed the small distance to her bed and gripped the side rails. "What hurts? What happened?"

"My ribs. I'm okay." She straightened, but wasn't able to hide the grimace contorting her delicate features. "We never officially launched the rooms. We sent out a newsletter and asked for volunteers to try a new feature of our site. The response was huge, and we rushed to get in as many people as we could. Not all the safeguards were in place and some things slipped through the cracks." She lifted her gaze and her rounded eyes filled with regret and turned the edges of her brown irises black.

"One of those people was Richard Pike?" He already knew the answer, but had to ask.

She nodded and the tears came back to cloud her irises. Dammit. Right now, he preferred the steel. She sniffed and the hair from her cheek fell across her eye and shielded her face behind a curtain of mangled hair. His fingers itched to push it back. He released his grip on the bed rail and flexed his fingers. Samantha sniffed and he lost all control.

Using the pads of his fingers, he swept the hair back and hooked it behind her neck. The tip of his index finger brushed against her soft skin and her eyes locked on his.

Beep, beep, beep.

The heart monitor beside her sped up, threatening to bring the nurse back to the room. He didn't care. His mouth went dry and he leaned forward; the urge to press his lips to the delicate curve of her neck pulsed through him.

Ring, ring, ring.

His phone chirped and broke the magic of the moment. What the hell was he doing? She was a victim he needed to help, not some chick he'd picked up at a bar for a good time. He dropped his hands and took a step back.

Samantha dropped her gaze to her blanket and smoothed it over her legs. His phone blared into the silence, but he checked the screen. He wanted to roll his eyes at his brother's number flashing there. He'd call him later. Now he needed to collect himself and get the information from Samantha so he could get on with his investigation.

"So Richard Pike was let into this trial run?" He fell back into his seat and picked up the paper and pen from the floor. "Did he meet these women in one of the rooms?"

Samantha kept her focus on the blanket as she spoke.

"No. He hacked into the system and stole the information of the women from one of the rooms. I'm sure you can guess which one." Her voice hitched on the last word.

An image of ropes and binds flashed in his mind. Yeah, he had a good guess. He sucked in a deep breath. "How was none of this in the report?"

"We made sure it was kept quiet. There was no real need for it to be known, and we deleted everything from the test run. It didn't hinder the investigation, and it saved us from a ton of bad press. It might seem harsh, but we needed to protect our assets."

Her admission was like a punch in the gut. She cared more about her damn company than the safety of the public. Maybe she was more like the women in the gilded world he'd grown up with than he'd first thought. Money was all that mattered. "Well, as long as you made your millions I guess things worked out all right. But Richard Pike has a history of targeting women who all have similar tastes just like the murderer I'm trying to find who is targeting women of similar looks." Rage burned hot in his blood and threatened to consume him. He shoved a hand through his hair. "How is this guy even out of jail?"

Samantha bit into her bottom lip. "His lawyer used Richard's agreement to get professional help to lessen his sentence."

He stood and his phone rang once more. Jack's name popped up on the screen.

"I need to take this call and it's important I find Richard Pike and ask him what he's been up to the past week. Is there anything else I need to know about before I go? Any other secrets that could lead to a killer?"

Her gaze lifted and jaw dropped for a second before she snapped it shut. "I have nothing else you need to know."

"Do you still have my card?"

"Yes."

"Call me if you think of anyone else who would want to harm you. Anyone else who's left you with a bad feeling or made you uneasy. I'll be in contact."

He didn't wait for a response as he burst through the door. He'd lost his cool, let her get to him with her vulnerability, and then she'd sucker punched him with the admission of how Richard Pike had stolen the information about his victims.

Dammit, how could she keep that quiet? All to protect her stupid company.

He stormed through the hospital and a blast of cold air streamed in through the automatic doors and smacked against his overheated body. For once, he craved the wind and the snow and the godforsaken cold that could beat down the flames of turmoil and lust Samantha Gates had stirred inside him in less than twenty minutes. He had a job to do, and he wouldn't let Samantha Gates get in his way of doing it. Now he just had to figure out how to protect her without letting her drive him crazy.

The news flashed across the television. The obnoxious voice of the perky reporter blasted into the room. Samantha Gates was expected to make a full recovery from the hit-and-run that had sent her to the hospital early this morning.

Shit!

Slamming a car into her body had been far more satisfying than expected. Not as much as shoving a knife in her black heart…but the rush was still there.

But now the crushing defeat stole any satisfaction away and left an aching need for release. Killing had become a drug, and the fix from earlier had been stolen. Good thing an entire list of potential dates was waiting on the computer. One click, one message, one invitation was all it would take to lure some dumb woman into the trap.

An image invaded the screen. Samantha curled in a ball on the street. But who was standing over her?

You've got to be kidding me! The same detective who'd walked out of her office. He was getting too close. He'd have to go, too. Ideas formed and adrenaline built. If this cop was around so much, the next trap would be two deaths for the price of one. That would make giving Samantha what she deserved well worth the wait.

Chapter 8

"Thanks for coming with me," Max said. "I don't have the energy to do this alone tonight." Max relaxed his death grip from the steering wheel of his police-issued car and rotated his neck to release some tension. He hated driving in New York. The drive from Manhattan to Queens had been long and brutal, but he didn't want to chance taking the subway back to the precinct late at night. The last thing he needed was to find himself stuck underground on the subway due to construction.

Jack cracked his knuckles as he glanced out the window. The strobing light from a streetlamp cast a shadow on his smooth skull. After they'd left the military, Jack had kept the close-cropped cut. "Glad to help. I don't get a chance to do this often enough."

"I'd hate being stuck behind a desk like you." He scanned the darkened sidewalk in front of the apartment building. Jack had tracked down Richard Pike's apartment, as well as his work schedule at a bar in Jackson Heights. He would have rather paid a visit to the guy earlier, but had been forced to wait until Richard was off work.

Jack's husky laugh vibrated inside the heated car. His broad shoulders shook with the movement and he rubbed a palm over the nearly visible light brown skin on the top of his head. "You'd just be pissed you couldn't figure anything out on a computer. You've always sucked with technology. But I have to admit, I'm thinking about switching things up. I need more action—to be out in the thick of things a little more."

"I can't say I blame you. If you want to really get crazy, I'm always looking for a good partner." Max reached for the handle and pushed open the door. "Let's get this over with."

A blast of cool air rushed to meet him and instantly sent a chill to his bones. Light flurries fell from the black sky. Horns honked and someone yelled out of an open window, as the scent of greasy French fries wafted up his nose and made his stomach growl. He'd worked through dinner, and the diner across the street mocked him with the pictures of dancing corn dogs and smiling waffle fries.

He skirted around the front of the car and met Jack on the sidewalk. They walked shoulder to shoulder— the width of them dominating the sidewalk—and Max pulled open the door to the shabby brick-faced building. A cloud of cigarette smoke hung in the stairwell. Someone must have thought it was too cold to step outside, but didn't want the stale smoke to linger in their own apartment. He coughed to expel the smoke from his lungs, and then held his breath as he jogged up to the second floor.

Music blared through the thin door of 2B. Max pounded on the scarred door. The thin wood rattled beneath his knuckles. No noise broke through the screeching music and Max glanced over at Jack, who shrugged. Max knocked again, applying just a bit more pressure than before so his fist wouldn't break through the wood. Heavy footsteps shook the dirty floor beneath their feet.

The door opened and the sound waves of whatever boomed from the stereo rained over him. "Can I help you?"

The man who opened the door had a thinner face and more facial hair than the picture in the file he had studied. The hair was a little longer, but still had the disheveled look of someone fresh from bed, even though every tousled blond strand was meticulously placed. The hazel eyes sparked with interest as he stood in the doorway, blocking the view of his apartment.

Max had his badge ready in his hand. "I'm Detective Green and this is Detective Stone," he said, nodding toward Jack.

Richard's eyes widened and he took one step back, his hand never leaving the round doorknob. "Why are you here?"

"We just have a couple of questions for you. Do you mind if we step inside?" Max asked the question, but he took one step forward to show Richard he didn't have much of a choice.

What Richard lacked in height he made up for in width. He straightened his shoulders and tried a pathetic attempt to make himself bigger.

It didn't work.

"What's this about?" Richard glanced past them around the dimly lit hallway.

"Like my friend said, we just have a few questions for you. I think we'd all be more comfortable inside."

Please, God. The haze of smoke had penetrated Max's brain, leaving him light-headed.

"Fine. But I've only got a few minutes." Richard turned and walked to the old stereo sitting on the laminate counter in the kitchen.

Max followed Jack inside and shut the door behind them. The music cut off, but the thud of a bass from the apartment next door beat against the wall. The musty scent of the old cigarette smoke stayed outside the apartment, but a new scent assaulted his nostrils. Like a wet dog had shaken itself dry and left the residual water clinging to every surface in the suffocating space. Max's gaze scanned the living room and kitchen. No clutter clogged the counter and no stray bits of dirt littered the old shag carpet. The cleanliness stood in stark contrast to the rest of the disgusting apartment building.

"I haven't done anything wrong. You can call my parole officer and ask him." Richard planted his bare feet into the cracked kitchen floor and folded his arms across his chest. The defiant set of his mouth added an edge to his looks. Richard didn't appear the slimeball Max had expected. He had blond surfer-boy looks a lot of women would find attractive. He had to make a killing in tips tending bar. As long as he kept his disturbing tastes to himself.

Jack stood in front of Richard and mimicked his pose. A laugh threatened to gurgle up Max's throat. Richard looked like a child trying to intimidate a much bigger, much stronger big brother. He coughed and pushed the laugh down, fixing a don't-mess-with-me snarl on his face. "Where were you Monday night?"

"Working. I work most nights. Except Saturdays and Sundays."

"Do you have someone to vouch for you?" Jack asked.

Richard's eyes turned to slits and his hands balled into fists under his biceps. "I can give you my boss's number."

"Okay," Max said. "What about this morning?"

"Sleeping. And no, there's no one to vouch for that."

Max nodded. "Write down your boss's number for us." He'd call. If Richard really was working on the nights of the murders, he'd be at a dead end.

The muscles above Richard's mouth twitched, but he grabbed a pen and paper from a drawer and scribbled on it. He thrust it toward Jack, who folded it and put it in his pocket. Max took one last glance around the apartment and his eyes landed on a backpack sitting on the floor beside the threadbare sofa. Frayed rope spilled from the top of the unzipped bag. His blood turned cold.

"Been doing some rope climbing lately?" His voice was as ice-cold as the winter blast in the Arctic.

Jack sucked in a sharp breath.

Richard marched across the room, bent over and zipped the bag shut. He stood to face them and his pale skin flushed red. "What if I have? I let you in here didn't I? I wouldn't have done that if I had something to hide. Now I think it's time for you to leave."

Jack caught Max's eye and held his gaze. He raised his brows in a way that could only mean one thing. It was time to go.

"I'll be calling your boss to check your alibi. If I find

out you lied to us, you can expect another visit. And next time, you won't be able to get rid of us so easily."

Max strode to the door and yanked it open, the ancient wood creaking on the rusted hinges. He walked into the cloud of smoke in the stairwell and pounded down the steps as fast as his legs could carry him. Pushing the glass door open, he inhaled deeply and the frost of the air stung his lungs.

A hand slapped down on his back. "Sorry, man. It would have been easier to have found your man right here and now, but we both know these things never work that way."

Dammit. Jack was right. What had he expected? Richard to confess to murder? He'd been around the block long enough. That never happened. He opened his mouth to speak, but his phone vibrated against his thigh. He grabbed it and held it to his ear. "Green here."

"You're needed in the Bronx." His boss's voice boomed through the speaker.

"What? Why?"

"There's been another murder. I'll send you the details. Head over there now."

Shit!

He disconnected, shoved his phone in his pocket, and met Jack's creased brow and narrowed eyes. "Want to go to the Bronx?"

Sunlight streamed through the gauzy curtains in the living room and landed directly on Samantha's face. Every muscle in her body hurt, as if she'd run twenty miles in a pair of stilettos, but she couldn't give in to the fatigue weighing her down. Someone was trying to kill her, and she needed to figure out who.

Sitting on the plush sofa in the living room, she balanced her computer on her lap and searched for information regarding a murdered woman at Columbia University. A picture of the woman Detective Green had shown her at the hospital dominated the screen along with an article detailing her death. She scanned the words for a date.

Emily Steele had been murdered last week. Before Jose was released from prison.

Questions spun in her foggy brain, and she picked up the letter she'd been sent to notify her of Jose's release. She grabbed her phone and called the number listed in the right-hand corner. If Jose was in jail when the first murder happened, could he still have had a hand in orchestrating the whole thing? The person she'd be contacting at the Department of Justice might not have the answers she sought, but maybe she'd be given the name of someone who did.

"Department of Justice. How can I assist you?"

"Hello," Samantha said. "I need information regarding a man who was released a few days ago. I have the notification of release right here. Jose Diaz."

"I'm afraid I can't offer you more information than what's already been sent in the letter." The woman's words held a hint of annoyance, as if calls like this were a normal, and unwanted, occurrence.

"What if it's a matter of personal safety? I need to find out if this man is a risk to me or my family."

The woman sighed. "If he was deemed a risk, he wouldn't have been released. But the prison he was released from would have more specific information. My advice? Call a lawyer and get into contact with the warden."

"Thank you." She disconnected then did a quick search for contact information for the prison Jose had been locked up in. If the warden wouldn't speak with her, she'd take the woman's advice and call her lawyer to help navigate the red tape. After locating the number, she put it in her phone.

Ding-dong.

Samantha strained her ears for who was at her door. Laurie would answer it, but hopefully her trusty assistant could get rid of whoever it was.

"Ms. Gates is not expecting company today." Laurie's stern voice seeped through the closed French doors. As much as she hated to mesh her two lives together, she couldn't stop working and she couldn't go into the office. So Laurie had come to her house instead. She'd set up in the kitchen without complaint, and had been busy ever since.

Samantha sighed and disconnected the call before anyone answered the line. The conversation would have to wait until she dealt with whoever had shown up at her house in the middle of the day.

"It's important we see her. We need to make sure she's okay."

She cringed. Only one person on Samantha's radar could inflict so much self-righteous condescension into two small sentences. And he was as far on the edge of that radar as she could possibly keep him.

Teddy.

The French doors flew open and Teddy breezed into the room. His wife, Margo, glided behind him as if the wind stream from his entrance carried her in. A deep part had been cut into the top of his hair, much farther to the side than his natural hairline. His lean swimmer's body was the perfect frame to show off the deep blue custom-made suit. The lighter blue tie around his neck was the exact same shade as his eyes—which were as sharp as the tongue he often used when he didn't get his way.

Margo with her bountiful blond waves cascading down her back stayed close behind him. At least worry filled her wide green eyes. She kept one hand clasped around Teddy's biceps and her heels staggered as his brisk pace carried her forward.

Teddy's eyes connected to Samantha's and he came to a dead stop, sending Margo crashing into his back. "You look like death. Are you wearing pajamas?"

Dammit, she couldn't stop the curve of her lips. She straightened against the plush back of the sofa and tried to keep the smile in place so a grimace wouldn't take over. Leave it to Teddy to tell her the truth about her appearance after being run down in the street. Love him or hate him, Teddy didn't mince words. "It's nice to see you, too. What are you doing here?"

Margo fluttered to Teddy's side like a baby bird unsure of its wings. "We had to see for ourselves that you were okay. My God, you could have been killed."

Samantha turned a genuine smile at Margo. No matter how much hostility simmered between her and Teddy, Margo had never shown her anything but kindness. Samantha missed her friendship with Margo, but Teddy didn't want his wife spending time with her after she refused to let him back into the company. As much as she'd tried to stay in contact with the other woman, Teddy's resentment had made it impossible for them to remain as close as they'd been in college. "As you can see, I'm fine. I just need a little rest."

"Exactly, you need rest. So why is your assistant here? You shouldn't be working."

The hairs on the back of her neck prickled as if a huff of cold breath had been blown on her skin. She shouldn't be surprised. It wasn't beneath Teddy to use her near-death experience as a way to try to weasel back into her company.

"I'm fine. I can work from home, and Laurie is here to help. Not to mention James. I have a village watching over me, so no need to worry." Margo winced at her harsh tone, but Samantha didn't care. She couldn't dance around the issue with Teddy. He'd take any opportunity presented to try to get his way.

He took a step closer and his sorry attempt at a smile twisted his lips into a snarl. His expensive cologne engulfed her nose and memories of college assaulted her senses. Not because they were bad…most of them were damn good…but because they were built on lies.

"Let me help you. No one knows the business better than I do. You can't do this alone right now."

A brittle laugh escaped her parched throat. "Absolutely not. You tried to sneak your way back in to *EternalMatch* before our public offering just so you could cash in. No way I'm letting you back in now. Not after everything you did."

Teddy didn't try to hide his disdain behind his well-honed mask of innocence. His cobalt eyes blazed with fury. "You mean after I helped you come up with the idea and work out the logistics?"

She met his glare with one of her own. "No. I mean when you refused to put up any money or do the actual work to get the company off the ground. You bailed because it wasn't worth the risk, and then came running back when things looked good. I won't let you latch on to something you turned your back on and bleed it dry for your own personal benefit. I've worked my ass off for this company and I won't see you ruin it."

"You wouldn't have a damn thing if it weren't for me. You'd still be penniless and living in the South Bronx, trying to keep your head above water."

"As much as I'm interested in hearing the rest of this conversation, I'm going to have to stop you right there and find out more about how Samantha used to live in the South Bronx."

The deep, gravelly voice made her stomach drop and nerves dance with anticipation at the same time. Laurie had been given instructions to let Detective Green in, but Samantha wished she had a heads-up that he was here. After their conversation yesterday, she'd hoped she wouldn't have to see Max again for a while. So why was her heart flapping around in her chest at the sight of his crystal-blue eyes and muscled body stepping into the room? He came to a stop beside Teddy, and his dark looks and leather jacket made Teddy look like a school-boy in the middle of a temper tantrum.

She took in the grown-out whiskers on his jaw and swallowed the pool of saliva in her mouth. "What are you doing here?"

"You and I need to talk. Now." The hard tone of his voice combined with the worry in his eyes made her shiver.

"Excuse me, but who the hell are you?" Teddy half turned toward Max and tried to look down his thin nose at him, but Max's equal height made it impossible.

"I'm Detective Max Green with the NYPD, and I need to speak with Ms. Gates alone."

So they were back to Ms. Gates? Gone was the compassionate man who'd held her hand and calmed her fear. A stab of disappointment pierced her already tender ribs.

"That's too damn bad, Detective. We're discussing something more important than whatever the hell you need." Margo pulled on Teddy's hand, but he yanked it away and shot daggers at Max.

"Well, unless it's more important than the case I'm working, I suggest you get the hell out of here. Ms. Gates can call you later."

Margo stepped up beside Teddy and her baby-doll mouth formed a perfect O shape. She blinked her unnaturally long lashes up at Max. "A case? Why would you need to talk to Samantha about that?"

His gaze stayed glued on her and she fought the urge to straighten her tousled hair. "Because she might have more answers for me than she realizes."

Chapter 9

A tug of satisfaction yanked at her ego as she watched Teddy's retreating form leave her house. She wished she could send Teddy away like the annoying rodent he was as easily as Max had. But he'd always managed to fester around her feet until she'd be forced to give him a swift kick in the ass. The door slammed shut and she forced her attention back to Max.

"What do you mean? What else could I possibly have to tell you?" Samantha smoothed imaginary wrinkles from her silk pajamas. If she would have known her town house would be freaking Grand Central Terminal today, she would have put something more respectable on.

Max clasped his hands behind his back and strode around the perimeter of the room. He skirted around the baby grand piano in the corner and ran a long, slender finger along the ivory keys. The sound bounced off the high ceiling and a smile lifted her lips.

He pulled his hand away and reconnected it to the other still lingering at the small of his back. "Another woman was murdered last night."

His words slapped the smile from her face. His casual tone and leisurely surveillance of the room had her mind searching for an appropriate response.

None came.

She sat on the couch and gripped the soft material so hard her fingernails threatened to puncture the fabric. A ripple of pain shot up her side, and she grabbed a throw pillow and held it against her to ease the pain the way the nurse had shown her.

"Where was she found?" Her small voice trembled and dread drenched her like the wailing gusts of a hurricane.

"Outside a nail salon in Melrose."

He wanted to question her about living in the South Bronx.

Every ounce of energy left her body and she swayed. Thank God she hadn't tried to get up. She squeezed her eyes shut and scenes played in her mind like pictures from a horror movie. She'd give anything for them to go away, but they'd branded themselves in her brain.

The darkness around her grew darker, as if something blocked the sun pouring in from the window. A source of heat radiated in front of her and chased the chill of her memories away.

But not the memories. Never the memories.

Light pressure on her knees dipped them down and helped to steady her. She opened her eyes and found Max's probing gaze right in front of her. He'd crouched down and placed his large palms on her kneecaps. His dark eyebrows almost met at the top of his nose and concern tightened the skin around his eyes.

His warm breath caressed her cheeks and his eyes searched hers. "What are you not telling me?"

She flinched at his words. Not because of the accusation, but the kindness and worry behind it. She didn't want to answer him. She didn't want to let him into the past she tried like hell to bury and leave behind. Dammit, for the first time in fifteen years all she wanted was for someone to wrap their arms around her and comfort her. After all this time, why did she want that comfort from Max? His reaction to her yesterday proved he'd not only never understand the decisions she'd made in her life, but he'd judge her for them.

Summoning all the strength left in her battered body, she pushed herself up and sidestepped away from the magnetic force field that drew her to him. The soft rug cushioned her bare feet and she grazed her fingertips along the side of the couch to steady herself. She kept her gaze fixed on the hot-pink polish on her toes. Here she was again. Trying to maneuver her way through a minefield. Which answers would give him what he needed and which ones would blow up in her face?

"I grew up in Melrose."

"Tough place for a kid." He straightened to his full height, but didn't attempt to move closer to her.

She laughed and it came out as brittle as glass. "That neighborhood was a tough place for anyone. I hated it so much. It's improved in the last few years, but for me, it will always be the place I wanted to escape."

"You've certainly moved up in the world." Again, the kindness in his voice caught her off guard. He was easier to deal with when condemnation coated his words. Silence hung between them for a beat before he asked, "Do a lot of people know you grew up there?"

"No. I've tried very hard to keep my past behind me. I don't want it to be another source of entertainment for people to discuss."

He took a step toward her and let his hands drop to his sides. "Why? We all have a past. Good or bad, it's what shapes us into who we are."

She crinkled her nose up at his clichéd words. "Spoken like someone with nothing but sunshine and rainbows in their rearview mirror."

"That's about as far from the truth as you could get," he said as he cupped his chin with his palm and chuckled. "But that's a story for another time. Right now, I need to know why the killer left a body in Melrose, besides the fact that you grew up there. Maybe it was a way of telling us they know a lot more about you than we thought."

Bile slid up the back of her throat and coated her tongue. "What was the name of the nail salon?" Not like it mattered. Hell, the place that held so many nightmares for her could have exchanged hands a dozen times. A dead body in Melrose was a message no matter where it was, but it couldn't be a coincidence if it was beside a nail salon. And if it was the same one...

Max grabbed a notepad from the inside pocket of his jacket and flipped through the pages. *"Polish Me Pretty."*

Her knees buckled and her vision blurred. Beads of perspiration broke out at the base of her neck. She reached her hand out to grab hold of the back of the couch, but her stupid cast banged against the tufted material. Her body swayed toward the ground and she tensed her muscles to brace for the inevitable crash.

Two strong arms encircled her waist and scooped her back to her feet. Samantha clung to his jacket and the supple material bunched in her tight fist. Tears clouded her already blurred vision and she buried her head in Max's shoulder. She couldn't fight her attraction to him right now—didn't want to. All she wanted were his strong arms around her, keeping her safe from the past barreling into her present. Her heart beat so hard against her chest, it threatened to break through her sternum.

"You're okay. I've got you." Max's hand skimmed up her spine, under her sheet of hair, and cupped the back of her head. His thumb swiped back and forth against the wispy hairs on her neck. Sweat probably coated his finger, but she didn't care.

"I'm sorry." She attempted to pull away, but he kept her firmly rooted against his hard body. Her broken wrist hung at her side, and she loosened her hold of his jacket with her other hand. Flattening her palm, she slid her fingers underneath the leather and pressed the heel of her hand against his beating heart.

"Just give yourself a minute." A beat passed with only the sound of his heavy breath against her ear. Finally, he asked, "Tell me about the salon?"

She pressed her forehead against his chest and squeezed her eyes shut. She had to tell him. "My brother was killed outside that nail salon fifteen years ago." The words rubbed against her dry throat like sandpaper, and she tensed as she waited for his response.

His hand dropped from her head and both arms came around her again. He tightened his hold and crushed her against him. Her ribs screamed, her heart ached, her mind raced…but she pushed everything away and melted against him. She let the tears in her eyes course down her cheeks and let this big, pain-in-the-ass man who was hunting down a killer comfort her in a way no one ever had.

A light tap on the open French doors had her lifting her head, but Max still refused to let her go. Laurie stood in the doorway with wide eyes and her bottom lip sandwiched between her front teeth. "Sorry to interrupt, Ms. Gates, but your mother is here."

Samantha transformed from a puddle of weeping mush to a rigid ball of tension in seconds. Anger ripped through him. Anger at himself for once again falling victim to her softer side and forgetting to conduct himself in a strictly professional way. And anger at her for obviously not wanting her mom to find her in his arms. It shouldn't ding his pride. Hell, she was nothing to him—at least that was the lie he kept telling himself. But her rejection sent him right back to the pain and humiliation of the woman he once loved turning her back on him.

She pushed away from him, but he refused to let her go. Her head jerked up to stare at him with pleading eyes and he tipped his lips up in a tight smile.

"Samantha! Who in the world are you holding on to, and why are you still in your pajamas? Either your boss is too lenient or you are doing a poor job with your work." A woman with dark hair swept into a tight bun breezed into the room with an older woman following along behind her.

Samantha's eyelids fluttered closed as if in silent prayer. She inhaled a deep breath and tried to hide the pain that twisted the muscles in her face. When she opened her eyes, the raw pain that melted her irises to black stole his breath and he dropped his arms to his sides. She staggered to the side before she straightened her spine, fixed a smile on her face and turned to meet the women.

"Hi, Mama. How are you? I didn't expect you this morning."

The woman behind Samantha's mom flinched and mouthed, "Sorry."

Max's gaze flickered from one woman to another. What the hell was going on?

A sharp gasp rang around the room and Samantha's mom hurried to her. "What happened to your hand? And your beautiful face is covered in bruises."

Samantha curled her hands into her mom's. "I'm okay. I was in a little accident, but it's no big deal."

"Why didn't you call me? Does Robbie know?"

Questions sprang to Max's mind faster than he could keep up. Wasn't Robbie the name of the brother who'd been killed? And why hadn't Samantha told her mom she'd been hit by a car and had spent the night in the hospital? Not to mention the fact that someone was trying to kill her. His own mother might drive him crazy sometimes, but there was no way he'd keep such important details from her.

"I called Mrs. Walsh and let her know I was fine. I didn't want you to worry." She nodded toward the other woman—Mrs. Walsh he assumed—and an understanding smile curved her lips.

"What about this man? Who is he and why is he disturbing you at work? You really should be busy cleaning this place, though why you're in your pajamas is beyond me."

Samantha glanced at him and uncertainty danced in her eyes like a flame through a shadow. An urge to help her swept over him, but he didn't know what was happening. His first assumption had been dead wrong. He couldn't trust his instinct when it came to Samantha.

She faced her mom again and said, "He's a friend."

Her mom's face wrinkled at the word and she spared him a glance. Pursed lips, narrowed eyes, obvious disapproval. "You shouldn't have friends bothering you at work." She drew out the word *friends* as if it were made up of three syllables instead of one.

Samantha circled the thick cast at her wrist with her good hand and twisted it back and forth as if trying to take off the hunk of plaster.

Screw it. He might make the wrong move, but he had to do something. She needed his help and he needed to move things along so he could talk to Samantha about the investigation. He wanted to hear more about her brother, and she still had to tell him about the asshole who'd been here earlier. He took a step toward her mom and extended his hand. "It's so nice to finally meet you. Samantha's talked about you a lot over the past month that we've been seeing each other."

A light brightened her dark eyes, and Max focused on that instead of the scowl on Samantha's face and the openmouthed shock from Mrs. Walsh. Samantha's mom brushed past her and wrapped her arms around him. "It's so nice to meet you. Please call me Maria. Samantha has never introduced me to a man she's dated before."

He cut his gaze to Samantha and the ashen panic on

her heart-shaped face had him doubting his decision. Maria released her death grip on him and, dammit, she had tears in her eyes when she stepped back.

He rubbed the sweat from the back of his neck and tried not to stutter from the fear the situation evoked in him. Hell, he'd rather face the barrel of a loaded gun than the teary eyes of a woman he'd just lied to. He had to get her out of here. "I'm Max. I needed to speak with Samantha about something important, and then I'll get out of her hair. I hate to be rude, but could you and your friend possibly come back another time? I need to get back to work, but can't until Samantha and I clear something up first."

"Yes, Mama, why don't you two head home and I'll come to see you soon. I promise."

Maria flashed him a wide smile and her head bobbed up and down like a fishing lure in the water. "Okay. I hope to see you again soon, Max. It was so nice to meet you. And, Samantha, you hurry this up so you can get back to work." She gave her daughter a kiss on the forehead, looped her arm through the crook of Mrs. Walsh's elbow and turned to walk through the foyer and out the front door.

Samantha whirled to face him and pressed a finger to his chest. "What the hell is the matter with you? You have no idea what you did."

Chapter 10

Samantha pinched the bridge of her nose and her lips twisted into a grimace. "I need a glass of wine, but I'll settle for coffee. Let's go to the kitchen." Her voice lacked the bite he'd expected, as if she'd swum a hundred laps and didn't have the strength to put more energy than necessary into her words.

"I don't know what just happened, but I'd kill for a glass of scotch." Her undignified snort brought a smile to his lips, and he followed close behind her through the French doors and around the corner to the kitchen. He doubted she'd offer the stiff drink, and Lord knew he'd need more than the pungent alcohol to erase the feel of Samantha in his arms—her small frame pressed against his body.

A low whistle vibrated his bottom lip, and Samantha's assistant glanced up from her computer. She sat at a dark cherrywood island that ran the length of the narrow kitchen, the light marble top mimicking the color of the cabinets. Stainless steel appliances gleamed from the sun shining through the window and a rustic chandelier above the table in the corner added a touch of charm. But the focal point was the fireplace, made from the same smooth wood as the island, on the far wall.

He'd kill to have a fireplace in his apartment and wished he could turn it on, but his quick perusal didn't spot a switch. He couldn't test his manhood by attempting to build a fire himself in the wood-burning fireplace. Not to mention, the addition of a romantic fire was the last thing he needed at the moment.

Samantha stopped beside the island and rested her palms on top of the counter, leaning her weight against it. "You can head home, Laurie. Some things came up, and I won't get much work done for the rest of the day."

The sheen of the marble counter reflected off Laurie's blue eyes as she studied Samantha. "Are you sure? I can stay."

Samantha shook her head and her thick, wavy hair whirled around her face. The little bit of natural texture gave her hair volume that her normally iron-straight hair lacked. His fingers itched to run through it. Instead, he shrugged his jacket off and draped it over his arm.

"I'll call if I need you. Thanks for coming today. I might need you here tomorrow. It just depends on how I feel in the morning." Emotion made her words heavy.

Laurie nodded while she packed her things. She lifted her bag and started toward the door that led God knew where in this maze of a house. "Okay. I'll see you tomorrow."

His gaze slid down the tidy counter until he spotted the coffeepot. He threw his coat on the back of one of the stools in front of the island. "Why don't you sit and fill me in on why your mom thought you were the cleaning lady while I make the coffee?"

Samantha hoisted herself onto a stool and he opened the cabinet above the coffeepot in search of the grounds. Bingo. He grabbed a bag of gourmet beans from the cabinet and glanced over his shoulder at her. "Do you have any beans already ground?"

"In the freezer." She rested her elbows on the counter and dropped her chin in her hand. "I can't believe you told my mom we were dating."

"I can't believe you didn't tell your mom you were hit by a car," he returned. He put the bag back in the cabinet, opened the freezer and took out the preground beans. "And didn't you mention yesterday your brother's name was Robbie? Why did she ask if you'd told him about the accident?"

Samantha's heavy sigh had him casting her a quick glance before he placed the grounds in the filter and filled the machine with water.

"Robbie's death broke my mom. She couldn't accept it, and her grip on reality is…tenuous."

The emotion in her voice punched him in the gut. He couldn't imagine dealing with the loss of his brother, even if he could be a dick, and then to lose your parent in a completely different way. "How old were you when he died?"

"Seventeen. He was my younger brother by four years. He followed me everywhere." A soft chuckle hummed through her words. "It used to drive me crazy. I'd give anything to have him back."

The fancy Italian coffee maker chugged to life and

he faced her, pressing his back against the hard edge of the counter and crossing his arms over his chest. "It had to be hard as hell."

She nodded. "It never gets easier. Especially when my mom brings him up as if he's still here. I've brought in a number of specialists, but anything she's tried has just made it worse. She refuses to take any more medication. Mrs. Walsh, the woman who was here with her, lives with her a few blocks away. We try to keep things as calm and familiar as possible. Change upsets her."

"So, she doesn't realize this is your house?"

"Sometimes she does. Sometimes a tiny glimpse of the woman who raised me comes back and she understands what I've done with my life and what's really going on. But most the time, she thinks I'm still the same girl who helped her clean houses to pay the rent on our crappy apartment. It's too hard to correct her all the time, so we just let her believe what she wants. I don't know if it's the right thing to do, but it's the easiest. I owe it to her to make her life as easy as possible."

"What does that mean? Why would you owe her that?"

Samantha bit into her bottom lip and color flooded her face. Max's instincts rose higher than the Empire State Building. She was still hiding something from him. He wanted to press her, but there were more important things to discuss right now.

When it was clear she wasn't going to answer his question, he asked another. "Who was the douchebag here earlier?"

The muscles in her face relaxed a little, but tension still remained. "Theodore Van Buren and his wife, Margo. He goes by Teddy."

"And he used to work with you?" No more water dripped into the pot behind him, so he turned and grabbed two mugs from the cabinet. Filling them both to the top, he carried them to the island, set one in front of Samantha and cradled the other in his hands. Heat seeped through the black ceramic mug, but he didn't mind.

Samantha took a sip of her coffee and wrinkled her nose. "Can you grab me the creamer from the fridge?"

"I should say no, but I can't refuse someone who's had such a rough day."

"Gee, thanks." She ran the pad of her finger around the edge of her cup as she waited for him to get the cream. "Teddy, Margo and I went to college together. Teddy and I studied computer science and worked on the concept of *EternalMatch* for a class project. We decided it could work in real life, but when it was time to invest time and money into the program, he bailed."

He handed her the bottle of liquid sugar he'd taken from the fridge and settled onto the stool beside her. "He didn't think it was worth the risk?"

She poured the cream into her coffee and the color went from black to tan. A shudder rippled through him and he took a sip of his own black coffee. He'd never understand the point of drinking coffee that tasted nothing like actual coffee.

"He's a spoiled brat and he's never had to work a day in his life. He didn't want to spend time developing the app. He wanted me to do the work and he wanted the credit, and I should have been honored someone like him would want to even be linked to someone like me."

Annoyance flared hot in his gut. Teddy was exactly the kind of person he steered clear of, and Samantha was…well, she was unlike anyone he'd ever met before. The combination of strong, self-made billionaire and at times soft, vulnerable woman enchanted him to the core. A feeling that left him helpless toward her charms and pissed him off at the same time. Being charmed by a woman like Samantha Gates was the last thing he needed, but dammit, he couldn't help it. "Sounds like a real peach."

She snorted again. "He's an ass."

He couldn't peel his eyes from her. Damn, she was cute as hell when she let her guard down. With her pajamas and messy hair and letting go of the air of professionalism that intimidated him. "What happened with the public offering?"

Samantha lifted her face and stared at him and the wheels turning in her head showed in her dark brown eyes. "*EternalMatch* had been successful for several years before the public offering. Teddy would come into my office once in a while and try to sweet-talk his way in. He wanted to work on new projects, or help develop new aspects of *EternalMatch*. I wouldn't allow it. Each time he'd come in, he'd be angrier. I see him and Margo at a lot of charity events, and it'd get more and more awkward every time. Things blew up before the public offering. He found out about it and wanted in before it happened so he could cash in."

"I'm sure he was pissed when the stock shot up and you made billions."

"That's an understatement."

The heat from the cup finally pierced through his

skin and he set his mug on the counter. He kept his gaze locked on Samantha's and asked, "Pissed enough to kill you?"

A biting chill swept up her spine and Samantha took a sip of hot coffee to beat it back. The sweet liquid slid down her throat. "Teddy is a lot of things, but a murderer isn't one of them."

Max's raised brows expressed his doubt clearer than anything he could say. "Are you sure about that?"

Her mind raced. Could she be sure of anything? Three days ago she was sure she'd never be in this situation. She measured her words carefully as she spoke. "Teddy knows a lot about me. About my past and my present. He hates not getting his way, and he can be vindictive. But murder?" She shook her head as the possibility washed over her like chunks of ice from a hailstorm.

"Has he ever been aggressive toward you? Scared you in any way? What about his wife? Do you know if he's ever been abusive?" He hurled the questions at her, each one hitting her like a piece of shrapnel.

The coffee in her stomach churned and she pushed her mug to the side. "I don't know much about his personal life. I see him a handful of times a year. Margo a little more because we serve on numerous charity boards together. She's never hinted at troubles in their marriage. He's never been forceful with me. He talks more about getting lawyers involved than getting his hands dirty."

"I know the type," Max said.

She tilted her head and studied him. Did he? Here she was spilling her life story to him—or most of it—

and she didn't know a damn thing about him. "Really? You don't seem like the kind of guy who'd spend time with people like Teddy."

"I didn't say I spend time with them—I said I know them."

She waited for him to elaborate, but he remained tight-lipped. He wasn't the one being hunted down by a criminal they needed to find. "Touché."

Max reached into his pocket for his phone and pulled up a picture. "I'm sure this follows pattern, but do you know a Stacy Rodriguez?"

Samantha glanced at the screen and a lead ball dropped in her gut. "No. Did she use *EternalMatch*?" The answer to her question was obvious, but she needed him to tell her.

"Yes."

The lead ball pulled her insides toward the floor. "Have you found the profile of the man she met last night, or do you need me to find him?"

"We already did. Just like with the other men, it was a dummy account. We can't figure out who these profiles belong to or where the person is logging into their computer. My buddy Jack is the best computer guy we've got and he's working his ass off to figure it out. But if there was any other clue, any piece of information you could give us to point us in the right direction, it could be huge."

"What else could there be? I swear, I'm telling you everything I can."

A beat of silence pulsed between them when a gleam of enlightenment sparked in his eyes. "Who killed your brother?"

All the air left her lungs and she gasped for breath.

The pain in her ribs be damned, she needed to suck in the air as quickly as possible to keep from passing out. An image of Jose invaded her mind. Dark hair with unruly waves crashing around his chiseled face, dimples that flashed whenever he smiled at her, a desperate desire to escape the life they had in the South Bronx.

The picture of the boy she loved vanished and was replaced by the angry young man sitting in the courtroom. A man sentenced to years in jail for punishment of a crime he'd never meant to commit. A crime that stole the life of her brother.

Raw emotion burned her esophagus and she struggled to clear her throat. "Jose Diaz." After so many years of keeping his identity hidden in her heart, saying his name was like a speaking in a foreign language, the letters clumsy on her tongue.

"Was he charged with murder?" Max's soothing tone was like a balm on her frayed nerves.

"Manslaughter."

The pupils in Max's eyes dilated as the impact of her words sank in. "Sam, is he still in jail?"

"No. He was released the same day Linda Hoyt's body was found." Her whispered words were louder than any bomb.

"What? Why the hell didn't you tell me this?" Max exploded from his chair. "Have you had contact with him? Would he want to harm you or seek revenge? How did he kill your brother?"

Samantha hunched her shoulders forward and tried to crawl into herself…to disappear. It didn't work. "I was getting my nails done and Jose came to get me. I didn't know he planned on robbing the salon. My brother came to find me, and when he walked in Jose panicked and the gun went off. It all happened so fast."

Max stopped his frantic pacing and his jaw dropped. "You were there?"

She nodded and fought to keep her composure. "Yes. I testified against Jose. That's the last time I've seen him."

"Shit." Max tunneled a hand through his hair, and mumbled sounds poured through his mouth. "I've got to find him. Dammit, Sam. This is huge. Why the hell didn't you say anything? I've been chasing my tail with dead-end leads with Richard Pike and asking questions about Teddy when this whole time you had a giant skeleton dancing around in your closet."

Anger boiled her blood. She had enough of his judgment. "He was in prison, Max. He wasn't released until the morning the second body was found and he was sitting in a cell when the first woman was murdered. And how could he have followed me? Known where I'd be yesterday? It doesn't make sense, and I can't have this leaked to anyone. My name...my mom's name... we can't go through it all again." Her voice broke and tears closed her throat.

"I'll keep this quiet, but I have to talk to him. He might have hired someone, or hell, some pissed off relative of his could have taken it upon themselves to make you pay for putting him in jail."

She dropped her head in her hands. "I had the same thoughts. I called the Department of Justice this morning, and the woman I spoke with said I needed to speak with the warden. I didn't get a chance to call before Teddy stormed in. But I...I can't believe Jose is behind this."

Max stared at her with hard eyes and an opened mouth.

She wrapped her arms over her middle, not knowing how to explain the conflicting emotions Jose still stirred in her gut.

"I have to go." Max strode toward the doorway of the kitchen that led to the foyer, his strides fast and furious.

She staggered off the stool and followed behind him as quickly as she could. Her mind raced with a million possibilities. Her bare foot touched down on the wooden floor of the foyer.

Crash!

She whipped her head toward the broken window that faced the street. Glass shattered to the floor and something flew into the newly formed hole.

"Get back!"

Max's yell barely penetrated her brain before he scooped her over his shoulder and ran in the opposite direction. He reached the carpeted floor of the living room and leaped through the air. They crashed behind the couch and pain shot through her body.

Boom!

A loud explosion pierced her eardrums. The lights flickered and plaster poured down from the ceiling. Max's hard body crashed down on her. Silence filled the heavy air and Samantha squeezed her eyes closed and waited for this nightmare to end.

Chapter 11

The gentle skim of strong hands brushed against her arms, her hair, her face. She waited for her body to scream out in agony, but instead adrenaline from the heat of those hands zipped through her veins.

"Sam? Can you hear me? Open your eyes."

She tried to smile at the long-forgotten nickname, but the muscles in her face wouldn't cooperate. The sound of the once familiar name on Max's lips wrapped around her like a warm hug. But why were his hands on her body? Not that she was complaining. It'd been a long time since a man had touched her. She just didn't understand how he'd gone from irritated with her to running his strong hands over her body so quickly.

A sharp stab pierced her side and her bones ached. Pain slammed against her skull. Max didn't change the pressure of his hands on her skin, but his touch morphed from a heart-pounding caress she craved to a fierce frisking of her tender arms.

A loud buzz vibrated her eardrums and she cracked open her eyelids. Nausea pitched high in her stomach. Smoke clouded her vision and she blinked to clear the bits of dust from the crumbling plaster out of her burning eyes. Panic puckered the lines of Max's face and he was so close she could see the tiny flecks of green that rimmed his sea-blue irises.

Something thick and dry coated her throat and she coughed to free it from her mouth. "What happened?" The words scraped her throat like razor blades.

Max's mouth moved and distant sounds came out as if caught in the rapid waves of a storm. She wrinkled her nose and leaned closer. He cupped her face with his hands and pressed his lips close to her ear. "Are you okay? We need to get out of here."

His warm breath tickled her ear and heated her blood. Her eyes searched his and her mind went into overdrive to put together the missing pieces of the last few minutes. "I'm fine, but I think I passed out." She shimmied under him. The bulk of his weight rested on his forearms pressed against the floor, but terror and pain be damned, the close proximity to him made her head swim.

"A bomb crashed through the window. We need to go. Now."

She craned her neck to take in the sight of her battered sofa. They had ended up behind the tufted piece of furniture she'd toiled over picking out for months, searching for the perfect piece for her private sanctuary. Now singed circles covered the gray material and tiny tatters splattered the once spotless couch.

The rest of the room hadn't fared much better, and a glimpse over Max's head to the foyer showed a broken window, shattered glass and heavy smoke clogging the entryway. A dark shape morphed in the midst of the debris and Samantha gasped. "Someone's in here."

Max lifted himself onto the balls of his feet, his legs bent low in a crouch. He reached into the holster at his side and pulled out a gun. "Stay here."

Where was she going to go? Her house was crumbling down around her, every muscle in her body hurt like hell, someone was in her house and she was laid out on the living room floor in her freaking pajamas.

Max stayed low to the ground and hurried to the wall. Pressing his back against intricate wallpaper, he sidestepped toward the foyer with his gun poised in his hands. Samantha kept her eyes locked on the shadowed figure lurking in the entryway. Her heart pounded in her ears and competed with the cacophony of buzzing that must be a side effect of the bomb.

"Hello? Is anyone inside? The police are on their way."

Relief had her tense muscles sagging to the ground. *James.*

Max swung around to face James with his gun pointed at his still-growing shadow. "What are you doing here?"

James stepped through the fog of debris and snarled at Max before lifting his palms in the air. "Why do you always have a gun pointed at me?"

"I believe you started that game," Max shot back. "Now answer my question."

"Ms. Gates had me park out front all morning. I was to keep my eyes and ears open."

Max pivoted to face her, his brows raised. "Is this true?"

Samantha used her good hand to push herself to her feet and groaned. She gritted her teeth together until the worst of the pain passed. "Yes. I haven't had a chance to hire anyone else I trust for extra security, and thought James would provide the protection I need in the meantime."

"I guess your plan didn't work, but let's discuss this outside. We don't know how much damage was done, or if someone plans on coming back." He hurried toward her and she fought the urge to cower away from his angry stride and glowering eyes.

She straightened her spine, and her head spun from the movement. She'd faced more intimidating men in her life, although for the life of her none came to mind at the moment. He reached toward her, and when she didn't move, he wrapped one arm around the small of her back and used the other to support her elbow above her cast. Melting against him, she matched his slow gait toward the doorway. He kept his face downcast, and she studied his profile as he led her out of the house and into the fresh air. James hurried out behind them.

Sirens called out their distressing song and blue-and-red lights danced against the overcast sky. The cold air stole her breath and she rubbed her hand up and down her arm as she descended the stairs of her town house and stepped onto the sidewalk. The chill of the steps soaked into her feet and tiny needle pricks pierced her skin, announcing impending numbness.

"James, hold on to her for a second. I'll be right back."

James's familiar form lingered beside her, but she

couldn't bring herself to relax into him the same way as she had Max. She kept her eyes fixed on the open door, waiting for him to emerge. He'd said they didn't know the extent of the damage, so why had he run back inside?

A police car screeched to a stop outside her town house with an ambulance behind it. The same grouchy detective who'd been in her hospital room the morning before stepped out of the driver's side and a younger officer she'd never seen jumped out of the passenger side. The wind made his cheeks rosy, and even the stressful situation couldn't dim the brightness in his eyes.

Seconds ticked by as they made their way toward her, and she tore her gaze from them and focused on the doorway again. Smoke billowed out in waves, greeting the frigid air as if the house were blowing hot breath into the afternoon chill. Where was he? She held her breath and tapped her bare foot against the cold-as-ice concrete.

A hacking cough preceded Max through the door and she let out a huff of relief. He covered his mouth with the crook of his elbow and walked toward her, his leather jacket dangling from his other hand. The jackass had gone inside to grab his coat. Words of scorn danced on her tongue and she opened her mouth to berate him, but he slipped the jacket over her shoulders and pulled a pair of cozy slippers from his back pocket.

Her throat closed as she slipped her tortured feet into the warm fleece lining of the polka-dotted slippers. She bit into her cheek to keep the tears in her eyes from falling. His arm came around her shoulder and he used the width of his body to block the wind. She glanced up at his tight-lipped mouth and something tugged at her heart. Something she hadn't felt since the first stirrings of young love so many years ago.

A young love that had destroyed her family and left her broken.

Max was a man who could cause her a lot more pain than a few bruised ribs. He could crush her heart if she let him inside her well-built walls. A bomb may have just crashed through her window, but she had a lot of practice at keeping people at arm's length. She needed to make sure Max didn't break down the walls she'd painstakingly put up over the last fifteen years. The result could destroy more than just her home...it could destroy everything.

Again.

"We need to stop running into each other like this," Caspano said as he came to stop in front of them. His partner halted behind him and his sharp gaze took in the destroyed window. "Do we need to call the bomb squad?"

Samantha shivered under Max's arm and he pulled her closer. He needed to get her out of the cold. "I don't think so. We need to go in and check out the bomb that flew in the window, but it's already gone off. I just got a passing glance, but it looked homemade. The bomb squad won't be able to tell us more than we already know. I'm guessing it was thrown in by a drive-by."

"I had just stepped out of the car when it happened," James said. "A white utility van flew by me as I ran into the house. It all happened so fast, so I didn't think to try and grab a plate number."

Intuition tingled the base of his tailbone. A white van had been caught on camera close to where the body had been found last night. All of the bodies had to have been transported to their prospective dumping areas. None of the women had been murdered where they'd been found. Max glanced up at the streetlights looming above the busy road and then back to Caspano. "Are there traffic cameras that would have an angle of the house?"

"Some. Not sure where they're directed, but they could have gotten the van." Caspano glanced over his shoulder and said, "Check it out, Skippy, and get back to me."

The officer behind him nodded and grabbed his phone. "Yes, sir."

"Skippy?" Max still couldn't remember the young man's name, but it sure as hell wasn't Skippy.

Caspano shrugged and not one hint of guilt tightened his facial features. The guy was such an ass. "You two were the only ones inside?" He directed the question toward Max, and he nodded. Samantha made no attempt to chime in. Hell, she was probably in shock.

"James is Ms. Gates's driver and he ran in after the bomb went off. I was able to get her out of harm's way, but she should probably head to the ambulance to get checked out. She may have a concussion." He dipped his chin toward the squad car and the two paramedics making their way up the sidewalk.

"No, I'm fine. I don't need to be poked and prodded." She glanced up at him and a gust of wind blew her unruly hair into her face.

He tucked a strand behind her ear and Caspano's incredulous stare burned a hole in his forehead. He didn't care. Samantha was his priority right now, not Caspano's opinion of his behavior. "If you don't want them to look at you, why don't you at least sit in the back of the ambulance while you figure out where to go? It's freezing out here."

"I can take you anywhere you need to go, Ms. Gates." James took a step toward her and clasped his hands in front of him.

"That won't be necessary," Max cut in. Someone close to Samantha, or at least someone who was able to dig pretty damn deep into her past, had tried to kill her twice in twenty-four hours and he didn't want her out of his sight. James was very low on his list of suspects, but he couldn't cross him off completely. Not yet.

James's big hands clenched into fists and his attempt to keep his cool in front of his employer was almost comical. "I don't believe I asked you."

"No, but you're the only witness we have. We need to ask you more questions, and Ms. Gates needs to wait until I'm able to see her to an undisclosed location where I'm positive she'll remain safe."

Samantha stepped away from his side and used her good hand to gather his jacket closer around her neck. "Excuse me?"

"Sam, you can't stay here. It's not safe."

"Go ahead and take her wherever she needs to go," Caspano said. "There's no reason for you to be here. I'll talk to the witness, Skippy's figuring out the cameras and I'll reach out if I need your assistance. I can get both of your statements later today."

"Like hell," Max said in a low growl. "I can't believe you're still turning this into a turf war. This is my case. I was here. I can handle it, with or without you."

Caspano rocked back on his heels and his chest rose on a deep breath. "Believe it or not, that's not what I'm doing. You need to take care of her right now. That's most important."

"I have a name," she said through clenched teeth. "And it's up to me to decide if I leave my house and to figure out where to go."

"Don't be stubborn. You're a smart woman. Staying in this house isn't a good idea. Someone threw a bomb in your window, for God's sake. What will they do next time? How far will they go?" Grabbing her shoulder, he turned her to face him and lowered his voice. "What if your mom would have still been inside? You can't tell me you'd want to jeopardize her safety by staying where she can easily get to you. You need to change your routine, and that means staying somewhere that no one would think to look for you."

"I'll go to a hotel. I'll grab what I need and head there now. I don't need to sit in the back of an ambulance until you're done working and have you hold my hand to the lobby."

The idea of holding her hand made his palms itch and heart race, but he pushed the idea from his head and focused on the problem. "No. Not a hotel. The city might be full of them, but anyone with half a brain would know you'd be at one of the best ones in the city and it wouldn't be hard to narrow it down. Not to mention people talking about seeing you going in and out of wherever you'd choose to go. It's too risky. I need to take you to a safe house."

"That might be a problem," the young officer said. He cut his eyes to Caspano as if seeking permission to speak, then shifted his face back to Max. "We moved a witness to the last available safe house in the city early this morning."

Caspano rubbed a palm across his mouth. "I forgot about that."

Samantha's shoulders dropped and a frown pulled down the corners of her mouth. "Then what do you suggest?"

Max fisted a tuft of hair in his hands and his mind raced. His eyes scanned the busy street and the small crowd gathering on the other side of the road. He had no clue where she'd be safe. She hadn't hired any security, and doing so now would only make her feel pressured to rush to hire someone. That could lead her to make the wrong decision. He had to keep her in his sights, and from where he stood, there was only one way to do that.

"You'll stay with me...after the EMTs take a look at you." He raised his brows, waiting for an argument.

Samantha shrugged, offering a small smile.

Good. She'd get her injuries evaluated and erase one worry from his mind. The second, more pressing, worry wouldn't be so easy to put to rest. How could he keep his fascination with this woman from growing when he wouldn't be able to get away from her?

Chapter 12

Max slid his key into the dead bolt of his apartment door and inhaled the garlicky scent of Chinese food from the restaurant below. The familiar scent mixed with his anxiety made his stomach churn. He shouldn't give two shits about Samantha's opinion of his apartment, but the differences between their homes were like night and day. He opened the door and let Samantha inside, following behind her with her suitcase. He watched as she stepped into the small apartment and let her gaze wander around the space.

She slipped her boots off her feet before walking into the living room. No grand foyer for him. He was lucky his one-bedroom apartment had enough room in his kitchen to store his bike. Every inch of the space was utilized, or he'd never be able to fit all his stuff inside.

"I'll put your bag in my room. The bathroom's tight,

but take as much space as you need. I'll sleep on the couch while you're here."

"You don't have to do that. I'm fine on the couch." She ran a slender finger down the exposed brick on the far wall and glanced out the window. "I love this. I wish my place had some of this charm. And the wooden beams along the ceiling are fabulous."

Pride puffed his chest at her words. Maybe she wasn't the type of woman who only wanted the glitz and glamor—the kind of woman who'd turn up her nose at someone who chose to uphold the law instead of become a titan of industry. The kind of woman his ex was when she'd left him broken-hearted. "Thanks. Go ahead and get settled. I need to make some phone calls."

She turned to face him and uncertainty danced in her eyes. "Are you sure this is a good idea?"

No. In fact, this was probably a horrible idea. He was a detective, not a babysitter. She had plenty of money to hire a professional security team, but dammit, he couldn't help but feel responsible for her. He bit back every bad reason for having her stay with him, including his ever-growing attraction for her, and fixed a smile on his face. Besides, he didn't have any other options. Even his lieutenant had agreed it was the best solution at the moment. "It will be fine. I have some solid leads and you shouldn't have to be here long."

She shook her head and one side of her mouth quirked up. "I can't believe I agreed to this."

He couldn't either. He blamed it on the pain pills she must be taking and had swooped in to grab what she needed the moment she agreed to his half-baked plan. James had been pissed, but he had no good excuse to not stay and give his statement to Caspano. He needed to run a background check on the driver so he could get rid of his lingering suspicions of the man. Samantha trusted him, and he could admit to himself half of his distrust came from how much he disliked the prick. But even a fool could see how devoted James was to Samantha—something she didn't seem to have much of in her lonely life.

Hell, he hated to admit it, even to just himself, but part of the reason he didn't like James was because he'd kill for Samantha to look at him with the same trust and kindness she bestowed upon her driver.

He turned his body to squeeze past her and walked toward the bedroom. "This is the safest place for you. No one knows you're here." He placed the Louis Vuitton bag inside the door and took a quick survey of the room. The bed hadn't been slept in last night since he'd been at the crime scene all night, but the covers were still tossed carelessly around the queen-size mattress. Dirty clothes littered the floor and a large plastic cup he always filled with water before bed sat on the dusty nightstand.

Oh well. Can't do much about it now.

He pivoted to face her again and she crashed into him. Reaching out to steady her, his hands skimmed the soft silk of her pajamas and he huffed out a laugh. A quick glance at his watch told him it was after 4:00 p.m. "Are you going to get dressed at all today?"

She glanced down and color stained her cheeks. A small groan purred from her throat and tugged at his groin. The sound reverberated through him and visions of that noise coming from her lips while beneath him with her legs wrapped around his waist flashed through his mind. "I can't believe I traveled to Brooklyn in my pajamas."

He chuckled and rubbed the silky material of the rose-colored collar between his fingers. "At least they're swanky-ass pajamas. If I'd been run out of my house after being in bed, I'd be walking around in a pair of boxer briefs."

She glanced at him through those heavy lashes he wasn't quite sure were real and the heat from the bomb earlier had nothing on the smolder in her eyes. She tucked her plump bottom lip between her teeth and it was his turn to groan. She broke eye contact and he trailed his fingers from her collar, up her throat and brushed the pad of his thumb over her lip. She met his gaze again and his pulse spiked. This woman had gotten under his skin in a matter of days in a way no woman had before.

At least not since his world had been turned upside down, and Catherine had broken his heart. His blood boiled at the memory of her deception, of being used for his family's money for years without being none the wiser. What a shock it had been when she'd called off the wedding. She couldn't accept he'd chosen a life as far from the Green Empire as possible and refused to be the wife of a lowly police officer.

He clenched his jaw and searched her face. Samantha might not need him for money or status, but her own wealth could jeopardize everything he'd worked hard to achieve—it could take the respect he'd been forced to earn through years upon years of sacrifice and dedication.

As if reading his thoughts, she pulled away and his

hand dropped to his side. "This isn't a good idea. Especially now."

Reality crashed down on him like a bucket of ice water, cooling his blood and clearing his head. What the hell was he doing? He needed to protect her and make her feel safe, not pounce on her the minute he talked her into coming to his apartment. He took a step away from her and rubbed the tension at the back of his neck. "I'm sorry. I overstepped."

Her gaze never left his and the grit and steel he'd grown accustomed to came back in her eyes and that damn mask he hated came back to contort the muscles of her face. "It's okay. Do you still need to make your calls? I don't want to keep you."

He scratched the hair at the back of his head and scrunched his nose. "Yeah. I should do that. Are you hungry? It's getting close to dinner."

Her pupils retracted as she widened her eyes. "I'm starving."

He smiled. Her hunger was at least one problem he could solve. "How about I head out while I make my calls and grab us dinner while you get settled in?"

"Perfect. Can you get some of the Chinese food from downstairs? It smells so good." She cast him a smile and walked past him to his bedroom; the door clicked closed behind her.

He stared at the barrier between them and fought the urge to fling the door open and kiss the hell out of her, even if it was the stupidest thing he could do right now. She liked the charm of his apartment, the cheap Chinese food smelled good to her and she didn't want him to touch her. She was full of surprises. What the hell had he signed up for?

* * *

Samantha pressed her ear against the door and waited until the gentle click of the front door told her Max had left. A sea of tension left her body and she dropped down on the bed. Her gaze darted around the unkept room. She'd never understand how people could live in such clutter, but at least the rest of his apartment seemed clean. More so than she'd expected. The bachelors she'd come into contact with would have lived in filth if it weren't for the housekeepers tidying up behind them.

Oh God, Max was a bachelor, wasn't he? He obviously wasn't married, but that didn't mean he was free and clear. Hell, he could be in a serious relationship. It was not like she'd ever asked him.

The look in his eyes and the tender brush of his fingers up her neck rushed into her brain and a ripple of pleasure coursed through her. No. He wouldn't have touched her like that if there was another woman in his life. She dropped her head in her hand. Dammit. What had she been thinking when she'd agreed to come here? Max had been so convincing that this was her only option, but she hadn't had her wits about her. She'd stay here tonight, and then find an alternative for the rest of the time she needed to keep tucked away. She might be safe from whoever was trying to kill her, but she was just as frightened of her growing attraction to Max.

A soft hum in her purse stole her attention and she grabbed her bag from the floor and retrieved her phone.

Laurie.

The desire to ignore the call almost had her hitting the decline button, but Laurie needed to know what had happened.

"Hey," Samantha said, the fatigue in her body coming through in her voice.

"What's going on? You're all over the news. Are you okay?" The concern in her assistant's voice had guilt rearing its ugly head at almost ignoring her call.

"I'm fine, just a little shaken up." That was an understatement. Her entire life had been stuck in a blender and pureed to hell. She'd fought hard to get to the point where she had control of her life and now it was slipping away. Worse yet, she didn't know how to make it stop.

"The news reported a bomb went through your window. Is that true? I had just left."

Samantha closed her eyes as the terror of earlier played on repeat in her mind. "Yes."

"Oh my God. First the car accident and now this?"

A lump formed in her throat and she fought back tears. They wouldn't help anything and she'd already cried enough today. "They think it was the same person who did both."

A sharp gasp rang in her ear. "What? Why?"

She shook her head, not wanting to get into the details. "A lot of stuff's happened. I need to keep my eyes open for a few days."

"Do you want to come over? You don't want to stay at your place, and your mom... This isn't something she'd be able to handle."

Since Laurie was responsible for so many aspects of Samantha's life, she was one of the only people Samantha trusted with details of her mother's health. Appreciation squeezed her heart. She was lucky to have an assistant who not only cared about her well-being, but her mother's also. It'd be so much easier to stay with Laurie, but she couldn't put her in danger. "I came to

Brooklyn to stay with the detective who's working the case until things blow over. Though I'm planning on looking for a different place to stay after tonight."

Interest hummed from Laurie's throat, and Samantha could picture the intrigue painted on her face. "The same detective who was at your house earlier? Was he there when the bomb went off?"

"Yes." The memory of his hard body pressed against hers as he'd lain over her on her living room floor was ingrained in her soul. He'd been tempting enough with his bright blue eyes sparking against his dark hair and constant stubble, but now he was even more dangerous.

She was caught up in her own thoughts for God knew how long when Laurie asked, "What aren't you telling me?"

Samantha sighed. One of the disadvantages of having an assistant she was friends with was not being able to keep secrets. Laurie knew her better than almost anyone. "Nothing. I'm tired and sore and scared out of my mind. Max is a good guy. I'm safe with him."

"Max?"

Samantha ground the heel of her hand against her forehead.

"You never call anyone by their first name."

She drew in a deep breath and her ribs didn't hurt quite as badly as this morning, although other muscles ached more after being thrown on the floor. The events of the last few days had bruised both her body and a bit of her ego, and all she wanted was a hot shower to melt away the constant pain that hummed inside her.

But she couldn't focus on the pain now. If she didn't want Laurie to see through her lies, she needed to measure her words with extreme care. "He's been around a lot the last couple of days and probably saved my life earlier. I've been forced to let my guard down with him, and I appreciate everything he's doing."

"So, is he like a bodyguard now, or something? I mean, is it normal for a detective to house the victim of a crime?"

Samantha rolled her eyes. "He's not a bodyguard. James had to stay at the house to speak with the police and Max didn't think I should be alone. This seemed like the best option for the night." She didn't add that someone had been stalking her and she needed to change her routine, or the original plan had been to stick her in a safe house. No need to worry Laurie more than necessary.

"Will Max be at the Heart Gala on Saturday night?"

Oh no. She'd forgotten all about the Heart Gala. How the hell was she supposed to attend when she was banged up and someone wanted her dead? She stood and rifled through her hastily packed bag. She needed a shower before Max came back. "I don't know if I'll make it." The idea of not seeing all her hard work come to fruition pained her. Hell, they'd raised more money for research for heart disease than ever before. But she had to be smart.

"No way. You have to go. You're the chair of the board for the hospital and we've put so much work into the event. There's only so much I can do on my own. You need to be there."

Samantha rubbed the tension building in her forehead. Laurie was right. They had worked for months to make this event perfect. Not attending wasn't an option. Even if just the thought of zipping into her tight dress made her wince. "You're right. I'll be there."

"Good. In the meantime, I'm here for you if you need anything."

Samantha thanked her then clicked off the line. Laurie would go through hell and high water to make her attend the gala. Truth be told, she didn't want to miss it. She'd put a lot of hard work into planning and they'd already raised a record amount of money…and that was before the impressive silent auction she'd managed to assemble. But was it worth risking her life by exposing herself at an event the entire city knew she would be at?

It would be if Max were with her. He'd cut one hell of an image in a black tuxedo, and for the first time in years she'd be able to walk in on the arm of a handsome man. A ball of nerves settled in her gut like a middle school girl about to ask out a crush. She'd talk to him about it tonight, and if he didn't want to go with her it wasn't a big deal. She'd get James to attend.

Disappointment crushed down on her. She didn't want James, or anyone else, there to protect her. She wanted Max.

Lord help her.

An idea formed, curving her lips into a smile. Going to the gala meant putting her at risk but could also mean drawing out the killer. With Max beside her, he could not only keep her safe but might also catch whoever was after her. And with this nightmare behind her, she could focus on the messy feelings building for Max.

Chapter 13

Okay, take a deep breath and get back in there. Be professional and polite and try not to shove your tongue in her mouth.

Max rolled his eyes at his own stupid pep talk and let himself back into his apartment. He was a grown man, not some horny teenager. He could keep his cool in front of a woman.

The steady *splish, splish, splash* of the shower rang through his apartment. He set the plastic bag full of food on the cluttered counter and faced the closed bathroom door. Steam billowed from the small crack between the door and the floor and rolled up the wall, forming tiny beads of condensation. Oh, shit. Samantha was in the shower.

Wet and naked.

Lust swooped into his stomach and squeezed his

guts. His stiff slacks tightened around his growing erection and he shifted his package, taking his focus off the delicious woman currently in his shower.

Maybe I'm not any better than a horny teenager after all.

His feet stuck to the wooden planks of the floor as if glued down. If she came out of the bathroom to find him staring at her it'd be creepy as hell, but he couldn't move. His shallow breaths quickened as anticipation zipped through his veins. Would she be wearing a tiny towel, or maybe a sexy robe? His imagination ran rampant, each image of her with wet hair and dewy skin more scandalous than the last.

Crash!

"Crap!" Samantha's shriek penetrated the thin door and he ran the short distance to the bathroom.

"Sam! Are you okay?" Either the pounding of the water drowned out his question or she'd fallen and had knocked herself out. Seconds ticked by without a sound except the steady fall of water beating down.

He turned the knob and relief flooded him to find it unlocked. Yanking the door open, he barged into the bathroom and walked into a dense fog of steam. Moist heat slid over his skin and invaded his mouth, expanding in his throat like a balloon. He squinted to see through the thick haze and spotted a crumpled form in the stand-up shower.

"Are you all right? Do you need help?" He dropped his gaze to his feet and trickles of perspiration formed on his temples.

"Don't look at me," she yelled, panic making her words pitch with hysteria. "Oh my God. This is so embarrassing."

He forced himself not to glance toward the shower, and damn if it wasn't the hardest thing he'd ever done. "What happened?"

"I slipped and then lost my balance trying to keep this stupid cast from getting wet. I'm having a hard time getting back to my feet with all my other muscles hurting." The slight catch in her voice gave away just how much pain she was in.

He chanced a peek toward the shower and sure enough, her cast hung over the lip at the bottom of the tiled basin. If she didn't get out soon, or at least turn the shower off, the cast would get drenched. "Just lie still and keep your arm outside the shower as best you can. I'm going to turn the water off and then help you up."

"No! I'm naked."

He laughed and wiped beads of condensation from the stubble on his chin. "I kind of figured that. I won't look."

He kept his gaze locked on his feet as he closed the small gap between the door and the shower. Damp steam coated the glass door that was slightly ajar, and he caught a glimpse of slick, toned calves before he angled his body away from the shower, reached inside and turned off the water. He grabbed the white towel she'd hung on the hook and tossed it in her direction. "Tuck this around yourself and then I'll help you to your feet."

"Thank you." The pitiful tone of her voice had him wanting to scoop her up and carry her into his bedroom.

Sweat clung to his forehead and he wiped it off with the back of his hand. "Damn, how hot was the water? This room is like a sauna."

She chuckled. "I like my showers hot. Opens up the pores. Okay, I'm covered."

Max pivoted and his shoes squeaked against the wet floor. Samantha had managed to open the shower door the rest of the way and he stared down at her. Brown strands of hair tangled around her face and the heat of the water made her cheeks glow bright red. All the moisture in his mouth evaporated and he coughed at the sudden dryness. He drew in a deep breath and the humid air fled inside and coated his cheeks.

He rubbed his palms together and raised his brows, gathering his courage to touch her bare skin. "Okay, let's get you out of there."

Crouching down, he placed his hands on either side of her shoulders and shifted her to a sitting position. Samantha placed her hand on his forearm and tried to pull herself up. She got to her heels and slipped. Her good hand grabbed a handful of his shirt, catching him off guard and pulling him forward. His balance wavered and he crushed her to him, twisting his body just in time for his back to hit the hard ground. The impact sent sparks of pain up his spine, but at least he'd taken the brunt of the fall. Samantha had been knocked around enough the last couple of days.

A hiss of air left his lungs and his arms fell to the damp tiles on the floor. He squeezed his eyes closed and winced, waiting for the pain to subside. "Sonofabitch."

"Are you all right?" The laughter in her voice made a mockery of her concern.

Max opened his eyes and the little bit of sticky air he'd managed to bring back into his body left again, but this time because her face was so close to his. Her dark eyes and even darker lashes hovered over him as her soft body molded against him. Water drenched his clothes, and the haze from the steam gave the illusion of trapping them into a cocoon of warmth…safe from the world and their actions.

Beads of water from her hair dripped down and ran over his face. Her lips parted and her narrowed gaze searched his eyes. He reached up and pushed the soaked strands behind her ear and she sucked in a breath. The thin wet towel saturated the front of his clothes and the wet material amplified the feel of her breasts against his chest. He stroked his thumb against her cheek and bit into the tender flesh of his mouth to keep from kissing her full lips.

Samantha's gaze lowered to his mouth and every muscle in his body tensed. She had said it wasn't a good idea for him to touch her earlier, but her heavy breathing and intense focus on his mouth said otherwise. But he couldn't take that leap, couldn't disrespect the boundaries she'd so clearly set up between them.

He dropped his hand from her face. Her nearly naked body on top of him was temptation enough. He didn't need to make this worse by caressing her soft skin. He shifted and braced his hands on her narrow waist, trying to position her so he could pick her up without the towel dropping. He glanced around the shower and searched for something he could use to pull them both up with.

Samantha traced a finger around his lips and his gaze shot to hers. She sandwiched her bottom lip between her teeth and indecision darkened her brown eyes. Damn, he'd never wanted to kiss a woman more in his life, but he didn't want her to regret staying with him. Didn't want to cross the line and get involved with a victim of a crime he was investigating. He wrapped his hand around hers, halting the motion of her finger on his lips.

"You said this wasn't a good idea." The humid air

mixed with his husky voice, making the words stick to his throat.

"It's not," she said in a whisper, and then pulled their joined hands from his mouth and pressed her lips to his.

Max groaned into her mouth and dropped his hands to skim the gentle curve of her spine. Her lips parted and his tongue probed inside her. She tasted of sweet coffee and woman. His head spun from one kiss, one taste, one damn moment of weakness. She'd knocked him off-balance in so many ways.

I'm screwed.

What the hell am I doing?

Her mind screamed at her to stop, but she couldn't pull away from Max. Hell, she didn't want to. As she'd stared down at him, she'd been drawn to his mouth like a magnet. It'd been so damn long since she'd been kissed. She was half-afraid she'd forgotten how.

Max's strong hands cupped her butt and molded her against him. The hard length of him pressed against her stomach and her toes curled. All thoughts fled her mind. She opened her mouth wider, giving him more space for that talented tongue of his to explore. Her nerve endings danced and tingling bursts of excitement erupted in between her legs. She wiggled against him, the tingling sensations building, and a moan of anticipation growled from deep in her throat.

Beep, beep, beep.

The shrill sound pierced her eardrums and she pulled away and stared down at Max. "What is that?"

Strangled breaths puffed from Max's open mouth and he squeezed his eyes shut. "Sounds like the smoke detector. I need to reset it to get it to shut up. I have to get you up. Hold the towel to your chest while I get you to your feet." Lust made his voice come out deep and sensual and sexy as hell.

On a whoosh of breath, Max hooked an arm under her knees as he pushed up on his other hand. She circled her arms around his neck. He got to his feet and twisted her so she lay in his arms, like a gallant hero saving a princess.

Or a groom carrying his bride across the threshold.

She rolled her eyes at her own stupid train of thought. The skin of his forearm grazed against her knees, and she summoned all her strength not to squirm. Smoke detector or not, desire still beat its desperate drum inside her body. She needed to get a grip.

"I'll put you down in the hallway so you don't trip again, and then I'll deal with the noise."

She nodded, even though her head rested beneath his chin. "All right," she said, the word squeaking from her tight throat. Reality crashed down on her and her brazen actions had embarrassment flooding her cheeks.

He walked out of the bathroom and set her on her feet. "Do you mind turning around while I go into the bedroom to change?" she asked, the blaring of the alarm making Max lean forward to hear her.

A flash of regret changed his light blue eyes the color of ice, but for only a second. He pressed his mouth together and nodded before turning his back on her. She fled to the safety of his bedroom and closed the door. Not wasting time, she dug into her bag and pulled out the first thing her hands landed on. The reason for the smoke detector going off was yet to be determined, and she couldn't run from the building draped in only a ratty old towel.

Dropping the towel, she pulled a sweatshirt over her head and stuffed her legs into a pair of yoga pants. Not clothes she usually wore around people outside of close friends and family, but she didn't have time to be picky. Besides, somehow Max had managed to see her at her worst several times in the last week.

The obnoxious beeping stopped and her shoulders sagged in relief. Max wouldn't have turned it off if there was an issue inside the apartment. She slipped socks on her feet and stepped out of the bedroom. A cloud of steam still lingered in the hallway, but not as thick as it had been in the bathroom. Samantha wandered into the hallway and turned toward the sound of rustling bags. Max rummaged around the kitchen, opening food containers and dishing out food.

She leaned against the doorframe. Uncertainty churned in her stomach and she struggled with where to put her hands. Dammit, why had she kissed him? Now that she'd tasted those full lips, all she wanted was more. "What triggered the smoke alarm?"

Max glanced up, and then returned his focus to the food in front of him. "Judging by the condensation dripping from the ceiling and the steam still hanging out in my hallway, I'm guessing it was the heat from the shower."

She wanted to die. It had been a hot shower, all right, but she'd never set off a smoke detector before. "I'm so sorry."

He chuckled and shrugged. "No big deal. Are you still hungry?"

Boy was she, but it wasn't for the food in front of her—it was for Max.

The memory of Max's large, hot palms on her naked skin flashed through her mind and her pulse spurred through her temples. She cleared her throat. "Yes."

"I don't have a table, no room for one. I usually eat on the couch. That okay?"

"Sure."

Max picked up two plates and carried them past her into the living room. He placed them on the coffee table, and then walked by her again to grab glasses of water from the kitchen. Her eyes followed his every move, and when he sat down on the couch, she willed her legs to move in his direction.

She forced a smile to her lips, but couldn't look him in the eye. What was wrong with her? She hadn't done anything bad, and it wasn't as if she were a naive girl. She was a woman who went after what she wanted, and right now, she wanted Max. She sank down beside him and her gaze landed on the wet shirt sculpted to his rock-hard chest. Her eyes flew to his. "You're all wet. Do you want to change before we eat?"

One side of his mouth quirked up in a smirk that had her heart racing. "Nah. I'm fine. I think I'll need to grab a cold shower anyway after we're done."

Heat spread out from her core and burned every inch of her body. She tucked a strand of wet hair behind her ear and busied herself by pulling her plate of food on her lap. "I'm sorry. I can be such a klutz sometimes."

His body leaned toward her and he cupped the back of her neck, forcing her gaze to his. The amusement he'd displayed a moment earlier was gone, replaced with drawn-down brows. "You have nothing to apologize for. Anytime you want to trick me into the bathroom and tackle me so you can give me a kiss, I'm game."

She widened her eyes and pushed at his chest, but he didn't let go. "I didn't do that." Her defensive tone had him laughing. She fought the curve of her lips, but lost the battle. Her wide grin matched his and she shook her head. At least he'd managed to break through the awkwardness.

"In all seriousness, I hope you didn't hurt yourself when you fell. You've been through a lot the last couple of days. I'm glad I was around to help. But if you decide you want to give that kiss another chance, I'd be more than happy to see where things lead."

Chapter 14

The heat from Max's hand branded the back of her neck and she dropped her gaze to the plate of Chinese food on her lap. He let his hand fall from her skin and she pushed the lo mein around her plate with her fork. Seeing where another kiss with Max would lead interested her too, but it was a horrible idea. Especially now. She was trapped in his apartment for the night, for God's sake. Maybe once the adrenaline of being hunted by a killer passed, she could explore what her true feelings were. Right now, the adrenaline that didn't seem to leave her body might be the only thing drawing her to her protector.

Tucking her feet beneath her, she slurped a slippery noodle into her mouth and shifted on the sofa. The plush cushions engulfed her, and she straightened her spine to keep from falling farther back into their welcoming embrace. She needed to stop letting him get under her skin. Twirling another noodle on her fork, she asked, "How were your calls?"

Max grabbed his water, took a long sip and set the glass down before he answered. "Good. Caspano took down all the statements and his lackey got ahold of footage from a traffic camera on your street. Since we know the time frame, it will be easy to track down the different vehicles spotted at the time of the bomb, or shortly after it was thrown."

James's words about the van flying past her house came back to her and she leaned forward, pushing into Max's space. The smell of his cologne wasn't as strong as earlier, probably from the shower, and mixed with the spices wafting from his plate. "Did they see a white van?"

Max took a bite of food and he squinted at her, as if unsure of what he wanted to tell her.

"Don't try to give me some lame excuse about not being able to tell me. I have a right to know."

He nodded and set his plate of hardly touched food on the coffee table. "You're right. You're in this all the way, and something I tell you might even knock loose a memory that could help. Yes, there was a van that matches the description James gave us. They ran the license plate and it's listed under the name Booker Harlan. Have you ever heard that name?"

Samantha twisted her lips into a side pucker and she searched her brain for the name.

Nothing.

"No." She dropped her fork on her plate and fell back into the couch. Screw it. She needed a hug, even if she could only trust the stupid couch to give it to her. She didn't dare lean into Max's strong arms for fear she'd never want to leave. "I don't know whether to be disappointed by that or not."

"Chances of you recognizing the name were slim. Unless you have connections to the mob."

Horror clenched her stomach. "What?"

Max ran a palm over his face. The Harlan name is well-known in my world, but they usually keep their business outside the city, mainly in Jersey. Do you know anyone who's gotten caught up with these guys? Or anyone from the mob?"

She shook her head, words and questions trapped in her throat.

"I doubted it, but someone who wants you dead has connections to the Harlans. After we eat, I'll dig into that a little more."

She nodded and tried to ignore the uneasiness in the pit of her stomach. "I don't know about you, but I've lost my appetite. Let's start now."

Max's lips hitched up in a smile. "Okay. I'll put the food away and then grab my computer."

She glanced around the small room until her gaze landed on a closed laptop on a stand by the window. "Mind if I have a crack at it?"

"Have at it." He crossed the room and grabbed the computer, bringing the screen to life and entering a password before handing it to her and collecting their dishes.

Shifting to tuck her feet beneath her, Samantha plopped the computer on her lap and opened her Facebook account. She typed the name Booker Harlan into the search box. Multiple names popped up, but only one with a location close by. She clicked on the name and scanned the limited information that littered the screen.

Max came back into the room and settled in beside her. "Looking at his social media. Smart."

She caught his eye and the intensity of his gaze made her squirm in her seat. "It still surprises me how much people share about themselves online. I'll never understand it."

Max raised his brows. "Luckily for you, huh?"

She couldn't help the smile that widened her mouth. "Good point."

"What'd you find," he asked, dipping his chin toward the computer.

She skimmed the screen. "Booker doesn't share a lot unless you're his friend. He lives in Hoboken and works for VB Enterprises."

Samantha's blood turned colder than the February wind howling outside. "Oh my God." Her voice shook and she rubbed her hand across her chest, as if it'd slow her rapidly beating heart.

Max twisted toward her. "What is it? My God, Sam, you're white as a ghost."

"That's one of the companies Teddy's family owns. That can't be a coincidence."

"Are you sure?" Max leaned over and opened a new browser window. He put the name of the company in the search engine.

"Yes. VB stands for Van Buren. Teddy runs a large chunk of it, but I'm not sure how much work he actually does. I was always under the impression he was more of a figurehead."

Max scanned the list of websites that came up and

clicked on one. "Wow, they dip their hands in a lot of pots, don't they?"

Samantha clicked on the drop-down bar in the corner of the screen. A list of companies popped up. "That's surprising."

"What?"

"They've changed the website. I don't deal with them a lot—I don't like to interact with Teddy if I don't have to, but I've kept tabs on them over the years. Teddy's father had a stroke a few years ago and Teddy was put in charge. It looks like they've either downsized or consolidated some of their corporations."

"How can you tell?"

She used the tip of her index finger to scan down the list. "These are the different divisions that are a part of their main company. Financial services, insurance, waste management…well that's new."

"And an odd fit with a swanky company like this," Max said. "Click on the waste-management link."

She did as he suggested. "It's a new acquisition. And look who the president of this new arm of VB Enterprises is," Samantha said.

"You'd think Teddy would have covered his tracks a little better. He can't be stupid enough to think we wouldn't find the link between him and the van. And why would Teddy employ a member of the mob?" Max leaned back against the couch and rubbed his jaw.

"Maybe he doesn't realize I have a traffic camera on my street." A chill swept over her and she wrapped her arms around herself. She and Teddy hadn't been on good terms for years, but she never thought he'd try to hurt her. There had to be another explanation.

"Or in the Bronx," Max said. "The same van was

used last night to dump the body outside the nail salon. I need to talk to Teddy, but not until I find Booker. If he's the hired help, he might be willing to talk. A guy like Teddy will be defensive the minute I step foot in his space. If I can have some dirt on him first, it could help."

"If it's him." Her voice was so low she could barely hear it. Max must think she was a naive idiot, but the idea of someone she'd known for so long wanting to kill her shook her entire view of her life.

Max set his computer on the floor and rested his hand on her knee. His thumb grazed back and forth against her pants. "He's the best lead I have, and I need to follow up on it. I know it's a lot to take in, but he makes the most sense right now. He's pissed he lost out on millions of dollars by you not letting him back into a company he thinks he's rightfully a part of. And now the van connected to a murder and the attack on your house is linked to a man who works for him. The blocks are stacking up against him. I need to consider him. And even though all signs point to Teddy at the moment, I still need to look into Jose. If only to cross him off the suspect list."

She drew in a deep breath and let the calming stroke of his thumb quiet her frayed nerves. "I know. You're right, though—he will be defensive and uncooperative when you step on his territory."

"I've dealt with worse."

"What if you ran into him and could ask him questions? Gauge his reaction on neutral territory?" She lowered her gaze and used the pad of her finger to trace a circle on the back of his hand. This was her chance to get him to go to the gala with her without making it sound like she was asking him out on a date.

"How could I do that?" The note of skepticism in his voice made her hold her breath.

"You can go with me to the Heart Gala Saturday night. I have to be there, and Margo's on the board, so Teddy will be there, too. You can keep me safe and ask him a few questions while you're there." Her heart beat in her throat and she could practically hear dread colliding with logistics in his beautiful brain. If he agreed to go with her, she'd put off finding a different place to stay…at least for another night.

She chanced a glance at his face and a cynical smirk took over his mouth. "All right. Tell me more."

The tires of Max's beat-up police car crunched on the gravel road that led to the landfill owned by VB Enterprises. The sun shimmered on the horizon, sending sparks of orange and pink swirling through the darkened clouds. Energy zipped through his veins despite the early hour…and his lack of sleep. Samantha might have been behind a closed door, but trying to rest with her so damn close had been torture.

For once, he'd been more than happy to be out the door at the crack of dawn. A call last night to the waste-management company Booker Harlan worked at had told him the man came to work early and could usually be found at the scale house at the dump. The rest of his schedule was up in the air, so Max had to get to the landfill in Jersey by sunrise if he wanted to speak with him. Trying the phone number he'd been given certainly wasn't working, and the home address he'd been given was vacant.

Samantha had still been asleep when he'd crept around his apartment in the near dark. Only the streetlights spilling in from the living room window had assisted him in getting ready. She'd promised to stay at his place all day if he went to some stupid gala event with her. She'd keep her promise, but he'd asked Jack to sit outside his apartment just to make sure no one tried to get to her while he was gone.

She'd played him. He didn't need to go to some damn gala to get the information he needed out of Teddy, and using her as bait was dangerous. But here he was again, agreeing to do something so far from his job description he was surprised he didn't have his lieutenant breathing down his neck.

He'd be pissed if he weren't dying to see her in a slinky black dress. The woman had one hell of a body. She shouldn't be covering it up all the time. And because of his agreement, she'd be safe for one more day while he was out chasing leads. Maybe Booker would be the ticket he needed to find the asshole responsible for three murders and two murder attempts on Samantha. Then he could enjoy himself tomorrow night at a fancy event with a beautiful woman on his arm.

If she'd still want him to go. Somehow, Samantha had become important to him over the last few days and he wasn't ready to let her go. At least not until they finished what they'd started in his shower last night.

He drove through the open gate at the entrance of the landfill. Piles of trash dotted the landscape as far as he could see, which even with little light was pretty damn far. The lane he drove down led to a lone building in the middle of the mounds of trash. A dozen bulldozers parked in an uneven line on one side of the building; an idling red truck sat in front of it.

Booker.

Max pulled up beside the truck and put his car in Park. He'd leave it on so the heat could keep pumping inside. Opening the door, he braced himself for the impending blast of wind that would beat against him. He stepped outside and the brutal breeze didn't just carry a nasty bite, it carried the putrid scent of rotten food and decaying garbage. Max cupped his gloved hand over his nose and hurried to the truck.

The smell seeped through the leather of his glove and invaded his nostrils. My God. How could anyone stand to work in this? He could only imagine how bad it would be in the summer's heat. He hustled to the driver's-side window. A man with black hair that curled around the top of his neck sat hunched over the steering wheel.

Max shook his head. No wonder Booker came here every morning. He must sneak in before anyone else showed up to grab a quick nap.

Using the hand not covering his nose, Max tapped his knuckles on the hard glass of the window. The man didn't even flinch. Max closed his hand into a fist and knocked harder.

Nothing.

A shiver ripped through him, as if someone had rested icy fingers on the back of his neck. He dropped his hand from his nose and flinched as the heavy wall of stench drifted unhindered up his nostrils. His fingers hitched under the door handle of the truck and pulled. The door swung open and another scent competed with the overwhelming smell of the landfill.

A scent he was all too familiar with.

He angled his body to the side and crouched down so the steering wheel and the man's head were slightly above eye level. Max glanced up into the glazed eyes of who he assumed was Booker Harlan. A bullet hole sat centered in his forehead and blood trickled down, splashing against the black plastic mat at his feet.

A glimmer of light at Booker's feet caught Max's attention and he leaned closer. A single earring sat next to Booker's booted foot. Max leaned forward and studied the large brown diamond.

He'd have to wait for the scene to be swept for evidence to figure out if the earring belonged to Booker, or maybe one of the victims Max was fighting to get justice for.

Dammit. He couldn't prove it just yet, but he was sure he was staring into the dead eyes of victim number four.

Chapter 15

The gun fell into the Hudson with a tiny *plop*. Thank God the river hadn't frozen over. No one would find it sunken beneath the frigid waters of the murky waterway. Not when Booker's worthless dead body would be found in Jersey.

Dammit. Nothing was going as planned. Turning from the river and blending into the crowds, fury hid behind an exquisite mask. The bomb had been a misstep. That's what happened when plans were rushed. It should have been bigger, more lethal. It should have taken care of Samantha and the annoying cop who followed her like a shadow.

Instead, it had sent Samantha into hiding and caused sloppiness.

Sloppiness couldn't be tolerated, so Booker had to go.

A shudder rippled over heavily covered skin. There'd

be hell to pay for killing Booker, so everything had to be taken care of before Booker's boss found out what happened. Getting involved with the mob might have been a mistake, but there hadn't been a choice. They were the only ones who could help clean up this giant mess.

It'd all be worth it soon.

But first, a fire had to be set to send Samantha out of hiding. Or at least have her fleeing the safety of her new champion. It'd be too hard to get to her with him around. No doubt she'd be at the Heart Gala. That stupid thing was one of the biggest events of the year, and Samantha fooled the public into thinking she was a saint by selflessly heading it up. It'd be too risky to take her out there. She wasn't an idiot. Samantha would make sure to have protection.

If only others knew her for the rotten person she really was. They would soon.

At least they would if Samantha didn't do as she was told. She'd pay for all of her sins…one way or another.

Max's blood thundered through his veins with the force of a flash flood as anger pulsed a steady beat in his temples. He'd spent all day yesterday chasing down leads and fighting to get through the bureaucratic bullshit the FBI had brought to the crime scene of Booker Harlan. And now, instead of working with Jack to get a glimpse of the financial reports of VB Enterprises, he was standing in his bathroom trying to straighten a stupid bow tie.

Gripping the pedestal sink with one hand, he pinched the bridge of his nose with his other and drew in a long deep breath. This case was turning into a nightmare. One lead led to another, to another, and then to the mob.

He would never burst through a federal investigation to get what he needed on Booker.

He had to figure out if Teddy had a mob connection. If he could get a good look at his financial records, he was confident he could find the money trail. He just needed to either finagle a warrant, sweet-talk the information from the FBI or get Teddy to slip up tonight.

Straightening, he ran a hand along his slicked-over hair. He normally didn't need gel to make sure the short dark strands stayed in place, but he had to get his hair cut. The longer locks rebelled against the unnatural part, but it couldn't be helped.

He gave himself one last glance in the mirror. It had been years since he'd been forced to go to an event like this. God, he hated them. He'd always been a fish out of water, constantly searching for a new way to jump out of the same damn stream everyone pissed in. At least he cleaned up all right. Even though he had no idea how Samantha had managed to get a tuxedo for him on such short notice…or how she'd gotten the right size.

Lifting his wrist, he checked the time on his watch and cursed under his breath. If they wanted to make it in time, they needed to leave now. He walked out of the bathroom and rapped his knuckles on the closed bedroom door. "Sam? Are you about ready?"

"Almost," she said.

"We need to leave if we're going to get there on time." He tapped the toe of his polished black dress shoe against the floor.

"A car will be here to pick us up in ten minutes."

He wasn't sure if he was relieved he didn't have to drive through the city or irritated she just expected him to go along with whatever plans she made. Especially

if the car she'd called would be driven by her annoying driver. "Why'd you do that? I don't want James to
know where you are." He couldn't keep the bite out of
his voice.

The door opened a crack and Samantha's flared nostrils and pursed lips told him how annoyed she was. "Do
you think I'm an idiot? I know how you feel about him,
even though I don't understand it. I called a service I
use sometimes and they're sending someone here, so
don't get your panties in a bunch."

He raised his brows and hitched up his lips at the
same time. "My panties?"

She waved away his amusement. "You know what
I mean."

He curled his fingers around the narrow edge of the
door and opened it a little bit wider. "Maybe I'm not
wearing any." He dropped his voice low and her gaze
shot up to his.

Her pursed lips morphed into a sly smile. "Maybe
I'm not either."

His gaze dropped from her face, but her body was
hidden behind the door. His grip tightened on the hard
wood and lust grabbed ahold of his stomach like an
iron fist. His mind searched for a witty comeback or a
smart reply…hell, any coherent sentence would be better than staring at her with his mouth open and what he
was sure was drool pooling at the corner of his mouth.
Just the thought of her bare rear end was enough to send
him into a stupor.

Samantha's laugh purred from her throat. "Down,
boy. Can I trust you to zip me up? I've been trying for
the past five minutes, but it's too difficult with the cast."

He swallowed hard and snapped his mouth shut.

"Sure." The lack of moisture in his throat made the word scratch against his esophagus.

The door swung open and Samantha stood with her back to him. Not a black dress, but red. Siren red. Samantha clasped the material together so only glimpses of bronzed skin peeked through the gaping folds that needed zipped. The floor-length dress had a slit up the back, but molded to her backside like a second skin.

Taking a step forward, he grabbed the zipper at the base of her spine and gently tugged it up. The soft hum of the metal teeth coming together caused a ripple of excitement to shudder up his back. Except he wanted to tug the zipper down and rip the dress off her. How she was able to still take his breath away in a dress that covered so much of her body was beyond him.

"All right. You're zipped."

She peeked over her shoulder and loose curls bounced around her face. She'd pinned one side back, which exposed her delicate jawline and the soft curve of her neck. Dark eye shadow and blacker-than-normal lashes made her brown eyes appear larger than usual, and a splash of pink on her cheeks reminded him of the way the hot shower from the night before had tinted her skin.

"You look beautiful." His chest squeezed, making his words small.

Her red lips curved, causing her cheeks to lift. "Thanks. I always feel so out of place at these things."

She turned to face him and he wouldn't have been able to move if his life depended on it. Warmth ran down him in a slow trickle, causing every nerve ending in his body to tingle with need. His gaze strayed from her face, roamed down her neck and followed the deep, deep dip of the neckline. My God, it had to stop just inches above her belly button. The sides of her full breasts played peekaboo with the red material keeping them tucked into the dress. He plunged his hands in his pockets so he wouldn't finish the game and release her puckered nipples from their confinement.

"Good God, woman. We better leave now."

Amusement brightened her face and she grabbed his hand from his pocket and checked his watch. "We still have five minutes before the car gets here. I have to get my clutch ready and my shoes on."

He shook his head, his eyes still locked on her. "You don't understand. If you agree to stay in my bedroom for one second longer, it will be hours before we get out that door." The words tumbled out of his mouth before he could stop them, but he couldn't bring himself to regret them. She tied him in knots, chipping away at the rough exterior he'd used as a shield since Catherine left him.

Understanding dilated her pupils and her gaze scanned him from head to toe. Was she actually considering staying? His groin tightened and stomach muscles clenched at the possibility.

Twisting toward the bed, Samantha grabbed a little black bag sitting on top of the bedspread and glanced inside. Apparently satisfied with what she saw, she locked the clasp with a little *click* and closed the distance between them.

The floral scent of her perfume consumed his senses and a little bit of his control slipped away. He brushed his finger down the long column of her neck and she leaned into his hand. Her skin was so damn soft.

A sigh shuddered from her parted lips and she

pressed the hard bag against his stomach. "We've got to go."

He nodded and took a step away from her. She was right. He was seconds away from peeling that dress off her and tossing her onto the bed. She had to get to the event and he needed to speak to Teddy. Depending on how the night went, they'd have plenty of time after. Time when he wouldn't be rushed and she wouldn't be distracted by other obligations. Time to finally get a taste of the fiery woman who'd wormed her way into some part of him. What he had to figure out was if he needed a taste to get her out of his system, or if she'd succeeded in achieving something only one other woman had ever done before…claiming a piece of his heart.

Samantha's phone rang from inside her clutch, breaking the spell weaving between her and Max. She reached inside her bag, grabbed her phone and glanced at the screen. The car service. "The driver's here."

Thank you, God. I can't resist him much longer, and I have to remain in control tonight.

Skirting around him, she crouched down to pick up her shoes and then sat on the edge of the bed. The smooth soles of her heels slid against her foot and she tried to grab the straps to wrap around her ankle, but she couldn't do it all with one hand. Stupid cast was always getting in the way of something.

She blew an annoyed breath through her lips and then peered up at Max. She'd been right—he looked damn good in a tuxedo. The hard lines of his abdomen couldn't be hidden by the starched white shirt and his broad shoulders fit the black jacket to perfection. He'd kept the black stubble on his jaw, which added a touch of danger to his cleaned-up clothing. James Bond had nothing on Max Green.

Clearing the lust closing up her throat with a cough, she regained her focus and asked, "Can you buckle my shoes? I'm sorry I'm such a pain."

Max's deep chuckle skimmed over her. Thank God she was already sitting or her jellylike knees would have buckled. He dropped to his knees in front of her and secured the straps she'd already attempted to bring together. She lifted her other foot and he closed his large hands around her arch. Heat shot from her foot, straight to her core.

His thumb grazed the tender skin on the sole of her foot and spark waves ricocheted inside her body. His blue eyes bored into her, the color darkened to the prettiest cerulean she'd ever seen. He was so close, his face inches from her own. His heavy breath skimmed her cheek and she braced her hands on the tops of his shoulders to keep herself steady. What was it about this man that threw her so off-balance? She'd been around handsome men before, but no one had broken through her walls and made her beg to break them all down.

Max kept one hand wrapped around the top of her foot and grabbed her shoe with the other. He gently guided her toes into the shoe, and damn if it wasn't sexy as hell. If he took this much time, spent this much attention, on her foot…she could only imagine what he'd do with the rest of her body. Her mouth went dry and she swiped her tongue across her chapped lips.

A low groan roared from Max and he lunged forward, taking her mouth in his. She wrapped her arms around his neck and pulled him close. Her knees parted so he could burrow his way closer, but her stupid dress wouldn't stretch.

Max growled at the unwanted barrier and leaned over her, lifting her up and then pressing her back against the mattress. His lips traveled from her mouth to her ear and nibbled on her lobe. The stubble on his chin scratched against her jaw. She shimmied under him and hiked her dress up so she could wrap her legs around his waist. Gala be damned. She wanted him now. She lifted her hips and Max's hand cupped her bare ass.

He hissed in her ear, his warm breath making her shudder. "I thought you were joking about the panties."

She laughed. "I never joke about panties."

A gentle hum sounded from the open clutch beside her and Max lifted his head to stare down at her. "Don't even think about it."

"It's probably the driver. Let me text him and tell him we'll be a little late."

Max lowered his lips to the base of her throat while she fished for her phone. His fingers brushed over her breastbone and against the side of her breast and she sucked in a breath. The pad of his finger traced a circle against her skin, wider and wider until it dipped inside her dress and skimmed against the tender tip of her nipple.

She found her phone and she crushed it against her palm. "God, Max." She moaned and cursed at the same time.

Her gaze flicked to her phone and her world went still. "Oh my God. Max."

The panicked tone of her voice had Max sitting up, the ice blue of his eyes back in place. "What's wrong?"

Her hands trembled and she lifted the phone for him

to see. He wrapped his hand around hers, steadying the shaking screen and read the text message out loud.

I'd rather leave you roses, to remind you of what I've done.

But you're nowhere to be found and are ruining all my fun.

I have some things to tell you, so go home tonight alone.

It wouldn't be wise to not comply, or the media will be most surprised.

Chapter 16

"I can't believe we're still going to this thing," Max mumbled. Annoyance crawled over him like a bug he couldn't swat off his skin. Chasing a murderer was one thing, but having the sicko sending threats to Samantha, taunting her, made him want to smash his fist through the window of the shiny black limo.

"What am I supposed to do? Just stop my life until this psychopath is found? I can't do that." The hurt and fear in her voice stomped down his irritation.

Not like there was much else to do now anyway. He hadn't been surprised when the text message she'd received was traced to a burner phone. Going to the gala was still the best place for him to talk to Teddy, and the threat had told her to go home alone. No one would be stupid enough to attack her at a major society event, and Samantha was right. Showing up could draw out whoever was torturing her so he could stop this tonight.

He reached over and squeezed her knee as the city lights blazed outside the car. "You're right. I just hate that I haven't put a stop to this yet. It's been two weeks since the first murder. I should have ended this by now."

Samantha turned her face toward him and the motion sent a wave of her perfume his way. The scent of lilacs and lavender floated up his nose and squeezed his heart. The lights of the city streamed through the window and highlighted the ashen tint of her skin. Dammit, she'd been so radiant before that text had come in. "Do you really think Teddy's behind everything?" Her eyes shifted back and forth as she searched for an answer.

He shrugged. "A lot of factors are pointing his way, and there aren't a whole lot of other options. If the FBI weren't chasing their tails with Booker Harlan's mafia connection, I might have been able to get a warrant to check into Teddy's financials, but even that's unlikely. I don't have anything substantial to bring to a judge."

"What about Jose? Have you found him?" Her words rushed out on a wave of eagerness, but he couldn't tell if it was from fear or a desire to know where he was.

"Yeah. He was easy to track down. I spoke with his probation officer this morning and am going to speak with Jose tomorrow. It's still a pretty big coincidence all this started around the time he was released from prison. And besides Teddy, he's the only one we've come across who could have an axe to grind against you."

She turned back toward the window and he studied her profile. The tight muscles in her face showed how hard she tried to keep her composure from slipping each time Jose Diaz's name came up. He wanted to know the rest of their story, even if it didn't have anything to do with his investigation. What had happened between her, Jose and Robbie had shaped Samantha's entire life. He'd read the case file, but he wanted her to open up to him…to tell him how she felt about what had happened.

Silence lingered in the tight quarters for a minute longer before Samantha asked, "Where does he live?"

"He's back in the Bronx." Jose had moved back in with his mother. Without a job, there was no way the guy could have afforded a place to live on his own.

She dropped her gaze to her clasped hands resting on her lap. "After all this time, he ends up back in the place he'd been trying so damn hard to escape."

He wanted to reach out and take her hand, touch her face…anything to let her know she could let her walls down with him. But something inside told him that was the last thing she needed. She'd carried a heavy burden for so long, he couldn't just rush in and take it from her. Samantha needed to hand it over to him, to trust him with it.

With his eyes fixed on her, he twirled the black cuff link at his wrist and asked, "Is that what he was doing that day? Trying to escape?"

"That's what he was always trying to do." A little laugh came out with her words. "Life was hell for us. We lived in the same building, and he'd help me take care of Robbie when our mothers were working."

Her words piqued his interest. He'd known she had been present at the time her brother had been killed, but he wasn't aware of how strong her ties were to Jose. "So you knew him pretty well?" He couldn't stop the rush of jealousy that whipped around his ribs.

She nodded and finally faced him. Tears shone from her heavily made-up eyes and a haunted smile curled her lips. "I'd known him since we were barely old enough to walk. We watched out for each other, tried hard as hell to keep out of trouble and swore we'd have a better life one day."

The stupid jealousy increased, pushing his organs against the lining of his stomach and making it hard to catch his breath. "A better life together?"

"Yes." The whispered word lingered in the silent car, its implication drowning out the sounds of the city beating against the outside of the limo. "That was the plan until Jose's mom lost her job. They had to move in with his grandmother and he was so angry. He wanted out, and he didn't want to wait. I thought I'd talked him out of it, but then he walked into that salon…"

Missing pieces of the puzzle started clicking into place in Max's mind. He was almost afraid to ask the next question, but he had to know the answer. "Had he talked about robbing a store before? Did he know you'd be getting your nails done that day?"

Samantha bit into the small space just above her chin. "I told him how stupid it'd be. How he'd get caught and just leave me to rot. How could we be together if he was in jail? He kissed my forehead, told me not to worry and said he'd see me later. When he walked in with a gun and I ran over to him, people thought I must have planned it with him. Everyone in the neighborhood knew we were always together. And then Robbie…" Her words trailed off and she returned her focus to her hands.

He couldn't take it any longer. Closing the space between them, he wrapped his arm around her shoulder and pulled her close to his side. "And then Robbie came in to find you. The little brother who used to always follow you around." He repeated the words she'd said to him a few days before.

She didn't have to answer, didn't have to acknowledge the accuracy of his words. "When Robbie came through the door, Jose panicked. He just pointed and shot. He loved Robbie as much as I did. It was all a big mistake. But Robbie died and Jose was the one who'd pulled the trigger."

"And you were the one left to pick up the pieces." He nuzzled his lips against her hair and the silken strands tickled his skin. "Is that why you changed your name? To distance yourself from the murder?"

"Partly. The police tried to paint me as an accomplice, a young girl swept up in the excitement of love and danger who got her brother killed. I didn't want that following me around the rest of my life. Especially after I entered the crazy world I'm in now. And my mom... she's already so messed up. She needs to be protected from all of it."

Understanding dawned on him. No wonder she hadn't wanted to help him when he'd stormed into her office and demanded answers. A wave of guilt washed over him as the limo merged out of traffic and pulled into a line of cars waiting to release their occupants. Max brushed his fingers up and down the pashmina she'd thrown over her shoulders, searching for the right words to make her feel better. "You've done enough to protect the people you love, Sam. I'm going to do what I can to protect you now, okay?"

Samantha pressed her lips to his cheek. He meant what he'd said. Samantha had been through enough and it was past time someone looked out for her. He'd still talk to Jose tomorrow, but a nagging voice in the back of his mind told him it'd be a waste of time. The car pulled up in front of a long red carpet stretched across the sidewalk and Max glanced past the horde of photographers and pedestrians and spotted the entryway of the grand hotel in the Upper East Side. If he were a betting man, he'd place all his chips on the person responsible for making Samantha's life hell being inside right now.

Max swung open the door and scooted out of the car and then grabbed the crook of Samantha's elbow to help her out. Another car pulled up behind them and a flurry of excitement rushed around them as people screamed for Samantha's attention. Max lowered his head, intertwined his fingers with Samantha's and led her down the red carpet.

"Oh my God. Maxwell! Is that you?"

Dread dropped in his stomach and he fought the urge to pick up Samantha and rush inside to avoid searching for the face that belonged to the sweet-as-sin voice behind him. His grip tightened on Sam's hand and he turned. Lights flashed around him and the mob of people searching for their best shot grew larger.

He pulled Samantha close to his side and fixed a smile on his face. His gaze found the light blue eyes that were more familiar to him than his own. "Hello, Mother."

"Maxwell?" Samantha said in a low voice from the corner of her mouth.

Max only had time to shoot her a quick scowl before a tall, elegant woman with raven-black hair that was swept up in a chignon wrapped her arms around Max.

His fingers slipped from hers and she wrapped her hands around her clutch, waiting to see how things unfolded. Max hadn't talked a lot about his family; he hadn't talked much about himself at all, but even if he hadn't called the woman mother, there would be no doubt who she was. Her blue eyes, strong jaw and wide mouth were feminine versions of Max's own features.

How had she not put two and two together before? The Greens were well-known in her social circle, even if she hadn't met them before. Mrs. Green's resemblance to Max was uncanny.

The woman stepped out of Max's embrace but kept her hands firmly around his forearms as she inspected him. "I had no idea you'd be here. What a pleasant surprise."

A man came to a stop beside Max's mother, his megawatt smile and hearty slap on Max's back evidence of his pleasure. "What are you doing here, son?"

Max raised his eyebrows and pulled his arms free from his mother's grasp. "I'm here with Samantha." He shifted his stance and placed one hand on her arm while the other stretched palm up in the air in front of her, as if offering her up to his parents.

She took a little breath and donned the mask she wore every day on her face. The one that didn't show fear, or nerves, or the huge ball of confusion that had just taken up residence in her brain. "Hello. I don't believe I've had the pleasure." She extended her hand to Max's mother, and then his father.

"It is so nice to meet you. Please, call me Edna." The warmth in the older woman's voice almost had Samantha forgetting about the cold air blasting against her exposed skin.

"And you can call me Frank, but how about we talk more inside. I don't know about you, but I know my wife has to be freezing. I couldn't talk her into putting on a damn coat. God forbid she be photographed in a designer coat." Frank rolled his sea-blue eyes, but the curve of his lips showed his humor.

Edna slapped playfully at the lapel of his black tuxedo. "Why buy the dress if no one will see it? But you're right, let's head inside."

The pair took the lead up the carpet and cameras flashed. Samantha raised her chin in the air just enough to make sure the angles of her face would be photographed properly. She hated the media, but had learned long ago there was nothing she could do to keep them away. It was easier to quickly give them what they wanted and get the best picture of her out there. A win-win for them both.

After Edna and Frank made it halfway down the carpet, she straightened her shoulders and took a step toward the entrance of the hotel. A tiny tug on her hand had her glancing up at Max. The tight set of his mouth and rigid bunch of his shoulders showed his discomfort, and his gaze darted around the crowd as if searching for a threat.

"Are you okay?" she asked.

"I don't like how many people are here. Can't we go in through the back?"

She laughed. "It's a little late for that now. People would throw a fit. Let's just give them a few pictures and get inside. Okay?"

Max nodded and they made their way down the walkway.

"Samantha! Over here! Let me get a picture."

"Who are you wearing? Can you take your pashmina off for a picture?"

"Who's the guy? New man in your life?"

"How are you feeling? Does your wrist hurt?"

She ignored the questions hurled at her, smiling and posing as she made her way toward the hotel. She'd never understand why people wanted to know the details of her life. Max led her past the photographers and through the doors of the hotel.

Her heels clicked against the marble floor and echoed off the domed ceiling. Clusters of people in beautiful dresses and perfectly tailored tuxedos stood around the lobby before making their way into the grand ballroom. She spotted Edna and Frank talking to a young man outside the double doors that led into the room.

"I really need to get inside. I'm late as it is. Do you want to speak with your parents while I look for the other board members?"

"I'm not letting you out of my sight. We'll head inside, and then I'll look for my parents once everything's situated."

Relief seeped into her tense muscles. She was so on edge and didn't want to wander around without Max. Whoever wanted her dead knew she was here, and regardless of if she played along with their game or not, there was no telling what their next move was. Having Max by her side made it easier to push the horror of the last week to the side of her mind and focus on what she needed to do tonight.

Still hand in hand, Samantha led Max into the ballroom and turned toward the front of the room where the board always sat.

"Well, well, well. Look who's here. With all the excitement surrounding you the last few days, I wasn't sure you'd show up." Teddy stood with a drink in hand, a smirk playing on his lips.

Max tightened his grip and the bones in her hand ached from the pressure. Max skirted in front of her, hiding her from the glowering stare of Teddy. "I'm glad we ran into you," Max said. "We need to talk. Now."

Chapter 17

"I don't have anything to say to you," Teddy said without tearing his gaze from Samantha's face. An ugly snarl took over his mouth. "You can't stop yourself from bringing the help along, can you?"

If they weren't at a fancy event with society's most elite members, including his parents, Max would have slammed his fist into the smug jerk's face. Teddy's upper lip curled to the side. "You'll have plenty to say to me when I ask you about Booker Harlan," Max said.

Teddy's gaze locked with his and his eyes widened for a fraction of a second. He clamped his lips together into a tight line and took a step toward him.

Max pushed Samantha even farther behind his back. Teddy wouldn't be stupid enough to hurt her here, but Max would sure as hell be certain to shield her from any threat he might make.

"What do you know about Booker?" Teddy spat out the question.

Max took a step toward Teddy, refusing to let the asshole intimidate him. "Quite a bit actually. I'm the one who found him dead at the landfill your family owns."

Blood vessels bulged on Teddy's face and a trickle of sweat dotted his impeccable hairline. His gaze flittered around the room. "I can't talk to you about this."

More and more people crowded into the room and a collision of colognes floated in with them, drifting along a wave of stilted air. Shoulders brushed past him and Samantha molded herself against his back. Her cast pressed against his upper thigh and her hand grabbed a handful of fabric from his jacket. "What can you talk to me about? The bomb that flew into Samantha's town house the other day? Or how about we discuss your whereabouts over the last couple of weeks?"

"I already told you that I don't have anything to talk to you about." Teddy's voice quivered and lacked the venom he'd spewed earlier. His toe tapped against the rich burgundy rug.

"Well, I'll be damned." Max groaned at the booming voice making its way toward him. Just his luck that every member of his family would be here tonight. Teddy whipped his head around, and a bit of tension seemed to drop from his shoulders. "Maxwell. I thought hell'd freeze over before I'd see you here. I didn't know you knew Teddy. And who is this ravishing creature behind you?"

Teddy faced Max again. His brows dipped down and a light show of confusion blinked on his stupid face. "Hi, Marcus. Good to see you, man. Do you know the detective?" Marcus stepped up beside Max and scrunched his hands on both sides of Max's shoulders, giving him the most painful massage on the planet. "The detective, sounds so stuffy," Marcus said with a laugh.

Samantha skirted to Max's side and stole Marcus's attention. He dropped his hands and ran a palm over his chest as if straightening imaginary wrinkles from the white button-down shirt. "Well, Ms. Gates. I was hoping to get a chance to speak with you tonight. I never dreamed I'd have to steal you away from my brother."

"Mr. Green," she said with an air of intrigue lifting her words. "I had no idea you and Max were brothers."

Irritation pulsed through him and he snaked his arm around the small of her back, curling his fingers gently against the side of her rear end. "I'll take that as a compliment. I don't like to advertise I'm related to this guy." He softened his words with a hoarse chuckle even as he pressed Samantha close to his side. He didn't like the fact they had any kind of history, no matter how innocent.

"This guy's your brother?" The disbelief in Teddy's voice had Max fisting his hands. How many times could one slime bag piss him off in less than ten minutes?

Marcus rocked back on his heels and his smooth-as-butter smile lit up his clean-shaven face. "Sure is. And I'm hurt, Maxwell. I tell everyone about my big bad brother, one of NYPD's finest."

"Well it was good to see you, Marcus. Let's catch up later. I need to find Margo." Teddy turned and fled in the opposite direction.

Max kept his gaze locked on his quick retreat. He'd find Teddy later. Their conversation was far from over.

"So, Ms. Gates, I must admit I'm surprised to see you with Maxwell. How do you two know each other?"

Samantha's lips curved into a sweet smile. "Your brother's been helping me with an issue this past week."

"Oh really? Police business, I hope." Marcus wiggled his blond eyebrows and his gaze dipped toward the low neckline of Samantha's dress.

Max's blood pulsed in his ears faster than the freight train he wished would breeze in and slam into Marcus. "Dude, I'm a homicide detective. Why would you hope that?"

Marcus shrugged as the meaning of his statement flew higher over his head than the crystal chandelier dripping diamonds from the center of the gilded ceiling. "I've been wanting to see you again for a long time, Ms. Gates. I just meant I hoped your involvement with my brother is purely professional." The words oozed from his mouth like pus from an open wound—disgusting and uncontrollable.

He opened his mouth, but Samantha said, "My involvement with your brother extends beyond the professional, but I'm so pleased to see you."

Damn, she was good. Even if her declaration hadn't been all-inclusive of their still-up-in-the-air status, at least she'd set his brother straight about where he could expect to stand with her.

Marcus dipped his chin and a sly smile curved his lips. "Ahh, I see."

"You don't see shit, and never have," Max said, stomping out any further comment on his interest in Samantha. "How do you know Teddy Van Buren?"

"How do you not?" Marcus asked. "His family and ours have mingled in the same social circles for years."

"Have I ever mingled in your social circle?" Max shot back.

"True. You never did quite fit in. He and Ms. Gates go way back though, don't you? College, right?"

"Yes." Her answer was just stiff enough for Max to sense her discomfort.

"It's a shame what they've been dealing with. I'm glad we've kept away from their business affairs all these years."

Adrenaline forced Max forward on his toes. "What do you mean?"

Marcus glanced around before leaning in close. "Teddy's been screwing the pooch. Word is he wasn't ready to take over after his old man had to step down a few years ago. Bad investments, questionable acquisitions. And there're these rumors about trying to get help in the wrong place. Between you and me, I don't know how much longer he'll be able to keep things going. And if rumors are true, he'll have a lot to say to you and your friends down at the station."

"Ah hem."

A light blush stained Marcus's pale skin and he dropped his gaze. Max and Samantha twisted to glance behind them and Samantha stiffened beside him.

Sonofabitch.

"Excuse me, but I need to borrow Samantha," Margo said with a smile so tightly fixed to her face she'd need a jackhammer to chisel it off. She smoothed back a piece of hair with only a slight tremble in her hand and pushed it behind her ear.

"Hi, Margo. Nice to see you." Samantha hoped the

guilt in her gut didn't smother her words as she stared at Margo with a wide smile.

Margo gave Samantha's words a nod of acknowledgment. "We really need to get the evening started, and we can't do that without the head of the board."

"I'll be right there. I want to make sure Max finds his seat." Samantha wanted to crawl under a table and die. She had no idea how much Margo had heard from Max's conversation with his brother, but she had to have heard something.

The edge of Margo's lips twitched and she circled her lips as if unhinging her smile, and then fixed it back into place. She nodded, turned on her black heels and headed for the podium set up in the front of the room.

Marcus let out a hiss of breath through clenched teeth. "Well, that was awkward."

"Probably not the first time she's heard this kind of talk," Max said.

A knot tightened in Samantha's stomach. "Trust me, it doesn't make it any easier."

Max relaxed his fingers against the dip of her hip and she glanced up into his understanding eyes. "You're right."

"Christ, I need a drink. That woman always gives me the creeps."

Marcus's declaration caused Samantha to wrinkle her brow. "Really? She's harmless as a fly. She drew the short end of the stick when she married Teddy. How such a sweet woman can put up with such a dirtbag is beyond me."

Marcus craned his neck in the direction Margo had retreated. "If the guys at my monthly poker game can be believed, she's not as sweet as you may think."

Max took a step forward, dipping his chin in Marcus's direction. "What do you mean?"

"I play with the guy she dated before Teddy. She saw him one night talking with his cousin, and she went nuts. Thought he was cheating on her. Put a baseball bat through the windshield of his brand-new Porsche."

Samantha twisted her neck to catch a glimpse of Margo, and then faced Marcus again. "That can't be right. I've never heard a word about Margo having a temper."

Marcus shrugged. "Money's pretty good at buying silence, but you could be right. The guy might just be pissed she found someone richer and better looking."

Max ran his long fingers along the side of his jawline. "Something worth looking into, though."

"You do that, and I'll go to the bar. I'll talk to you two later." Marcus winked at her and then walked toward the bar at the far side of the room.

Samantha stood on her tiptoes and peered over the crowd pouring toward their seats. Round tables with white linen tablecloths dotted the center of the room. She was scheduled to give a brief speech before dinner, and then a live auction and dancing would follow. If she had her way, she and Max would be long gone before the band had finished for the night.

Grabbing Max's hand, she maneuvered her way through the throngs of people congesting the limited space between the tables. "Why didn't you tell me about your family?" she asked over her shoulder.

Max leaned closer, his body molding against hers and the heat of his breath tickling her ear. "I didn't know it was important to you."

Samantha stopped and whipped toward him. He collided into her and wrapped his arms around her back to steady himself. The desire to just stand there and soak in his scent was hard to resist, but she pulled away and stared up at him. "You didn't think I'd want to know who your family was?"

"I didn't think it'd be important that they were rich." His rough tone had her taking a step back.

"Of course it isn't, but it's just funny you didn't think I'd know who they were."

Max rubbed a rugged hand over the jagged edges of stubble on his cheeks. "I've spent years trying to get out of their shadow. I never wanted the life they lead, and it's taken a lot of time to be my own man. Even now, I get flack for being their son. It's annoying as hell."

His words slammed into her gut. If he didn't want to be a part of his parents' world, would he want to be a part of hers? The two weren't all that far apart. She didn't have time to waste thinking about that right now. The curls she'd spent hours perfecting bounced around her face as she shook her head, and she fixed a fake smile on her lips. "Deep down, we're just two kids trying to run from our pasts."

She turned away from him so he couldn't see the wheels turning in her mind and made her way toward the front of the room. Samantha found her table front and center, exactly where she hated to be, and was more excited than she should be to find Laurie already seated. Her assistant provided a welcome distraction from everything going on in her life right now…including wrapping her mind around her feelings toward Max.

The long column of Laurie's silver gown extended down her legs as she stood. She reached her arms toward Samantha, placed her hands on Samantha's biceps and leaned in to give a quick kiss on both of her cheeks. She pulled away and worry sparked in her blue eyes. "You look horrible."

"Gee, thanks. Just what I want to hear before standing up to speak in front of a room full of people." Samantha smoothed her palm over her hair and hoped she'd kept it in place instead of messing it up.

Laurie winced and wrinkles rippled along her smooth alabaster skin. "Sorry. You look beautiful, but tired and a little beat-up. I'm sorry I made you come."

Samantha sighed. "I didn't have a choice."

"It's nice to see you again, Detective." Laurie shifted her attention to Max and appreciation replaced the worry in her eyes.

Max smiled and kept his gaze fixed above Laurie's plunging neckline. "Good evening. You look very nice."

A light touch on her arm had Samantha twisting around. "Are you ready?" Margo asked, her usually light voice tight with tension.

Samantha nodded and turned back around to shoot Laurie a warning look. "I'm leaving Max in your care for a few minutes. Can I trust you?"

Laurie's Cruella de Vil cackle had Max grabbing Samantha's hand, and apprehension shone from his eyes. Samantha burst into laughter.

"I'll take good care of him."

Max bent close and whispered, "Should I trust her?"

Samantha grinned. "Not even a little."

Max laughed and his warm breath tickled her ear. He pressed a kiss to her temple and little shivers of excitement rushed down her spine. She pulled away to fall into step beside Margo, and the empty space on the other side of her was like a giant hole without Max to fill its void.

"I'm surprised to see the detective with you tonight. Are you two dating?" The inflection in Margo's voice made Samantha smile, as if they were teenagers spilling secrets at a slumber party. And the fact that Margo only wanted to discuss trivial stuff with her made her want to confide in the woman she'd once considered a good friend.

"We're getting to know each other." That wasn't a lie. She'd learned more about Max tonight than she had in the few days she'd known him. She'd never met his parents before tonight, but she knew who they were. A million questions mounted in her mind for Max.

Teddy stepped up beside Margo and she stopped short. The scowl from earlier hadn't left his face. "I want to leave."

Margo placed a palm on his lapel and gave him the same patronizing look a mother gave a tantruming toddler. "We can't leave until after dinner. Now excuse us for a second. Samantha and I were in the middle of something."

Teddy took a step back and crossed his arms over his chest, his glare never leaving them. Margo leaned closer to Samantha, her eyes bright with interest. "I shouldn't ask, but I can't help myself. Will you be getting to know each other later at your place?"

Heat spread to Samantha's cheeks and words sputtered in her mouth like a dying engine trying to start. The question had caught her completely off guard. "Umm, no. My place is a spectacle right now. I won't be staying there for a few nights."

Margo's white teeth clamped together inside her

O-shaped mouth. "Oh, that's right. Silly me. I forgot. I'm so sorry about all that. You poor thing."

"It's okay," Samantha said, taking a step toward the podium. She needed to escape before Margo tried to hug her. The last thing she wanted was the woman's pity, or to be drenched in her god-awful perfume. "I really should get this speech over with."

Margo gave her a nod before leading Teddy to their seats. Samantha took a deep breath and stepped behind the glass podium positioned in front of the opulent room. Five hundred sets of eyes focused on her and she braced her hand on the stand. Her sweat-slicked palm slid across the smooth surface and she mentally counted to ten to slow the pounding of her heart.

Clearing her throat, she fixed a plastic smile on her face. Conversations stopped like a giant ripple in a pond—starting at one end and growing larger until most of the talking stopped. The tinkling of glasses and rustling of fabric as people hurried to their seats filled the space. "Good evening, everyone, and thank you so much for joining us tonight. I have had the privilege of being on the Heart Board for several years, and this is by far the most money we've ever raised. That wouldn't have been possible without all of you."

She clapped her moist hand against the side of her cast and the audience followed suit, sending waves of applause around the room. She glanced at Max and he beamed at her as his large hands pounded against each other. Pride swelled in her chest. She'd done this, or at least played a huge part in putting this all together.

The double doors at the back of the ballroom burst open, jerking Samantha's attention to a man in the hotel's tailored, gray three-piece suit and red tie. Frowning, he hurried up the narrow aisle between the round tables.

Samantha's heart thundered in her chest, and she sought Max's gaze. She didn't know what was going on, but the urgency in the man's pace set her on edge. Something wasn't right. She just hoped the man barreling toward her wasn't here to carry through on the threat from earlier. If so, time was running out for her to take cover.

Chapter 18

Samantha steeled her nerves as sweat gathered at the back of her neck. She shifted her gaze from Max to the man charging toward her. A hushed murmur rose around the room, and Samantha licked her suddenly dry lips.

Max rose and rushed to stand in front of her, blocking her from the wide-eyed hotel employee. He reached behind his back and gestured for her to go to him.

She stepped away from the podium and positioned herself behind him, slightly to the side. Needing an anchor to hold her steady, she flattened her palm against the small of Max's back. Fixing a smile on her face, she tried to convey a calmness that didn't exist.

The man, Ronald according to his name tag, came to a halt in front of Max and frowned. Leaning forward, he kept his voice low. "I'm sorry to interrupt, but a gas leak has been reported inside the hotel. We need to evacuate immediately."

Max stiffened beneath her touch. "Who called in the leak? Is it verified?"

"The caller claimed to be staying here and smelled the leak while walking in a hallway upstairs," Ronald said. "We've made the necessary calls, but can't take any chances. We need to get everyone outside as soon as possible."

Agreeing with Ronald, Samantha nodded. Even though a feeling of unease crept over her skin. Did someone really think there was a gas leak inside the hotel, or was someone playing with her? Trying to get her in a vulnerable situation because she hadn't come to the gala alone? Was showing up with Max enough to alert whoever was after her that she didn't intend to go along with the instructions sent to her before leaving her apartment? "I'll make an announcement."

"Thank you. I have staff positioned in the lobby to assist in getting everyone where they need to go as quickly and smoothly as possible." Ronald dipped his chin then clasped his hands behind his back.

Shifting to face her, Max grabbed her hand. "Make the announcement then we need to get out of here. We aren't following the herd. It's not safe."

His words proved she wasn't crazy to think this could all be a ploy. She squeezed his hand then took her place back behind the podium. She took a deep breath and cleared her throat. "Please excuse this inconvenience, but I've been informed there is a suspected gas leak inside the hotel. We need to evacuate immediately. Please stay calm and move quickly, but with care to those around you, as you grab your things and head outside."

The soft murmurs turned into irritated mumbles and gasps. People shot to their feet, clutching bags and jackets as they fled toward the doors.

Max extended a hand toward her.

She laced her fingers with his and hurried along behind him through the throng of people. She glanced around for Ronald, but he'd disappeared in the crowd. Her pulse raced. Maybe he hadn't even worked for the hotel. Panic gripped her gut, and she struggled to keep pace with Max as he swiped her bag from the table and weaved through the crowd pushing toward the exit.

As if he could read her mind, Max picked up his pace. A tall figure came forward from the shadows of the burgundy curtains by the bar and Max pushed her behind him. She peered around his broad shoulders as the menacing shadow came toward them. Max's free hand landed on the side of his hip where he kept his gun tucked away. His body coiled tighter than a spring ready to snap, but instead of a spring, he was a hunter ready to attack. A hunter ready to protect her in a moment's notice.

The figure stepped away from the darkened space beside the wall and the low overhead lights showed off the all-American good looks of Marcus. The easy humor from earlier had faded and a vein pressed against the thin skin on his temple as he marched toward them.

Max's body relaxed and Samantha stepped out from behind him.

Marcus stopped and ran a hand through his Ken-like blond hair. "What a shit show. I called my car and my driver is waiting for you by the back door outside the kitchen. I figured you wouldn't want to waste time waiting for someone else to come pick you up, and you need to get out of here faster than I do."

Gratitude took away the sharp edge of fear and Samantha leaned forward to press a kiss to Marcus's cheek. "Thank you."

She pulled away and Max nodded once to Marcus before picking up his hurried pace toward the door. He pushed his way past the clustered groups of people and they spilled into the lobby. The glass doors to the street stood to their side. Bellmen ushered guests to safety, but Max steered Samantha away from the slightly more organized chaos.

Ronald appeared, a frown pulling down his thin lips. "Ms. Gates. I've been informed you have a car waiting for you outside the kitchen. I'll show you the way."

Anxiety zipped through her veins, but she followed along behind Max. Trusting his instincts and knowing he'd keep her safe.

Ronald walked in silence, cutting through the small groups of people who loitered in the halls. They passed a dining room, and the mouthwatering smells of roast beef and garlic floated to Samantha's nose. Her stomach growled at the reminder of the dinner she would miss, but she pressed forward. Her feet ached from the quick pace, but she wouldn't complain. The quicker she was out of here the better.

Their guide stopped in front of a set of double doors and he pushed them open. "Walk straight through to the back."

"Thank you," Samantha said.

The kitchen was empty, the silence of the eerie space buzzing around the stainless steel appliances. She kept her head fixed on Max's broad back as he led her through the maze of silver tables and gas stoves to the back door.

He pushed it open and for once she didn't mind the rush of cold air that greeted her. A black town car idled in the darkened alley and Max hurried over and opened the passenger door. He held a hand to her to stop while he poked his head inside.

The wind blew and snow whipped up and coated her exposed toes. She wrapped her arms around herself to fight the chill creeping into her skin. Dammit, she'd forgotten her pashmina. Max reemerged from the car, closed the door and then opened the back door for her to crawl into. She didn't ask questions, just vaulted herself into the warm car and went limp against the smooth leather seat.

Max slid in beside her and closed the door. His arm went around her shoulders, she collapsed her face into the stiff fabric of his jacket. A sob caught in her throat as all the emotions from the past few days welled up inside her. Allowing herself to give in to everything she felt, she let the sob escape her as she finally let the dam burst free.

Max sat on the couch and his gaze followed her as she paced the short length of his living room with her cell phone pressed between her ear and shoulder. Her hands moved through the air like she was performing a damn shadow puppet show, the constant motion needed to morph shadows into mystical creatures for others' amusement.

But nothing was amusing about this situation. As soon as they'd gotten back into the safety of his apartment, Samantha had made calls to board members about how to save their abandoned event and he'd called his contacts. Jack was still trying to dig up enough dirt on Teddy's financials to get him a warrant and Caspano was working his butt off trying to find out if the reported gas leak was a setup. Neither one of them had gotten any answers.

Max loosened his bow tie. His fingers worked the knot and let the black fabric hang on either side of his neck. Not letting his eyes roam from the lean lines of Samantha's body, he unbuttoned the top few buttons of his shirt and then tossed his cuff links on the coffee table.

Samantha finished her call, threw the phone on the coffee table next to his cuff links, and a tiny grunt of frustration gurgled from her throat. She picked at the pins securing part of her hair back and threw them on the ground. A wildfire of waves fell around her face.

Max stood and gathered her in his arms. He brushed the silken strands off her cheek and pushed them behind her ear. He let his thumb linger on her jawline as the rest of his hand cupped the back of her neck. "What did you find out?"

"We'll put all the auction items on our website and try to get online bids. We still raised a lot of money tonight, but we could have gotten so much more with everyone there, bidding in person." Her red-rimmed eyes pierced through him like a sharp dagger. He stroked his thumb up and down her tightened jaw until the muscles relaxed. "I'm so frustrated. When will this ever stop?"

"You know this shines a spotlight on Teddy as suspect number one, right? He was at the gala—he knew you weren't alone." He fought the anger pulsing through his veins. Samantha needed calm reassurance right now, not a barely restrained, angry cop. "I don't buy a random gas leak the same time you were at the hotel."

Her shoulders drooped. "It doesn't make sense. The text said to go home alone. How would he know I wasn't planning on doing that?"

Max shrugged. "I don't know. Maybe seeing me with you rattled him and made him speed up his plan. Whatever his reasons, he'll pay."

Samantha sagged against him, as if the weight of the evening had finally worn her down. "If you're convinced it's him, will you still talk to Jose tomorrow?"

Max dropped both hands to the center of her back and dragged the tips of his fingers along her spine. "Yes. A bigger case needs to be built against Teddy, and I need to tie up all the loose ends. I'll make sure to see Teddy tomorrow, too. I need to talk to him about Booker Harlan and the van that showed up at two crime scenes. According to my contacts, the FBI still hasn't found it. I'm going to run a search tonight for all the properties Teddy owns where he might have stashed it."

"I just want this god-awful night to be over," she said, her voice muffled against his chest.

"Come on," he said. "Let's get you to bed. Once you're settled, I'll get some work done."

He led the way to his bedroom and she pushed past him to step inside. He hovered near the doorway. He wanted to follow her in, sweep her off her feet and finish what they'd started earlier. But a lot had happened since then, and he needed to get as much information as he could on Teddy tonight.

Samantha stopped at the foot of the bed with her back to him. She shifted, reaching her hand behind her, and released an irritated breath.

He took one step forward. "What's wrong?"

She glanced over her shoulder at him, a lock of dark brown hair falling across her face, and his heart stopped beating. Even with mascara trailing down her face and puffiness around her brown eyes, she was the most beautiful woman he'd ever set eyes on. "The stupid zipper. I can't get it down all the way. Would you mind?"

Saliva pooled in his mouth and he swallowed hard to keep the drool from escaping from the corner. He didn't trust his voice, so he moved into the room without answering her question. Moisture slid over his palms and the sound of his dress shoes slapping across the hardwood filled the otherwise quiet space.

Wiping the sweat from his hands on the thighs of his pants, he slowly lifted his hand to the top of her dress and pulled the zipper down the slight curve of her back. Samantha shifted her weight from one foot to the other, as if his light touch was enough to make her squirm.

His mind flashed to their earlier encounter and his fingers tightened on the zipper. His gaze dropped to the rounded shape of her butt below his hands. His fingers itched to skim over the smooth skin of her rear end again. Keeping one hand on the base of her spine where the zipper had stopped, he raised his other hand to graze his knuckles against the soft flesh of her back.

Her sharp intake of breath egged him on.

His knuckles rose to her neck and he turned his hand, flattening his palm to the shape of her neck. "Is this okay?" he asked, his mouth pressed against her ear.

"Yes." Lust made her word thick and he chuckled against her neck.

Dipping his fingers under the fabric of her dress, he slid the sleeve from her slender shoulder and leaned forward to press his lips to her supple skin. He traced the delicate curve of her neck to the rounded top of her shoulder.

A low moan rumbled deep in her throat and she turned to face him. His lips found hers and he cupped her face in his hands. She pulled away and his arms fell to his sides. He wanted to reach for her, pull her back into his embrace, but the wicked gleam in her eyes stopped him. Her tongue swiped a wide circle around her mouth and all the blood from his head dropped to his dick.

She slipped her fingers under the sleeve still in place and slid it down her arm and over her cast. She wiggled her hips just enough for the siren-red dress to drop to the floor, pooling at her feet like a puddle of wine. Lifting her leg, she stepped away from the dress and stood in front of him with nothing but the black heels attached to her feet.

All thoughts fled his mind and he released a primitive growl. He closed the distance between them, scooped her into his arms and deposited her onto his bed. Samantha lifted herself up on her elbows, thrusting her bare breasts toward him. Like a prowling panther stalking its prey, he came over her, his weight on his hands and his knees spreading her legs apart.

Nothing else mattered right now. Not Teddy, not the alleged gas leak, not the fact that this woman had completely knocked him off-balance and created a need for her so strong within his soul it scared him to death. Right now, all that mattered was him and Samantha and showing her exactly what she did to him.

Tonight, she was his.

Chapter 19

Max braced himself on his hands on either side of her; his face hovered inches above hers. Samantha's warm, slow breath caressed his skin and he dipped down to capture her mouth with his. Her full lips molded to his and she fisted the front of his shirt in her hand.

"I think we need to even the score a little," she said, pulling away. She slid her fingers to the buttons of his shirt. A groan of frustration gurgled from her throat and she yanked the fabric to the side, sending a freed button skittering across the floor.

"Easy," he said with a low chuckle. He pushed off the soft mattress and shifted back to sit on his knees. The muscles in his thighs stretched tight, one on either side of her slender hips.

Samantha's eyes followed his every movement. "I wish I could take your clothes off, but I'll settle for watching." She chewed her bottom lip and heat smoldered from her heavy-lidded eyes.

One side of his mouth slid up into a smirk. "Don't expect a show."

Her wide mouth opened and she laughed, making her body shudder beneath him. "If you were putting on a show, I'd expect you to put on a uniform."

His smirk transformed into a grin and he hurried to unbutton his shirt and yank it off. Samantha grazed the tip of her finger along his chest. "Better, but you're not done yet."

Max shifted his legs as he undid the clasp of his pants. He pulled the heavy material and his boxers over his ass, down one leg and then the other. He threw them to the floor and then repositioned his legs to the sides of her hips once more. His erection throbbed as it jutted forward and Samantha's eyes widened as she took in the sight of him. He scooted backward and she reached out to stop him. "Where do you think you're going?"

"Honey, we need to take our time. I plan on keeping you awake all night."

He edged off the bed and landed on his knees. The cold from the floor shot up his bones and he shuddered. Grabbing her still-parted legs, he pulled her gently toward him.

"Eek! What are you doing?"

Max rose high enough for their eyes to meet and his hands skimmed up her toned calves to the soft skin on the insides of her thighs. "Just lie back and relax."

Lowering himself, he let his lips follow the same path his hands had taken. Placing small, slow kisses up her butterflied legs. Her knees trembled with each touch. His mouth reached the apex of her legs and he blew a gentle breath into the pink folds. Samantha moaned and ground her hips against the bed. He placed one hand on her stomach to keep her still and placed the other on the inside of her thigh. His thumb caressed her clit and he used his tongue to dive deeper into her heat.

Samantha grabbed a handful of his hair and lifted her hips, letting him probe deeper inside her. Her moisture coated his tongue and fueled his lust. His pulsing erection begged to be inside her, but he fought the all-consuming need to crawl on top of her and take his own pleasure. He pushed his face closer and stroked his thumb harder, faster against her. Her muscles danced on his tongue and her legs went slack. "Oh God, Max."

He lifted his head and grinned. Samantha's breaths came out in sharp gasps and her breasts heaved up and down. He stalked toward her and lowered his mouth on one delicious nipple. A sharp gasp rang from Samantha's mouth and she reached forward to wrap her hand around his dick.

He growled and glanced at her. "I won't be able to keep this up much longer with you touching me like that."

"I want you now." Lust made her voice deep and husky. She lifted her head off the pillow and her orgasm added a soft glow to her cheeks. Her dark curls had turned to a whirlwind of hair, strand after messy strand contorting into every direction. "Do you have condoms?"

Screw it. He was on a short leash that was about to snap at any time. Leaning to the side, he plunged his hand into the top drawer of his nightstand and pulled out a condom. He ripped it open with his teeth, pulled it on and shifted his weight on top of her.

Samantha reached down to take the length of him in her hand and guided the tip of his erection to her slippery folds. He pushed forward, but she didn't take her hand away. His eyes met hers and she smiled, shaking her head. Using her hand, she grazed the tip of his penis against her...up and down, up and down. Each stroke caused tiny eruptions of pleasure to dance in his nerve endings.

"Dammit, Sam. I'm going to come before I ever get inside you. You're killing me."

She laughed, released her grip and rolled on top of him. Lowering herself onto him, he groaned as her warmth wrapped around him, her muscles expanding little by little as he fit into her. She rolled her hips, her breasts jiggling with the motion. He reached up and cupped her breasts in his hands, using his thumbs to rub the hard nipples into stone-sharp pebbles.

She rolled faster, her back arched, the moonlight illuminating her golden skin. Her breathing intensified and her muscles squeezed around his dick as she reached climax one more time. Dropping her beautiful breasts, he gripped her hips and rocked her hard against him. His heart pounded out a fast beat he tried to keep up with and sweat trickled down his temple. He grunted and growled as the last spiral of pleasure took hold of him, sending him into a euphoria of release.

"Holy shit," he said. His hands fell to his sides and he collapsed against the bed. Samantha stayed seated with him still inside her. She leaned over and the touch of her nipples against his chest was almost enough to make him rebound and take her again. Her hair tickled his bare skin and he wrapped his arms around her back, pulling her close against him.

Samantha kissed his cheek and then rested her head on his shoulder. Her heated skin mingled with his sweat and the steady thump of his heart fell into rhythm with hers. "That was amazing."

He had no words. He'd been with plenty of other women before, but nothing compared to what he'd just experienced with Samantha. He skimmed his hand along the ridges of her ribs and realization hit him like a knockout punch. "Did I hurt you? I got so carried away, I forgot about your injuries."

"Trust me—I'm fine." A yawn muffled her words.

He chuckled. "You sound tired. You should try to get some sleep."

She rolled to the side and the absence of her wrapped around him caused his heart to lurch. Her head stayed in the crook of his arm and she smoothed a palm against his chest. "I know you have work to do, but will you stay with me until I'm asleep?"

"You bet your sweet ass I will. You might want to take these heels off first, though."

Samantha laughed. "You know I can't take these stupid things off by myself."

"You're helpless."

She slapped his chest and he captured her hand, trapping it against the matted hair on his pecs. "Will you help me?" Her voice was small and his gut told him she wasn't just talking about her shoes.

"Honey, I would do anything you wanted me to."

Sitting up, he unclasped her shoes and threw them to the floor. He stood and the cold air cooled his sweaty skin. "I'll be right back." He hurried to the bathroom to clean off and grab her a washcloth. The longer he was away from the warmth of her naked body, the stronger the need for more of her grew inside him.

Stepping back into the bedroom, he glanced at her delectable body laid out on his bed like a tasting platter just waiting to be devoured. Her mouth opened on another yawn and he clamped his teeth together to stomp out the desire stirring inside him. She needed sleep. He crossed the room and knelt down beside her. Her darkly colored lids drifted shut, as if the weight of them was too heavy to keep open. A whisper of a smile danced on her lips and sleep lulled her under.

He sighed, placed the folded washcloth on the nightstand beside her and covered her naked body with the bedspread. His body ached to feel her against him, but he had work to do. He had to track down any real-estate holdings under Teddy's name and check with Jack and Caspano about anything they might have found. And when that was done, he'd come back to the beautiful woman in his bed, pull her into his arms and never let her go.

Sunlight flooded through the uncovered window and poured over Samantha's face. She stretched her arms above her head and winced. Her bruised ribs ached as if someone had smashed a hammer against them. She reached beside her and the empty space pricked at her heart like a bee sting.

She sat up and the covers pooled around her, exposing her bare skin to the subtle chill sneaking through the room. Goose bumps puckered her arms and she hurried across the space to grab some clothes. Waking up without Max by her side left a gaping hole in her gut, but he must have a good reason for leaving her alone. She needed to find him.

The old hinges of the door squeaked and cold shot up her toes as she walked into the living room. Max sat on the couch, hunched over with his eyes fixed on his computer screen. She tugged at the hem of her sweatshirt and rubbed the bottom of her foot up and down the soft cotton material covering her calves.

She ran her tongue over her teeth and cringed. She should have run into the bathroom and at least brushed her teeth. Maybe she could creep away before he noticed her and scrub last night's makeup from her face.

"So what's it going to be? Are you going to come in or what?" The laughter in his voice made her smile.

"Are you working?" she asked and walked toward him. Max scooted over on the couch and she sat down, chancing a glimpse at his lit-up computer screen.

"Yeah." He turned toward her and the smirk on his face was so damn sexy she had to lean forward and kiss him. The dark stubble on his jaw scratched her skin and he grazed his flattened palm over her back. She pulled away quickly. They'd gotten pretty damn familiar last night, but she still didn't want him to taste her morning breath.

Dropping his hand from her back, he faced the computer and lifted it onto his lap. He leaned against the cushions of the couch and draped an arm around her shoulder and she leaned into him. The scent of coconut shampoo drifted through her nose. "I found a ton of properties under Teddy's name, as well as the rest of his family."

Samantha scanned the list of properties lighting up the screen. "Doesn't surprise me. They own vacation houses all over the world, but most of them are close enough for a quick weekend getaway. I'm not sure how often he goes to any of them. He's a city snob, and I can't picture Margo leaving Manhattan unless it was to some elegant spa or five-star European hotel."

"What about their place on Martha's Vineyard or the house in the Berkshires?"

"I'd see him visiting the Vineyard a lot more than the Berkshires. Teddy in the woods brings up a lot of laughable images, no matter how luxurious the house."

"Interesting," he said, scratching his skin. "The house in the Berkshires is one of the properties in his name, not his parents'."

She shrugged. "Maybe he likes the quiet."

The scent of coffee floated in from the kitchen and competed with the freshly-showered scents lingering on Max's skin. She glanced at the coffee table and a half-filled mug sat on a black coaster. "I'm going to grab some coffee. Do you want a refill?"

"No thanks. I need to head out and talk to Jose." He clicked out of the window on his computer and set it back down.

She straightened. "Are you going now?"

"Yes. I want to talk to him and Teddy today, and my sources are saying Teddy might be hard to find. The FBI is squeezing him tight about his connection with Booker Harlan, and the guy staked outside his penthouse last night reported he never went home." Max stood and stretched his arms over his head before leaning over and grabbing his coffee mug. He drained it and set it back down.

"You can't leave me here alone. Let me go with you." Panic settled into her bones. Never in her wildest dreams would confronting Jose be her best option, but staying at Max's apartment alone like a sitting duck was a much worse idea.

Max ran a hand through his hair, scratching at his scalp and causing the straight strands to stick out in all directions. "You've got to be kidding me. You want me to take you along to interview the man who killed your brother and is your suspected stalker?"

Anger and frustration pushed her to her feet and she jammed her index finger into his hard chest. "And you want me to sit around, twiddling my thumbs and waiting for the next attack…by myself? You already told me Jose is all but crossed off your list of suspects, and we both agreed whoever's after me knew I attended the gala last night with you. Do you really think they won't look for me here?"

His hand trailed from the top of his head to the back of his neck. "You're right, but maybe I can get Jack or Caspano to come watch you while I'm gone."

She crossed her arms over her chest. "To babysit me? I don't think so. I don't trust them. I trust you, and you might as well give up and agree because I'm not backing down."

Max growled his frustration out through clenched teeth. "Dammit. Why do you have to be so stubborn?" His hard tone softened and she let some of her tension slip from her tight neck.

"I'm not stubborn. I just know when I'm right."

Max lifted her chin toward him. "You stay in the car and you don't talk to anyone. I don't need a lot of time to cross Jose from my list and there's no reason to put yourself in his path."

She nodded, but he kept his fingers clasped to her chin.

"Promise me you'll stay in the car." His blue eyes bored into hers.

"I promise." What the hell did he think she was going to do? Going back to Melrose and seeing Jose again was the last thing in the world she wanted to do. But if it was between that and keeping herself from being caught in some madman's trap, she'd take her chances with Jose.

A shudder rippled through her. Fifteen long years had passed since she'd laid eyes on the man who'd killed her brother...the man she'd once loved.

Dear God, don't let that streak end today.

Chapter 20

Warm air wheezed through the rattling vents of Max's car. The heat mingled with the cold air taking occupancy in the space. The cold air was winning, even though they'd arrived in the Bronx five minutes ago. Samantha hadn't spoken a word, her mind spinning about what the morning could hold. She kept her gaze out the window as the familiar streets and buildings crawled by in the slow-moving traffic.

How could she be gone from the neighborhood she'd grown up in for so long and feel as though she had just left yesterday? Chills swept up and down her covered skin, and she lifted her hand in front of the vent to steal more warmth.

"Are you all right?" Max asked.

She drew in a deep breath and winced at the dull ache in her ribs. Forcing her eyes from roaming over the crowded streets and familiar buildings, she turned to focus on Max. "I'm nervous."

Max captured her airborne hand and placed their entwined fingers on her knee. "You have nothing to be nervous about. I'll run up to the apartment, ask a few questions and come right back down."

She offered him a weak smile and then turned toward the window again. Light flurries rained from the gray sky. The closer they got to the apartment where Jose was staying, the more run-down the buildings became. The sidewalks were mostly bare, but a few people scattered here and there. Worn coats, tattered clothes, shadowed and sunken eyes.

Her heart lurched.

She used to be one of them.

Max pulled the car to the sidewalk and parked in the fire lane. Letting go of her hand, he turned to face her and lifted her chin with the tips of his fingers. The dark stubble on his face had grown, shadowing the sharp angle of his jaw even more and making the blue of his eyes more pronounced. "I'll be right back. Lock the doors as soon as I get out. Call me if anything strikes you as off or you need anything."

"Okay." She pasted a weak smile on her face and hoped it hid her trembling nerves.

He leaned forward, pressed his lips to hers for a quick kiss and stepped out of the car. She locked the doors and then watched his hunched form brace the cold and step into the building in front of her.

Her gaze drifted to the clock lit up on the dashboard—9:10 a.m. Would Jose be home? When they were younger, he used to attend church with his mother every Sunday. Most weeks, her family would go with them.

They'd sit in the same pew and keep their heads ducked down together, whispering during the long mass. Both of their mothers would demand their silence, but Robbie would snicker behind his hand and fight to get in on their conversation.

Shifting to face the street, she swept her gaze up and down the sidewalk. The building she'd grown up in was only a few blocks from here, and memories assaulted her. Maybe it hadn't been such a good idea to stay away from this part of her past. The exile hadn't helped to heal any of her wounds; it had just pushed them to the far part of her mind she never dared to explore.

A part of her mind that was screaming at her now.

An older woman ambled around the corner with two grocery bags dangling from her hands. A bright scarf covered her head and she bent slightly at the waist as she struggled to keep her gait steady.

A gust of wind whipped down the street and rattled the windows of the car. The woman took a few steps backward. She lifted her hand to shield her face and the reusable green bag fell to the ground. Large red apples rolled away from her and a carton of eggs spilled open.

Samantha reached over to turn off the car and remove the keys from the ignition, and then jumped onto the sidewalk. Her booted feet left imprints in the light dusting of snow clinging to the frozen concrete and she bent over to pick up the trail of apples. The ache of her ribs from the long stretch toward the ground had her bending her knees to pick up the last few pieces of fruit.

"Thank you, dear. That wind came barreling around the building and all but took my breath away."

The familiar lilt of the woman's voice stirred a million emotions inside Samantha. She sucked in a sharp breath and the frigid air burned her lungs. Slowly, she rose to her full height, which wasn't much, but still enough to stand a few inches above the older woman. She stared into the weathered face of Jose's mom and tears sprang to her eyes.

"Samantha?" Mrs. Diaz asked in a shaky voice. The second bag of groceries fell from her hand and she covered her wide mouth with a trembling hand.

Samantha nodded, unsure of what to say as a million thoughts collided in her brain. None of them made it to her mouth. This woman had once been as much a part of her life as her own mother. She had loved her and hoped to one day be a part of her family.

Before she'd sent her son to prison with her testimony.

Before any words sprang to her mind, Mrs. Diaz shot her arms forward, grabbed her by the shoulders and pulled Samantha into a fierce hug. Samantha melted against her and let the heavy floral perfume engulf her. A smile touched her lips. She used to hate hugs from Jose's mom. Her perfume would cling to her skin and linger for days.

But now it smelled like home.

Mrs. Diaz pulled back and her hands tightened around the cashmere coat draped over Samantha's shoulders. Tears misted in the older woman's eyes, darkening the color of her brown eyes, but there was no denying the excitement that dilated her pupils. "It's been so long, my child. What are you doing here?"

Samantha sniffed, but her snot had frozen into the inside of her nostrils. "I had something to take care of this morning." What else could she say? Samantha had helped put her son behind bars once; she couldn't confess the real reason she was here was to make sure Jose wasn't trying to seek revenge on the part she'd played in his downfall.

"But it's been years. I haven't seen you since…" Mrs. Diaz's voice trailed off and she dropped her gaze.

"I know." Emotion clogged Samantha's throat and the words escaped with a tiny squeak. "It was easier to stay away. I didn't know if you'd want to see me."

Mrs. Diaz's gaze shot up and she reached her hand to cradle Samantha's cheek. Her icy fingers threatened to freeze to Samantha's exposed skin. "My dear child, I have never blamed you. I have been nothing but proud of you and everything you've accomplished. I'm just sad I never got to be a part of it."

Samantha's shoulders drooped and tears streaked down her face. This woman had lost so much, and Samantha hadn't even reached out to make sure she was all right. Fear and guilt had made her turn her back on the people she'd once cherished. "I'm so sorry."

Mrs. Diaz's thin lips curled into a smile. "You have nothing to apologize for. Now will you come have a cup of coffee with me? I want to know all about your exciting life. I've kept a close eye on everything you've done."

Panic kept her feet glued to the sidewalk and her mind blank. Max was upstairs right now. Was he speaking to Jose? And how much did Jose's mom know about her current life? Had she informed Jose about it, as well? She needed to find a way to politely refuse Mrs. Diaz's offer without hurting her feelings.

"Mama?"

Samantha widened her eyes and her heart beat an erratic rhythm in her chest. She tore her gaze from Mrs.

Diaz and searched behind her just as a man with short brown hair and bulging muscles sculpted under a dark brown jacket rounded the corner.

Their eyes locked and Jose stopped so quickly, the rest of his body wobbled from the abrupt change of motion. The lack of movement of muscles on his face gave no evidence to what this unexpected encounter meant to him.

All the moisture in Samantha's mouth evaporated and her vision tunneled. She stumbled to the side and Jose ran to her, brushing his mom to the side and catching her in his strong arms. Her knees buckled and she swayed against him. She lifted her face and the heat from Jose's breath skimmed over her skin. His intense stare penetrated her gaze, leaving her exposed and vulnerable, but she couldn't look away. He might no longer be the long, lanky teenager she'd once known, but she'd have recognized him anywhere.

A door opened and closed behind her and heavy footsteps pounded against the ground. A low growl pierced through the heavy haze threatening to swallow her.

Max.

"What the hell is going on?"

Jose Diaz stood on the sidewalk with his arms around Samantha and she was…what? Letting him? Hugging him back? She sure as hell wasn't trying to get away from him. Jealousy ebbed through Max, heating him from the inside out. Small flakes of snow fell on his burning skin, and he half expected steam to sizzle from the impact.

Samantha straightened her spine and stepped away from Jose. The man looked just like the picture the parole officer had shown him. Close-cropped dark brown hair, medium height, one hell of a build.

No doubt from lifting weights during all his free time in prison.

His gaze swept up and down Jose and then trailed over to Samantha. The curls from the night before had turned to soft waves that hung around her face and her naturally bronzed skin was as white as the flurries falling from the sky. Her wild-eyed stare darted from face to face as if shock had stolen her ability to make sense of the situation.

He wanted to ask her why she'd gotten out of the car, but now wasn't the time.

He dropped his chin toward her and asked, "Are you all right?"

She nodded, but her jerky movements and rigid stance told him otherwise.

Shifting back around to face Jose, he pulled out his badge and held it high in the air for the other man's inspection. "Jose Diaz?"

"Yes." A hint of fear lingered behind the acknowledgment.

"I need to speak with you. Now."

The older woman stood in front of Jose with her hands fisted on her wide hips. "What's this about? My son's done nothing wrong since he's been home."

Max fought to hide the smile that tried to lift his lips. The woman's maternal instincts had her trying to block access to her son, but Jose stood a good six inches above the woman. Max trained his gaze on her as he spoke. "I'm not saying he did. I just need to talk to him about some things that have happened since he's been released from prison."

"What things?" Jose asked. Frustration turned his words sharp.

"Things concerning me," Samantha said, her soft voice muffled by the brisk breeze.

"I told you to stay in the car," he said under his breath, but louder then he'd intended.

"If I remember correctly, nobody tells Sam what to do." Jose's easy use of her nickname made his blood boil and Max ran his tongue over his teeth to keep his temper in check.

He narrowed his eyes and tightened his grip on his badge. "Maybe they should when her life is in danger."

Jose's brown eyes turned to steel and he glanced first at Samantha and then to Max. "What do you mean?"

"Now that I have your attention, why don't we go upstairs and continue this conversation?" Max tried to keep his tone calm, but the clipped words belied his internal conflict.

"Oh *Dios mio*," Jose's mom said. "Please, everyone come upstairs and I'll make coffee. Jose, please pick the groceries up and carry them upstairs."

"Yes, Mama." Jose bent to pick up the fallen food at his feet.

Max grabbed Samantha's elbow and twisted her toward the car. He pressed his mouth close to her ear. "Why did you leave the car? Why was he holding you?"

"I hurried out to help when she dropped her bag." A hitch in her words made her stop to catch her breath. "I was in shock when I realized it was Jose's mom. She and I had always been so close, but I was afraid to see her after Jose went to prison. I just left her behind like everything else."

"Anyone would have done the same thing," he said. "But what happened with Jose?"

"I almost passed out when he came around the corner. If he hadn't caught me, I would have collapsed." She glanced over her shoulder and he followed her gaze back to Jose.

"I don't want you around him." The man was too far away to hear him, but he lowered his voice anyway.

She faced him and a myriad of emotions swam in her eyes and yanked on his heart. "I can't go back in the car now. I've already seen him, and his mom, and maybe I was wrong for staying away. I need to face my past, and all the mistakes in it."

Her words were like a vise clamping down on his gut. Facing her past meant not only staring into the eyes of her brother's killer, but apparently sitting down and having coffee with him. That was crazy. What would that prove?

The vise tightened. Maybe she wanted more than to just face her past. Maybe seeing Jose again, seeing the man she used to love and had planned a future with, had eased her fears enough to open her heart to other possibilities.

Whatever her reasons, Max would be by her side through it all. Even if being in the presence of a man she once loved would be uncomfortable as hell. She needed support right now, not his stupid insecurities, and he had to show her that he was the man who could give her everything she needed—because God help him, when the threat to her life was over he had no doubt he needed Samantha to be a part of his life.

Chapter 21

Tension sizzled in the air louder than the teakettle's shrill whistle screaming in the kitchen. For once in her life, Samantha didn't want the artificial buzz of caffeine zipping through her veins, so Mrs. Diaz had offered to make her tea. She wasn't much of a tea drinker, but maybe the heat of the warm liquid would break through the numbness that had kept her emotions paralyzed and brain murky. As if she'd been slowly making her way out of a pit of quicksand ever since she'd laid eyes on Jose.

Taking a shallow breath, she tore her gaze from her lap and found Max pacing, probably wearing a hole through the thin carpet in the living room. He hadn't stopped fidgeting since they'd stepped inside the cramped apartment. He'd jammed his hands in his pockets and the tinkling of loose change rang as loud as church bells in the otherwise silent room.

He'd been pissed when he'd spotted her in Jose's arms, but now something else lingered behind his blue eyes. A shadow had moved into them, darkening the irises that were usually alive with light.

She chanced a peek at Jose from the corner of her eye. He stood with his back to the only window in the room, his broad form keeping the limited sun from sneaking its way into the gloomy space. Samantha couldn't keep her gaze from roaming over his unfamiliar body and up to his still-familiar face. A shiver ran down her spine. How could someone look so similar to who they once were and so different at the same time?

"Does anyone want cream or sugar?" Mrs. Diaz asked as she buzzed into the room carrying a serving tray with four steaming mismatched mugs. She set the tray on the end table beside the threadbare floral sofa, and no one answered as they grabbed their mugs and hurried back to their places.

Everyone except Max, who stopped his panther-like prowl across the room long enough to trap Jose in his blank stare.

"Thank you," Max said. "But I really just need you to answer a few questions."

Jose's large hand wrapped around the mug and he stared directly into Max's eyes. "I'll tell you anything you want to know. Especially if it will help keep Sam safe."

Her chest tightened. After everything that had happened, did he really care about her safety? It was hard to imagine.

Max nodded and took out a small notepad and pen from the inside pocket of his unzipped leather jacket. "I'm going to be blunt with you. Someone has been stalking Samantha and using the information they've gained to kill three innocent women, and is now trying to kill Samantha."

A sharp gasp had Samantha turning toward Mrs. Diaz. The older woman sank down beside her on the couch and clasped her hand over Samantha's. The firm leathery skin gave her a sense of strength she'd missed from her own mother for years.

She turned to face Mrs. Diaz and gave her a sad smile. "I'm okay. Max is protecting me."

"Max?" Jose asked from across the room. He said the name as if it filled his mouth with a vile taste and he couldn't wait to spit out.

Max cleared his throat. "Have you kept tabs on Samantha while you were in prison?"

Samantha's mind flashed back to what Mrs. Diaz had said outside and her heart pounded wildly in her chest.

A whisper of a smile lifted Jose's lips. "It's hard not to follow her life."

"I need you to be a little more specific," Max said, annoyance causing his nostrils to flare.

Jose shifted to face Samantha and her muscles clenched. "For the first few years, Mama would tell me about where you went to school and what you were doing. I didn't want to know. I was pissed that you were out there and I was in hell. It took me years to accept that I'm the one who put myself in jail. I tried to rob that stupid nail salon. I'm the one who shot Robbie. I'm the one who ruined the plan. I never even apologized to you or your mom for what I did."

Tears stung her eyes and Samantha bit into her top lip to keep them from falling. Mrs. Diaz's grip tightened on her hand. Samantha forced herself to meet Jose's gaze head-on. She'd imagined this moment a thousand times, but never dreamed it would actually happen. Never dreamed she'd hear Jose apologize and see nothing but regret in his deep brown eyes. A million words sprang into her mind, but her throat was so tight, she could only nod in acknowledgment of his words.

"I never stopped telling Jose about the wonderful things you accomplished. You were always like a daughter to me, and I was proud of you. I wanted him to see what he could have done if he hadn't been such an idiot, and what he can still do if he keeps his life on the right path." Mrs. Diaz's strong and steady voice held so much conviction, no one could doubt her words.

Max kept his lips pressed together in a firm line, his gaze flitting from son to mother and back again. His tight jaw and rigid stance screamed his discomfort to the room, but Samantha was too bogged down with emotion to worry about it.

"Do you know where Samantha lives?" Max's sudden question brought the attention back to him.

Jose rubbed the back of his neck. "Manhattan, right? Far cry from the Bronx. You really made it." He chuckled and the pain that darkened his eyes was like a dagger to her heart.

She couldn't handle it. Couldn't handle sitting across the room from the boy she'd once loved, and who'd killed her brother and their dreams all in one day. Knots tightened in her stomach and she struggled to draw a breath into her constricted lungs. Jose didn't want revenge on her for ruining his life. He wanted to go back in time and fix all the mistakes he'd made.

But some things could never be undone.

And never be forgiven.

Samantha came to her feet and her gaze found Max's narrowed eyes. Her heart continued to race and sweat beaded on the thin hairs at the back of her neck, behind the curtain of hair that brushed against the tops of her shoulders. Her chest rose up and down as she struggled to take a breath and heat poured through her, flooding her cheeks. Panic throbbed through her body, leaving her mind blank of the words she desperately needed to say to get the hell out.

Max took a step toward her, concern finally chasing the shadows from his eyes. "Are you all right?"

She opened her mouth to speak, but nothing came out. Reaching her cast-free hand up, she rubbed at her collarbone as if she were rubbing a magic lamp and a genie would appear and speak for her.

But she didn't need a magic genie. Max's long legs strode toward her and he cupped her cheek in his cool hand. His touch was like a soothing balm over her heated skin. Dropping his chin, he said, "I need to get you out of here. Say goodbye and let's go. I'll wrap this up later."

She nodded, his nearness giving her strength, and turned toward Mrs. Diaz. "I'm so glad to see you, but I need to go."

The lines in Mrs. Diaz's forehead deepened. "What about the person after you?"

Jose took a step forward. "If you came here to find out if I'm the person trying to hurt her, you came to the wrong place. I've caused her enough pain to last a lifetime. I'd never intentionally harm her. Not then and not now. I'll always…" Jose's voice trailed off and he hung his head.

Jose's words hit the stiff shield of armor she'd wrapped around herself until it all fell to the floor, leaving her exposed and vulnerable. She closed her eyes against the pain and sadness engulfing her like dark clouds gathering together before a tornado strikes. She needed to be anywhere but here when the tornado hit the ground and took her out at the knees.

"I'll be in touch. Thank you for allowing me to speak with you." Max pressed his fingers to the small of her back and pushed her gently toward the door.

With one hand on the brass knob, she glanced over her shoulder at Jose. Their eyes locked and a moment of understanding passed between them. Jose didn't want to kill her. He'd changed a lot over the years, but she still knew him. And he'd never hurt someone he still loved.

Max followed Samantha out the door of the apartment building. The frigid air whipped at his face and cooled the flames burning inside him. He wasn't sure if it was jealousy or frustration that made his blood burn hot, but he was glad for the dropping temperature bringing him back down to reality.

Samantha had bent over, elbows on knees, and hung her head the moment her feet had hit the sidewalk. People passed by without so much as a glance in her direction. Too bothered by the cold or their own damn problems to notice a woman in turmoil. Max walked up beside her and rubbed his palm up and down her back. The soft cashmere of her coat was like butter against his chilled skin.

He gave her a few minutes to catch her breath and said, "Let's get you in the car. It's freezing out here."

Her shoulders shuddered and she drew in a deep breath. Straightening, she stumbled to the side of his car as if he'd just picked her up from the bar after having a few too many drinks. He stayed close, her elbow clasped in his hand, and shut the door after she'd folded her legs into the car. He jogged around the front bumper, stopped to fill his lungs one more time with the brisk air and then hurried inside.

"Do you want to talk about it?" he asked and started the car. The old engine chugged to life and cool air rattled from the vents. They hadn't been out of the car too long; hopefully the air would turn warm quick.

"I don't even know what to say. Everything that just happened was just so…unexpected," she said, her voice hollow.

He wanted to gather her in his arms and comfort her, ease her away from the shock that lingered in her eyes. But he couldn't get the image of Jose holding on to her out of his head—or the glance that had passed between him and Sam. He wasn't an idiot. There was no mistaking the look of longing that haunted Jose's eyes.

The look on Samantha's face had been more difficult to discern.

A soft buzz vibrated against his thigh and he pulled out his phone. *Jack.*

He'd have to wait to get the answers his heart needed from Samantha. A murder investigation took precedence, and she needed time to gain her bearings. He could at least give her that.

Answering the phone, Max made sure the call wouldn't transfer to his speakers and said, "Hey, Jack. What's up?"

"Teddy still hasn't been home and the FBI has taken over his office. He's nowhere to be found. An account's been uncovered that links him to money laundering and some other very illegal activity. Most of which started the same time he bought the waste-management business."

"Shit," Max said. Samantha turned curious eyes toward him, but he kept his gaze fixed on the busy street, waiting for a chance to merge into traffic. "So I can get my warrant, but the feds will already have everything, and it looks like he skipped town."

Jack's deep breath blew through the speaker and rattled Max's eardrum. "Sounds about right. He owns a few places in the city that are being canvassed, but no luck."

"What about his wife? Where's she?"

Samantha's gaze all but burned a hole into his cheek and he glanced her way, holding a finger up for her to wait, and then turned back to the congested road.

"I don't know. Word is Teddy left the gala alone last night. She could have met up with him somewhere, or maybe has a place of her own nobody knows about."

"How is that possible?" A gap opened and he nudged the nose of his car into the lane of traffic. Horns blared around him, but he didn't care. He needed to get out of here and come up with a new game plan. Heading uptown to Teddy's penthouse wasn't an option any longer.

"Could you ask Samantha? She might have some ideas where Teddy would have gone. Hopefully he's still in the city, or we're screwed."

"She's right here. I'll ask her and get back to you if we come up with a plan. Have you been in touch with

Caspano at all?" Caspano's ability to link Teddy with the called-in gas leak was almost a moot point, but the more ammunition to use against Teddy the better. If the feds were able to lock him up for fraud or money laundering…fine. But he wanted to take him down for murder.

"Not yet. I'll give him a call now."

"Let me know what you find out." Max clicked off the phone, in too much of a hurry to tell Jack bye, and tightened his grip on the wheel. The coolness of the leather seeped through his skin. "Teddy is gone and the FBI has moved in to his office to take his computers and anything else they can use. No one knows where Margo is either."

Samantha pinched the smooth skin on her forehead. "This nightmare is never going to end."

"You said earlier that Margo doesn't like to leave the city. Do you know where she'd be? Is her family in New York?"

"No, I think they live somewhere in Jersey. But it wouldn't be hard for her to get there."

"Would Teddy try to hide there?"

She shook her head in slow motion, as if not confident of her answer. "I'm not sure, but I don't think so. Wouldn't that be an easy place to find him?"

"Maybe. I don't know how many agents they have looking for him. They might be more focused on gaining evidence at this point. Anywhere else you can think to look?"

"We could try Margo's office space. It's on the Upper East Side, just a few blocks from mine."

A car pulled out in front of him. He slammed on the brakes and horns erupted behind him. He hated driving in the city. He swallowed hard, pushing the brief moment of panic down his throat, and collected his thoughts. "Why would Margo have an office? I thought she didn't work? And a property like that didn't come up when I ran my search, not even a rental."

Samantha shrugged. "She doesn't have a job, per se, but she works her ass off on multiple charity boards. She'd need a space to work, and it never struck me as odd that she'd want a space separate from their home."

"Would it be listed under a different name?"

"Probably her legal name."

Interest heightened his anxiety. "What do you mean? Her legal name isn't Margo Van Buren?"

A small smirk erased some of the tension from Samantha's face. "She didn't take Teddy's name. It was a big source of gossip at the time. He was pissed she didn't want to be a Van Buren. Honestly, I think everyone was curious about why she didn't change it. The Van Buren name opens a lot of doors. I suppose those doors were open to her simply by marrying Teddy."

"So what's her legal name?"

"Margo Silverman."

He didn't give a damn about what Margo's name was. He needed to get to her office and pray to God she was there and had some answers for them. Once he found Margo, hopefully she could lead him to Teddy and maybe then he could find the missing piece to the puzzle.

And then he could dive deeper into Samantha's reunion with Jose. Images of her naked in his bed the night before flashed in Max's mind and a fist-like grip squeezed his heart. Did last night mean as much to her as it did him? Or had that been a one-night stand, a welcome distraction from the pain haunting her life?

Something inside told him getting the answer would be a game changer.

Chapter 22

Here was the over-the-top, smack-you-in-the-face display of wealth Max had expected to see in Samantha's office. Hell, he'd expected it in her Upper East Side town house. But both spaces had been warm and inviting. Margo Van Buren—or Silverman, whatever the hell her name was—hadn't opted for a cozy office that made everyone feel welcome. The space looked more like a shrine to herself with black-and-white portraits of Margo covering the walls. She'd gone for an all cream-colored palette that made him terrified of bringing a drop of dirt into the pristine room.

Hell, even a snowflake would mar the perfection around him. The white wouldn't be the same color as the soft carpet that padded his socked feet to perfection or the tufted sofa dominating the middle of the room. God, he hated taking his shoes off anywhere other than his own apartment. What kind of person made everyone who entered their office take off their shoes?

The answer was obvious. Margo Silverman was that person. A huff of irritation shot from his nose.

Samantha had surprised him by slipping into her public persona and erasing all signs of distress the moment she'd stepped out of the car and approached the doorman as if they'd been friends forever. She'd even remembered his first name, although she'd mentioned she'd only been to Margo's office a handful of times.

He shook his head, recalling the look on the man's face as Samantha Gates addressed him by name. Pride and excitement had danced in his eyes, making it laughably easy to make their way to the private elevator that led up to Margo. Add the power of his badge with Samantha's charm, and the doorman had been like very pliable putty in his hands.

Max would place money on any table in Vegas that Margo would be pissed to discover her doorman had not only told them she was there, but had granted them such easy access.

Margo displayed no evidence of it now as she sat behind the antique desk, her bright red lips lifted in a wide smile. "Well, this is an unexpected surprise. How are you today, Samantha? I'm so sorry for what happened last night, but I'm glad no one was hurt." She closed a notebook on her desk and walked over with an outstretched hand to greet them.

Samantha straightened her spine and tilted her chin in the air just enough to put her confidence on full display. It didn't matter that she still wore the tight yoga pants and sweatshirt she'd thrown on after rolling out of his bed this morning. Samantha belonged in this world just as much as she'd fit into the run-down apartment.

"Sorry if we surprised you," Samantha said before he could jump into his litany of questions. She squeezed Margo's hand, probably out of pity since it still hung in the air, and then dropped her arm to her side. "No one knew where you were, and I figured you came in to get some work done. We tried to call, but no one answered. We thought we'd stop by and see if we got lucky."

The muscles in Margo's face remained passive, but her pupils dilated for an instant. She rubbed her palms against the gray slacks hugging her thighs. "My phone died and silly me forgot I didn't have a charger here. I don't usually work on Sundays, but there was a lot of work to do last night and today after the way things ended at the gala. Especially when the chair of the board is rushed out the back. I've worked all night uploading auction items to the website."

"Thank you for your dedication," Samantha said. Her voice rose a bit higher than usual, cluing Max in to her lack of sincerity.

Margo didn't notice.

"Have you seen Teddy since last night?" Max asked.

Margo stiffened and Samantha cast him a glance from the corner of her eye. He raised his brows at Samantha and then studied Margo. He didn't have time for tact. The more hours that passed, the farther Teddy could be if he'd gone on the run.

Margo smoothed a hand over the tight ponytail giving her a free face-lift. "No. He disappeared into that chaotic crowd. You saw how badly he had wanted to leave, and then with everything that happened with that ridiculous gas leak scare, he took the chance to get out of there as fast as possible." Her voice trailed off and she dropped her gaze to the floor.

"Are you aware he is being investigated by the FBI right now?"

Her gaze snapped up to meet his and horror etched fine lines in the corners of her eyes. "What do you mean? Why would they be doing that?"

Suspicion danced in his gut. Teddy wouldn't be MIA if he weren't scared about a federal investigation landing on his doorstep. How could a wife be so removed from her husband's life? He chose to ignore her question and ask one of his own instead. "Does Teddy own or have access to a white utility van?"

A brittle laugh shot out of Margo's mouth. "Teddy? Own a utility van? This must be some sort of joke. The man barely knows how to drive."

"Margo," Samantha cut in with a low, soft voice. "This isn't a joke. Will you please search your memory for anything that could help us? Anything that jumps out at you about Teddy. I know he's your husband and I hate to ask you to do this, but it's important."

Margo pressed her lips together and stared at them with wide eyes. "Do you think Teddy's done something? Do you think he's the one who's trying to hurt you?"

Silence passed for a beat and Margo shook her head, her blond ponytail swishing from side to side with the motion. "I know you two have had your differences, but you can't honestly believe he'd want to hurt you?"

Samantha reached out and grabbed Margo's hand. Margo's green eyes locked on their clasped grip, as if she didn't understand the gesture. "We have to look at anyone who has a motive," Samantha said. "Please. Do you know if he'd have access to a white van, or has he mentioned anything to you? Has he been acting differently lately, going out at night without telling you where he'll be?"

Margo shifted her eyes to the ceiling and backed away from them toward the couch. The backs of her knees collided with the cushion and she sank down, covering her mouth with her hand. "He'd never do anything to hurt anyone." Her words came out muffled from behind her palm.

Max sighed. They weren't getting anywhere. "Where would he be right now? Is there a place he likes to escape to when he needs to get away?"

Margo dropped her hands to her lap and bit into her lip like a child fighting to keep in a secret. She lifted her gaze and tears turned her green eyes glassy. "He's been spending a lot of time remodeling our home in the Berkshires. That's been a little odd to me since he's never really liked going there. Over the last couple of months, he's become obsessed with hiring people to fix the plumbing and install a better satellite. He seemed happy doing it, so I didn't ask many questions."

Excitement clamped on to Max's stomach lining and he pitched forward on his toes. "So, he's hired a lot of maintenance crews?"

Margo cocked her head to the side like a dog trying to understand its master's words. "Yes. Why?"

Samantha clasped onto Max's arm. "Because maintenance crews drive vans."

"We need to go. Now," Max said.

Samantha nodded her agreement.

Margo held up her palms in frustration. "Stop it. You both are wrong. I'm sure Teddy is somewhere close by, not traipsing around in the Berkshires in the cold. If there's a problem, I'll call him and ask him to come and talk to you. I'm sure he can fix this whole mess with you and whatever nonsense is going on with the FBI."

Samantha's jaw dropped and she watched Margo maneuver her way to her desk. How could she be so naive? She picked up her phone and Max said, "I thought your phone was dead? Do you have a landline?"

Margo giggled and the sound grated against Samantha's nerves like nails on a chalkboard. "I swear, sometimes I amaze myself. I'm afraid I can't call him. I've never bothered to get a landline here since everyone has a cell phone these days."

A lead ball dropped in Samantha's stomach. Was Margo covering for Teddy, or just that much of an idiot? She'd offer her phone, but Max insisted she turn it off after she'd received the threatening text message the other night. She did have a landline at home, but it wouldn't do her any good right now.

"Take mine," Max said, cutting into her thoughts. He walked toward Margo, his phone stretched toward her. "Just make sure you don't tip him off that we're here."

She hesitated, but only briefly, before she took the phone. Her fingers made quick work of pressing numbers onto the screen and then lifting the phone to her ear.

Making sure Margo was out of earshot, Samantha turned Max to the side and said, "I want to go with you. What if he's still in the city? I don't want to be here by myself, and I don't trust anyone else but you."

"And if he's there, I don't want you anywhere near him while I'm trying to arrest him. He's dangerous, and cagey men take a hell of a lot of chances. I won't risk your safety." He brushed his knuckles against her cheek and she leaned into him.

She kept her gaze locked on his and tried to read the expression. His drawn-down lips and puckered brow could be a sign of concern…or something more. "I don't like being away from you."

A flash lightened his eyes to the color of clear blue water and his lips curved up. It was all she needed. They might not have talked about what had happened last night, but they didn't need to. One look told her everything she needed to know.

A sigh escaped her lips and excitement squeezed her heart. If Max needed her out of the way so he could do his job, she'd stay. Then he could come back to the city with this nightmare behind them and get on with trying to have a real relationship.

"I'll stay," she said and his eyes narrowed.

He glanced over his shoulder toward Margo, and then back into her eyes. "That was easier than I expected. Why the about-face?"

She shrugged and dropped her gaze to her toes. Maybe she'd read too much into his expression. Max might not be on the same page, and it was best not to give away too much until they talked. "You're right. It would be dangerous, and it's better for you to focus on your job and not worry about me. Besides, I have work to catch up on. I'll call James to pick me up and we'll swing by my place to grab what I need. He's as good as any bodyguard I could hire."

The pinched expression told Samantha exactly what Max thought about that, but she didn't see any other option. Max might not like James, but she trusted him with her life. And if Max was going to be out of town, James was the next best thing.

"He's not answering." The whine in Margo's voice cut into their conversation and made Samantha wrinkle her nose. A whining child was annoying enough, but a grown woman should never make that noise.

They faced Margo, and Margo's unexpected nearness made Samantha take a step back in retreat. Tears hovered on Margo's long lashes and any attempts at deflection of Teddy's crimes were erased from her smooth-as-silk skin.

"I need to go." Max yanked his phone from Margo's clasped fist and handed it to Samantha. "Call James. I'll wait until he gets here."

Samantha cradled the phone in her palm and pulled up James's contact information before pressing Send. James answered on the second ring.

"Hello?"

"James, it's Samantha. Do you remember where Margo Silverman's office is?"

"Yes, Ms. Gates. Are you okay?" The concern in his deep baritone voice soothed her frayed nerves.

"I'm fine. I need you to pick me up and stay with me for a few hours." Her gaze followed Margo as she chewed on her thumbnail and kept her chin tucked to her chest, oblivious to the world around her. Maybe if she'd woken up and looked around, she'd have seen what a sick bastard she was married to before he'd turned into a murdering lunatic.

"Okay. Is your house cleared?"

"Yes, but we won't be staying there long. I haven't been back since the explosion, and I assume it's still a mess. I'll need to swing by there and grab some things."

She glanced at Max for confirmation. They hadn't exactly discussed her waiting for him at his home. He nodded and relief washed over her.

"I'm not far. I'll be there in ten minutes."

Samantha clicked off and handed the phone back to Max. "Go now. James will be here soon and you don't have time to waste."

Max flicked a cautious glance toward Margo. "You are not to contact Teddy under any circumstance. He is dangerous and he needs to be stopped. If I find out that you tried to warn him in any way, I will arrest you for obstruction of justice. Do you understand me?"

"I couldn't even if I wanted to," Margo said, her voice growing more childlike every time she spoke. "I don't have a phone."

Samantha waited for more—another declaration of Teddy's innocence, interest in how Max knew how to find their house in the Berkshires, anything—but nothing came.

"I'll go down with you and wait for James in the lobby," Samantha said.

Margo turned to face the magnificent skyline dotted against the gray sky. Her shoulders dropped forward. Teddy had done a lot to try to destroy Samantha's life, but she'd been through worse and come out stronger. Hell, if Teddy hadn't started this sick game, she'd have never met Max. Never opened herself up to the possibility of finding love again.

But Margo's life was about to be destroyed in a different way. Once news broke about his murderous pastime, as well as whatever the FBI had found on him, the life Margo had known for so long would go down in flames. She wasn't sure Margo would survive it.

A prickle of pity pierced her heart as she headed toward the door, but she shook it off. She couldn't concentrate on Margo and whatever waited for her when this was all through. Samantha was still living in this hell, and it was beyond time to put an end to it. She needed to move on with her life without worrying about what lurked in the shadows.

She just hoped she'd be moving on with Max by her side.

Chapter 23

Samantha had to pay today. The FBI was closing in—squeezing, suffocating, smothering the life from the plan. Now it was time to act. Even if the new, half-assed plan was risky…it had to be enough. There wasn't time to come up with something better.

Blood rushed furiously through narrow veins and adrenaline spiked. Today was the day when Samantha would pay for all of her sins. The day she'd come face-to-face with her worst nightmare.

Shaking hands gripped the phone. The plan had to be set in motion with exact precision or it'd never work.

Taking a deep breath to calm the quivering excitement, the now-steady finger pressed the familiar number to the high-end floral store on the Upper East Side.

"I'd like to place an order for a delivery—I need it sent out as soon as possible."

* * *

Samantha's heart sank. She ran her fingertips along the scarred wall in her foyer. Gone was the beautiful mirror that had lined the wall and reflected light into the small space. Instead, tattered drywall hung in its place. Streaks of darkened soot ran down the paint, as if the house were crying for the beauty that had been so violently ripped away.

At least the shattered glass had been removed.

Turning a wide circle, she forced herself to face the rest of the destruction. Broken windows, marred hardwood floors and ruined furniture stared back at her. Emotion welled up in her throat, but she refused to let it blossom. Things could have been a lot worse.

She could be dead.

"Ms. Gates?" James interrupted her musings, his weight shifting as if he was unsure of what to do. The door stood open and a gust of wind blew through the foyer, stirring around loose debris that cluttered the once pristine floors. "Would you like me to grab your things for you, or keep watch downstairs?"

She didn't want him here at all. She wanted to be transported back in time to when her home provided her the only place of peace and solace in the whole damn city. But she couldn't tell James that. As much as it sucked, she needed his protection with Max chasing after Teddy.

"I'll run upstairs and grab what I need. You can stay down here, but shut the door. It's freezing and it might take me a minute."

James nodded and closed the door. Samantha turned to climb the two flights of stairs to her room. Her computer was in the living room, but she might as well pick up some more clothes to take to Max's. A wicked smile played on her lips. Maybe she'd grab something sexy to celebrate finally bringing in Teddy.

Ring, ring, ring.

With a sigh, Samantha turned on her heel and hurried toward the kitchen. Only one person ever called her landline on a Sunday. Her fur-lined boots slapped against the tile floor in the kitchen, and a rush of joy trickled through her. At least this room had gone unscathed from the bomb.

Samantha picked up the receiver and sank into the soft cushioned chair at the table. If her mom wanted to have a lengthy conversation, maybe she'd turn the fireplace on.

"Hi, Mama. How are you?" She forced a cheerful note to her voice and propped her feet up on the chair beside her.

"Oh my goodness, honey! You should see these beautiful roses someone sent me. Was it you? You know how much I love roses. But the poem you wrote was a little odd. You could have just had them sign your name. Really, writing was never your strong suit." Her mom's words came out on a rush of excitement.

Samantha's back went rigid and her feet fell to the floor. A prickle of fear stole her breath. She had to choose her words carefully. She couldn't clue her mom in to the terror seizing her heart. "What does the card say? They might have written it down wrong."

"Roses are red, violets are blue. Don't go away because I'm coming for you." Light laughter filled the speaker. "You're so silly. You should have just brought the roses with you when you stopped by. Four roses aren't too hard to carry. But it was a nice surprise."

Four roses. The last roses she'd received had two roses, one for each woman murdered. Two more victims, two more roses. Fear threatened to steal her voice, but she couldn't let it. Teddy wasn't in the Berkshires. He was in the city. And he was going after her mother.

"I would have brought them, but I got caught up. I'm sending James over, though. He wanted to say hi since he hasn't seen you in a while. I'll try to stop over later, okay?"

"Okay. That sounds lovely."

Samantha hung up the phone and scrambled to her feet. "James!" Her voice echoed through the room.

Heavy footsteps pounded toward her. James ran into the kitchen, a gun pointed in her direction. Samantha dropped down in a crouch behind the chair. She peeked over the top. "What the hell are you doing?"

James's panicked gaze skirted around the room, his gun trained in front of him. "Are you okay? Is someone in here?"

"No one is in here but me. Drop your gun." She stood and her legs were the consistency of cooked spaghetti noodles. She leaned against the chair for support. "I need you to go see my mom. I think Teddy is going after her. She just got roses with the same kind of weird message that I've been getting."

"I can't leave you here," James said, shaking his head.

"I'm not giving you a choice. She's in danger, and you're the only one who knows how to get to her. If you don't go, then I will." She pulled herself up to her full height and prayed the bravado in her voice hid the frantic beating of her heart.

"What if it's a trap? What if he's trying to lure you over there?"

"Even better reason why I should stay here. He won't hurt her with you there. Bring her and Mrs. Walsh here, and then we'll all go to Max's to wait. I need to call him and tell him about this, though. Teddy might not be where Max thinks he is."

James secured his gun in the holster hidden behind his dark gray jacket. "I still don't think—"

"I don't care what you think. You need to go. Now. Make sure my mom is safe." She hated the whine that cut through her shrill voice, but they couldn't waste any more time. Teddy could be moving in on her mom at any moment. She couldn't lose her.

A heavy sigh lifted James's broad chest. "Fine. I'll be right back."

She sank back into her chair as she watched him hurry out. The thin skin around her temples pulsed along with the rapid beat of her heart. If something happened to her mom, she didn't know what she'd do. The sharp talons of terror ripped into her soul.

She needed to call Max. If her mom had just gotten flowers, Teddy wasn't in the Berkshires. He was lurking in her neighborhood, ready to pounce. A chill swept over her as she cast a worried glance around the empty town house. She'd have Max come get her. He shouldn't be too far outside the city yet.

She grabbed the phone to place the call, her muscles relaxing at the thought of just hearing Max's deep, soothing voice.

Ding-dong.

Her pulse raced as fast as the thoughts in her frantic mind. Someone was at the door. Should she answer it?

Creeping out of her chair, she walked toward the front door on awkwardly bent legs. Thick sheets of plywood had been secured over the shattered windows, but she didn't want to chance anyone spotting her through the thin strip of glass around the door. Even her shadow could be more than enough to clue whoever was out there that she was inside…alone.

Ding-dong.

Fear churned in her stomach, mixing with the sudden arrival of bile sneaking its way up her throat. She had been stupid to send James away, but what other choice did she have? Taking a deep breath, she bent her head close to the tarnished floor and peeked up through the sliver of smudged glass on the side of the door.

A bright ray of sunlight squeezed through the gray clouds and shone down on sleek black boots, long, gray-cloaked legs and blond hair pulled into a tight ponytail. Margo's face was shrouded in shadows, but the whites of her eyes were clear as day against the gloomy sky.

Samantha's pent-up breath whooshed from her lungs and the crazy rhythm of her heart returned to normal as she stood to open the door. A gust of wind whipped inside and rattled the makeshift windows. Margo's wide eyes and trembling chin had the knots in Samantha's stomach tightening.

"What are you doing here?" Samantha leaned on the doorjamb, narrowing her eyes and taking in Margo's zombielike demeanor. Her unblinking eyes stared past Samantha and her rigid muscles showed no sign of recognition, as if she'd ingested some sort of substance.

The words cut into Margo's trance. She twisted her gloved hands in a tight circle. "Can I come in? I need to tell you some things. I thought… I can't…" An onslaught of tears cut off her words and she pushed past Samantha, gaining an uninvited entrance into the house.

Tension pounded against Samantha's skull. She didn't have time to deal with Margo's theatrics, but maybe she'd thought of something useful.

Or had stopped trying to protect a husband who wasn't worth the sacrifice.

Choosing to believe the latter, Samantha closed the front door against the fierce whistle of the wind and followed the sound of cabinets closing in the kitchen.

Porcelain teacups rattled in Margo's shaky hand and Samantha cringed. Margo set the cups on the marble countertop and went back to searching through the cabinets.

Samantha took a seat on a stool in front of the island and pinched the bridge of her nose while her mind raced. She'd let Margo take her time finding whatever she was looking for while she called Max. If Margo wanted to ask for help, she would have. Maybe Margo needed a minute or two to collect her thoughts to spill whatever she'd come over here to say. Grabbing her phone, she pressed the receiver to her ear and tried to remember Max's number.

Clinks and clanks echoed around the room and water flowed from the refrigerator. The microwave door opened and closed, and the gentle hum of the machine bit into the silence of the room. The door opened and closed again, and seconds later the sound of something pushing toward her had Samantha lowering her hand and staring down at a cup of tea.

Margo sat with a cup poised in her hands; a floral-edged saucer sat in front of her. "I need to talk to you about Teddy. I didn't want to believe…couldn't accept it…but I can't hide from the truth anymore."

Samantha lowered the receiver and hesitated. A quiver shook Samantha's body and she grabbed the tea Margo had set in front of her. A shot of whiskey would be better to calm her nerves, but she'd settle for the chamomile she always kept on hand. The hot liquid burned her tongue, but she forced another long sip through her lips and waited for it to soothe the rushing blood in her veins. She waited for Margo to go on; the drawn-out silence drove her to the brink of insanity. Margo needed to spit it out. Then she could let Max know about her mom and Margo's confession at the same time.

Margo's shoulders lifted on a deep breath. "He really went off the deep end when you wouldn't let him back in the company last year. He's always been pissy about it, but when he found out about the initial public offering he'd miss cashing in on, he lost his mind."

Samantha set the cup on the matching saucer in front of her and shook her head. Tan drips of tea trickled over the side and she swiped them away with the pad of her finger. "He didn't do anything to help with the company. How did he expect to walk in and get a major payday from it? And why would it matter? His family has more money than the whole state of Rhode Island."

Mimicking Samantha, Margo set her cup down and pushed it away. "Not anymore. Ever since Teddy took over the company, they've hemorrhaged money. He blames you. All he talks about is how you're the reason we're in this mess and how he'll make you pay for taking everything away from him."

The knots from earlier looped around her organs and

squeezed them tight. Although she and Max already figured out that Teddy was responsible for turning her life upside down, it was horrifying to actually hear the truth from Margo.

Max!

"I need to call Max." There was still time to reach him before he got too far away.

A sad frown pulled Margo's lips down like a kid whose favorite toy had been taken away. "I'm so sorry, Samantha. I never thought he'd take things this far. I should have said something. I should have stopped him." Tears made her words come out tight and tugged at Samantha's sympathies.

She wanted to reassure her it wasn't her fault, but she couldn't waste time. Max had to know what was going on...but where was her phone? Thick fog rolled over in her mind and her vision tunneled. She patted the cool marble around her for her phone, but her fumbling hand found nothing.

Dammit, what was wrong with her? Her blood pounded against her skull as she tried to remember Max's number. The harder she tried to focus, the more intense the pounding became. Samantha stood from the stool and her legs gave out. She grabbed for the top of the stool, but her palm slid from the seat and she crashed to the hard floor. Her blood crawled through her veins with the speed of a lethargic snail. A dull ache thudded through her side as her ribs registered the pain, even though her mind had a hard time catching up.

"Oh my goodness," Margo said and jumped off her stool. "Let me help you up."

Margo bent down and hooked Samantha's arm around her neck. Her other hand snaked around Samantha's waist and she lifted her back to her feet with an ease Samantha would never have guessed. Samantha opened her mouth to speak, but no words came out. Fear trembled inside her. What the hell was happening?

Margo walked toward the door at such a clipped pace, Samantha had no choice but to drag her feet along beside her. She tried to jab her elbow into Margo's side, but the muscles in her arm wouldn't cooperate.

Hell, none of her muscles cooperated. Her mind screamed into a haze of confusion, but she kept stumbling along beside Margo, unable to stop herself from being dragged to God only knew where.

Margo opened the door wide and dread curdled in Samantha's stomach. A white utility van sat on the street outside her house.

No, no, no.

She peddled her feet backward and Margo's harsh laughter cut into her murky mind. "Don't make this harder than it has to be."

Her eyeballs—the only thing that seemed to be working—darted from side to side. This was New York City; there had to be someone who saw a woman in danger. Someone had to help her. But it was a cold, gloomy Sunday afternoon and her street was quiet except the honking of cars echoing off the tall buildings surrounding her. A few stragglers walked with their hands stuffed in their pockets, heads down.

A man bounced off her shoulder and her bumbling brain screamed at her hand to reach out and grab him. Margo laughed and pulled her arm tighter around her waist. "Sorry about that, sir. My friend had a little too much to drink last night and she's a little out of sorts this morning."

The man huffed in their direction and hurried along his way. Of course no one would think Margo—the picture of polished perfection—was in the middle of kidnapping her. Desperation pumped through her, but there wasn't a damn thing she could do to stop Margo.

Propping Samantha's body weight on her hip, Margo opened the back of the van with her free hand. She shifted to the side and laid Samantha down on her back. Margo jumped into the van, grabbed Samantha's hands and pulled her the rest of the way in.

Beads of sweat dotted Margo's forehead and dropped down on Samantha's cheek as she bent over. Her bloodred lips curved into a wide smile. "Well, that was tougher than I thought it'd be. I'm not used to lugging around dead weight. That was Booker's job. But now you're here, and I don't want to hear your whining once the drug wears off. I'm not sure how much tea you actually drank."

Margo reached behind her and pulled out a gun.

Samantha widened her eyes and fought against the invisible demons holding her down. A whimper escaped her barely parted lips and the drug threatened to pull her under.

Margo maneuvered her grip so the butt of the gun rested snug in her palm, lifted it in the air and brought it down hard on Samantha's temple.

Pain exploded in her head and her eyes drifted shut. Margo's gleeful delight rang in her ears as her body went lax and she fell into the blessed relief of oblivion.

Chapter 24

The annoying drone of Max's GPS led him down the long lane that snaked through the barren tress, their branches whipping wildly into the somber sky as if to warn him away. The days were short this time of year, but driving into the foreign patch of woods sent him farther and farther into the darkness. If the neon light on his dash weren't showing the time, he'd think the sun had set instead of it being late afternoon.

The mouth of trees opened up and exposed him to the sheer ridiculousness of Teddy and Margo's house. Hell, *house* didn't even begin to cover it. The two-story brick colonial was double the size of his entire building. Who needed all that space?

He gazed up at the monstrosity of a house through his windshield. It might be a beautiful home, but uneasiness took hold of his gut as if he were about to walk into the Bates Motel. No matter how shiny the house, a monster still lurked inside. He slowed the car to a stop under the portico and parked next to a silver sports car.

Teddy's car.

After opening the door, he swung his legs out the side and stretched his tight muscles. Too much time wasted in the car driving to the middle of nowhere. Anger pulsed through him and he flexed his hands. What he wouldn't give to wrap his hands around Teddy's neck. He took in a deep breath of country air, filling his lungs in an effort to calm his nerves.

Okay, one point for the middle of nowhere. He glanced around and a prickle of apprehension did a tap dance along his spine. Something wasn't right, but he couldn't put his finger on it. He spun in a wide circle, taking in the width of the house and the expanse of snow-covered woods around it.

No maintenance vehicles.

He walked along the smooth-as-silk concrete he'd driven on. No mud or tracks stained the driveway. Margo said Teddy had been here remodeling the place. No sign of that lingered anywhere, but maybe the projects had been finished and the evidence cleared away.

Only one way to find out.

Not even a loose pebble littered the walkway to the front of the house. The snow had finally stopped falling, but the bite in the air threatened to take a chunk out of his nose. He quickened his pace to the front door and pressed a freezing finger to the doorbell.

The sound of bells chiming echoed from inside. Max waited, and when no one answered, he fisted his hand and pounded against the heavy door, the contact sending spikes of pain through his arm.

The door swung open, the force causing Max to take a step backward. Teddy stood in the doorway with bloodshot eyes and a tumbler of amber liquid in his hand. Resignation and annoyance clouded his blue eyes, beating out the anger Max had expected to find.

"What the hell are you doing here?" Teddy didn't wait for an answer. He turned and walked into the house, leaving the door wide open for Max to enter.

Max closed the door behind him and took a moment to let the heat of the house warm his frozen bones. Turning his head, he looked for where Teddy had disappeared. The sound of a crackling fire called out to him, and he followed the noise down the hall and turned the corner to find Teddy sitting in what he assumed was the den.

Dark wood met worn leather, and a laughably large television took center stage in the room. No frilly knick-knacks or decorations interrupted the masculine space. Max spied one framed picture in the far corner, but focused on Teddy instead. His disheveled blond hair spoke of a sleepless night. Teddy stood by the drink cart and refilled his half-full tumbler to the top before sitting down in a wingback chair near the fire.

Keeping his hands pressed to his sides, Max made his way in front of Teddy. He didn't take the empty seat beside him. He needed to be on his feet in case Teddy made a run for it.

"Did you come to arrest me? I figured they'd send a federal agent to do that, not a murder cop." For the first time since they'd met, Teddy's voice didn't hold an ounce of contempt. Only weary defeat.

Max narrowed his eyes and studied the broken man in front of him. "Why hasn't the FBI found you yet?"

Teddy shrugged, his eyes never leaving the dancing flames in front of him. "I guess they haven't been looking hard enough. They only got their hands on what they wanted this morning. They'll probably start looking soon, not that I made it all that difficult. Hell, even you were smart enough to find me."

There was the sliver of dislike Max had come to expect.

"What are they going to find?" Max had a good idea, but if Teddy was feeling chatty, he'd let him speak.

A low growl of pain gurgled from Teddy and he threw his glass against the red brick beside the fire. The glass shattered and liquid flowed down the wall. "Damn, Margo. I should have never listened to her. Things took a hit after my dad's stroke and she thought she was so damn smart. Said there was no way anyone could tie the mafia to my company. Said her damn daddy had worked with the Harlans for years and no one had been the wiser."

Teddy hung his head and scratched a hand back and forth over his face. He laughed a rough, hard, humorless laugh. "Who the hell talks about the mafia these days? We don't live in an Al Capone movie, for God's sake. I didn't think it was a big deal. And now I'm the one who'll go down for this."

Max's sixth sense went on high alert. Margo had connected Teddy with the mafia? He sank down on the edge of the seat to get a better read on Teddy's face, but kept his weight pressed on his toes just in case. "So you needed to get your company out of the toilet and your wife hooked you up with the mafia. How does Samantha fit in? Why go after her now, a year after the company made its billions?"

Teddy's head whipped up and frustration made all his muscles tight. "Are you kidding me? You came all the way here to talk to me about Samantha? I already told you. I have nothing to do with what's going on with her. I have enough problems on my plate right now."

Max opened his mouth to speak, but his phone vibrating against his thigh cut into his thoughts. He pulled it out and glanced at the screen.

Caspano.

"I have to take this," he said as he got to his feet.

Teddy gave a dismissive flick of his wrist, his gaze fixed once again on the flames.

"I found Teddy. He's at his place in the Berkshires." Max walked toward the front of the den, blocking Teddy's only path to escape. He rested his hip on the built-in shelves flanking the doorway and let his gaze take in the few mementos Teddy had displayed.

"I'm sure the feds will be happy to hear that, but we have a bigger problem. Samantha's missing."

A violent shake ripped through him and he knocked a picture to the floor. Panic threatened to crash through him like a tidal wave, but he fought to stay calm. James was with Samantha. This had to be a mistake. He crouched down to pick up the picture and he crushed his fingers around the silver frame. "What do you mean she's missing? She's with her driver in the city. He was supposed to take her to my place."

"He called a couple of hours ago to report her gone. New guy took the call, not realizing the extent of the situation. I just came across it. She's been gone for hours. James contends that Samantha made him go to her mother's house after the mom received roses and a weird note. When he got back to her house, she was gone."

He squeezed his eyes shut, willing the freight train barreling through his brain to slow down so he could think. It didn't make sense. Teddy was here. Why would he send Samantha's mom flowers, and where would Samantha have gone?

He opened his eyes and his gaze locked on to the picture in his hands. Margo and Teddy stared up at him with wide smiles on their perfect faces. Margo's blond hair whipped behind her as if caught in a windstorm. Max zeroed in on Margo's exposed ear and the world fell out from beneath him.

A chocolate diamond stud adorned her ear. Just like the one from Booker's truck.

"Dude, are you there?" Caspano's gruff voice penetrated his thoughts.

Max shot to his feet and his fingers threatened to break through the glass. His heart thundered in his chest and guilt burrowed into his gut. How had he missed this? "I need you to look up any properties listed under Margo Silverman. Now! I know who has Samantha."

A sharp stab of pain sliced through her head and a low groan rumbled in her dry throat. She tried to use her fingers to rub away the loud thud tapping against her skull, but her arm wouldn't move. Her eyes opened into slits and the tiny bit of light coming through a dirty window ripped into her brain. Closing her eyes again, she took a breath to gain her composure, and tried one more time to move her arms.

Nothing.

Fog rolled around inside her head. Her body rattled and shook as if being jostled around in the back of a car.

Samantha's eyes flew open. Margo. The drugged tea. The white van waiting outside her house to carry her away like a hearse transporting the doomed to their final resting place.

Reality crashed into her at a startling speed, making the nausea in her stomach grow more intense with every second. Saliva filled her mouth and the acidic taste of bile traveled up her esophagus.

Just breathe. Don't panic. Air in through your nose, out through your mouth. Don't let her win.

She lay flat on the floor with her good hand wrapped against her cast, her ankles tied together with a rough rope that cut into her tender skin. Wisps of wind made their way through rusted holes speckled along the side of the van. Goose bumps ran up and down her arms. She didn't have her coat on, and the heated air that rattled from the vents in the front of the van wasn't finding its way to her.

Samantha let her gaze wander around the empty space. The seats had been taken out, leaving the steel floor exposed. Dark red spots stained the floor.

Blood.

Refusing to look at the evidence of Margo's crimes—crimes she no doubt planned to commit again with Samantha—she lifted her eyes to the ceiling. Pictures and dating profiles of numerous women lined the top of the van. Brown-eyed women with dark brown hair and tanned skin stared down at her. Samantha gasped, the sound ringing around the small confines of the van.

"Oh look. You're awake." Margo glanced over her shoulder before returning her focus to the road. "I was afraid I'd hit you too hard and would miss out on having a little bit of fun with you. You've been out for hours."

Hours? Where the hell is Margo taking me? She couldn't waste time trying to figure it out. She needed to concentrate on getting out of here. Twisting her good hand, the rope Margo had used moved against the bulky cast on her broken wrist.

"I have to know," Margo continued. "Had you figured it out at all? I mean, you and that dreamy detective of yours were spending so much time chasing your tails and tracking down dear ol' Teddy. Did you even stop to consider his poor, ditzy wife?"

"I've never thought you were ditzy." Samantha kept her eyes on the rearview mirror and tried to keep the muscles in her face relaxed. She didn't want Margo to see the strain caused by rotating her wrist as fast as possible to get the rope loose. "I've always considered you a friend."

Margo snorted. "Please. I know what people say about me. They've always underestimated me. Even you—hell, my own parents never thought I'd amount to anything more than a trophy wife. So I used those assumptions, the weakness heaped on my shoulders, to make myself stronger. To allow people to only see what I wanted them to. But not anymore. Now I take what's mine, letting no one get in the way. Not Teddy, and especially not you."

Samantha had to keep her talking. Had to keep Margo's focus on herself and not on the frantic motion of Samantha's hands as she tried to ignore the pain ripping into her skin. She tried to pull her ankles apart, but that rope was too tight. The cast had made it difficult for Margo to tie the rope tight enough to keep her hands together. Freeing her good hand was her only chance at escape. "How will Teddy be blamed for murder? How can you make it look like he's the one behind everything?"

Margo's hard green eyes met hers in the mirror and every muscle in Samantha's body tightened. She held her breath, not daring to move. "I had you believing it, didn't I?"

"Yes." She hated the shake of her voice, but she couldn't stop it. Margo was dangerous, and no one knew where she was.

Or who had her.

Margo's eyes went back to the road and Samantha's gaze drifted to the ceiling again. This time, she spotted a newspaper clipping with Richard Pike's picture on it. "Why do you have an article back here about Richard Pike? Do you know him?"

Margo's eyes met hers once more in the reflecting glass and they were colder than the constant stream of air gushing in through the cracks of the old van. "Who do you think gave me this brilliant idea?"

Chapter 25

Samantha's blood turned cold, cutting off the only source of heat keeping her body from freezing. She averted her gaze from the collage of victims, targets and Richard Pike staring down at her. "You took inspiration from a sadistic stalker? Why?" This time, the quiver in her voice was from rage, and she clung to it, let it roll around her body and fuel her need to get away.

A tiny glimpse of Margo's slim shoulder shrugged over the back of the driver's seat. "He had a good plan, just didn't execute it well enough. People are so stupid these days. They post every little detail about themselves online and are so quick to believe they can find their soul mate through a dating app. Pathetic."

"What about the thousands of people who have found their soul mate online?" Not only was Margo slamming the business Samantha had poured her blood, sweat and tears into, but she was completely disregarding all the people who'd used dating sites to find the loves of their lives.

"Lowlifes just trolling the streets for a good lay." Margo's voice grew harder than the cold floor under Samantha's ass.

Margo's upbringing might have conditioned her to look down her narrow nose at other people, but that couldn't be the reason she'd gone off the deep end. "But what's the point of all this? Why do you hate me so much? Why murder those innocent women?"

The van turned and Samantha's strung-up body slammed against the wall. She continued to struggle with the restraints on her hands. A tiny gap opened up and she pressed her thumb and pinky together and tried to pull her hand through the opening. Her skin burned and blood leaked through her scratched skin.

"I couldn't risk going after you right away. I needed to practice, and what better way than with women who looked just like you. It was fun figuring out where to dump their bodies to freak you out, and they made it so easy. I'd show up where they were supposed to meet the men they'd been talking to. You know, the men I pretended to be when I found them on your stupid dating site. Then I'd rush in to comfort them when they thought they were stood up. Blabbering idiots downed drink after drink, not even stopping to question if a nice lady would slip something in them."

Vomit shot into Samantha's mouth and she choked it down. Those young women had all been murdered, their lives cut short, just because they resembled her. Logic told her it wasn't her fault, but the ache in her soul said otherwise.

"You've taken everything from me. I've lost my money and my husband all because you were too damn selfish to let Teddy have what was rightfully his. If he'd gotten the money he deserved from your little company, VB Enterprises wouldn't have suffered like it has. It wouldn't have turned into a black hole that's sucked all of our money from our bank accounts." The van lurched forward, as if the venom in Margo's words fueled the speed faster.

Samantha took a second to weigh her words. How could she use logic with an irrational lady? "Teddy walked away from *EternalMatch* years ago. He didn't want to put any time or money into it. I did all of that, Margo. You know how Teddy is. Too lazy to lift a finger if he doesn't know it will land on gold when it comes back down."

"Don't talk about Teddy like that," Margo snapped, her words hard and defensive.

Samantha tried to melt against the wall and continued squeezing her hand through the rope, but the width of her hand wouldn't budge through the tight space. Tears burned her eyes and she bit into her lip to keep from screaming.

Margo's earlier words circled in her head and her body went lax as she returned her focus to the front of the van. She softened her voice and tried to add a hint of sympathy when she asked, "What do you mean you've lost your husband?"

A huff of breath puffed from Margo. "Just another lowlife searching for a good lay online instead of putting his dick where it belonged."

Shock vibrated Samantha's core and her mouth fell open. "Teddy's cheating on you?"

"I found him at our house in the Berkshires with some whore. I left before he saw me, and after I did some digging, I found his dating profile on your stupid little app. He needs to pay for screwing around on me, and you need to pay for providing him the opportunity."

Samantha's mind spun faster than the tires barreling toward God only knew where. Teddy despised *Eternal-Match*'s success, and her, so why would he use it to find another woman? She couldn't focus on that now. She needed to keep her mind centered on Margo and the giant bag of horrible ideas she'd stored in her brain.

"I'm sorry he's cheating on you, but that's not my fault. If Teddy hadn't used *EternalMatch*, he would have found another way to find a different woman."

"If you had let him back in the company, he wouldn't be losing his fortune and wouldn't be depressed enough to look elsewhere. All I've heard from his whiny mouth for years is how you stole from him. That you were too big of a bitch to let him have his share." Margo clicked her tongue. "Trash can leave the Bronx, but you can never change who you are. No matter how much money's in the bank."

Betrayal burned her veins. Margo had once been a close friend, one she'd confided in, and Samantha had been stupid enough to believe Margo had liked her for who she really was and hadn't looked down on her because she hadn't been born with a silver spoon in her mouth. Regret filled Samantha. Margo had spouted a lot of nonsense, but what she said was true. She wasn't trash, but she did have a past that she'd fought too long to forget. No more. If she got out of this, she'd be proud of where she came from.

But first she had to survive.

"How long has Teddy been cheating on you?"

A beat of tense silence passed before Margo answered. "Right after Richard Pike was arrested."

"You've been planning this for a year? How do you expect Teddy to go down without taking you down with him?"

Exhaustion made her body heavy. She fought between the need to save her energy and the need to free herself. Shifting onto the side of her hip, she lifted her knees to her chest and rested her head on the hard knobs of them. Her arm turned, and the rope slid over the tops of her wrists, but didn't budge over her knuckles.

Samantha sucked in a breath and willed her heart to stop beating so damn loud.

"Easy," Margo said. The sound of her loud voice drowned out the drum beating against Samantha's chest and a little bit of the tension digging into her shoulders loosened. "I'm going to kill him."

"What?" Samantha couldn't help but shout the question and Margo's emerald eyes flashed back at her from the rearview mirror.

Samantha stopped moving, stopped breathing, stopped the flurry of adrenaline from pumping through her veins.

"I don't have a choice."

Samantha met her hard stare with one of her own. "You always have a choice."

Margo shook her head and put her attention back on the road. "Not this time, and if everything works out, both of you will be dead and I might even have a shot at your sexy detective. Booker's dead—that was a pity, but I can't just sit around and mourn a man I didn't even love. He served his purpose...and then some. My only intention at first was to take down the company Teddy and his family built before I made Teddy personally pay for his sins. Teddy never second-guessed how I knew someone involved with the mafia. He only cared about how it'd affect his bottom line. But one thing led to another, and Booker proved himself very useful to me. I was almost sorry I had to kill him, but I'm ready to move on."

Max.

"Max won't believe you. He'll know you had a hand in this."

"We're about to be in the Berkshires any minute. I'll kill you, make sure to leave your body somewhere Teddy would have been dumb enough to dump you, and then I'll kill Teddy. I wasn't lying when I told Max that Teddy was up here. We'll just make sure to go to a different house so our paths don't cross with your man. Detective Green will be heading back to the city by the time I'm done with you, and I'll call, a frantic mess. *Detective Green. Come quick! Teddy came after me. It was self-defense. Please help.* He won't be able to resist a rescue, especially when I tell him Teddy told me what he did with poor Samantha."

Giving one more yank, Samantha pulled her hand free. Tears hovered over her lashes, but she held them back. She closed her eyes, running Margo's sick plan over in her mind. It could work, but there was one thing Margo wasn't aware of. James knew she was missing. Word would get to Max. He'd unravel Margo's perverse scheme, but would it be in time?

The van came to a stop and Margo cut the engine. Samantha fought the urge to try to get a glimpse out of the filthy window. She wouldn't be able to see much anyway, and she couldn't risk letting Margo know she'd freed her hands. Taking Margo by surprise was her only hope.

Twisting in her seat, Margo turned toward her. Her lips curved up and the bloodred lipstick that colored her full lips held a sinister quality that hadn't been there before. "We're here. I need to run in the house to grab some tools. I have plans for you before I kill you."

Samantha bit into her cheek to keep any emotion from playing on her face. She wouldn't show the fear that was eating away at her stomach lining, she wouldn't show the hatred burning in her veins and she wouldn't show Margo that she'd finally met her match. She'd never backed down from a fight in her life, and she didn't plan on starting today.

Max clicked off the phone and stormed over to Teddy. He grabbed him by the shoulder and spun him away from the fire.

Teddy wobbled, the alcohol in his system playing havoc with his balance. He jerked away and swatted Max's hand. "Get off me."

"Where would Margo take Samantha?" he demanded.

Teddy reared back, puzzlement crinkling his eyes, and a sneer twisted his lips. "What the hell are you talking about? Margo and Samantha don't socialize outside of charity events. I'd never let her spend time with that ungrateful woman."

Max leaned forward, grabbed a fistful of Teddy's shirt and hauled him to his feet. "Samantha is missing and your wife sent me on a wild-goose chase to the middle of nowhere to find you. She said you'd been doing a lot of remodeling and would have access to a utility van. A van that was used to transport murder victims to their dumping place."

Teddy's head shook back and forth and confusion made his stupid face pinch together. "I haven't done any remodeling. Why would she say that? She's the one who's had workers constantly out at her house."

Max drew his eyebrows together and pushed his face farther in to Teddy's. "Her house? Isn't this her damn house?"

"Yeah," Teddy stammered, Max's insistent anger finally penetrating through his haze of intoxication. "But she bought another place here about a year ago. Just on the other side of the woods behind this house. When it came on the market, she insisted it made sense to buy it. That it was a smart investment. She wanted to buy under her name...her legal name. Said she had some money saved up and wanted to feel like she was doing something for our future."

Max's phone buzzed again. He threw Teddy back down in the chair and clicked on the line.

"Margo has a couple of properties listed under the name Margo Silverman," Caspano said. "One in Jersey, one in Miami and one—"

"In the Berkshires," Max finished. "Teddy just told me. Shoot me the address. Sounds like it's on the other side of the woods from where I am, but I don't know how deep they are."

"Consider it done. Are you sure Margo has her?" Doubt crept into Caspano's voice, but Max ignored it.

"Positive. She's the one who hooked Teddy up with Booker Harlan and his mob connections. She's the only other person who would know so much about Samantha's past, as well as have a score to settle with her. I may not know every reason she'd be delusional enough to think she has to go after Samantha, but I'll damn sure find out."

"I'll call the local police department up there and send over backup. If she's as dangerous as you think she is, you don't want to go in there without someone covering your back."

Caspano may have been a thorn in his side the last few years, but the guy was a good cop who'd come through for him more than once in the course of this investigation. "Thanks, but I won't promise to wait. I've got to go."

He clicked off and turned to find Teddy standing inches from him, his hands fisted in his hair. "You think Margo wants to kill Samantha?"

Max nodded. "And I think she wants to set you up for it."

"But why? I've never done anything…" His voice trailed off and he dropped his hands to his sides. The pale color of his skin took on a yellowish tint and he pressed his hands to his stomach, as if trying to keep whatever was in there inside. "She knows."

Max took one step closer. "She knows what?"

Teddy stared at him with wild eyes filled with regret. "I cheated on her. I brought a woman here. Only a couple of times, but Margo acted different afterward. More…polite with me. I thought it was all in my head, but she bought that stupid house right afterward."

"How many ways can you mess things up?" Disgust swirled in Max's stomach as the pieces to the puzzle all clicked in place like a Rubik's Cube. "I don't have time to deal with you."

"I'm coming with you," Teddy said and grabbed a jacket that had been tossed over the back of a chair. "Maybe I can talk some sense into her before she does anything stupid."

"She's already killed four people."

Teddy closed his eyes and swallowed hard, making his Adam's apple protrude from his neck. "Dear God."

"God can't help Samantha now, but I can." He turned to leave and a firm grip grabbed his shoulder. He spun back and found himself looking into clear, determined eyes.

"She's my wife. I'm coming."

"Suit yourself." He didn't have time to argue, and if he said no, Teddy would be stupid enough to get behind the wheel and drive himself there. He didn't need to worry about a drunk jerk on the road right now.

Quickening his pace, he fled toward the front door with Teddy at his heels. Moisture fell from the sky. Not snow, but a freezing rain that stuck to his skin and chilled his bones.

He prayed Samantha wasn't outside, that she was safe and warm and that this was all a big misunderstanding. But his gut told him otherwise. Samantha was in danger, and if he was right about Margo bringing her to the Berkshires to frame Teddy for her murder, then he was her only chance for survival.

Chapter 26

The driver's door slammed shut and Samantha counted to twenty before she bent over and worked at loosening the rope tied around her ankles. Margo had taken off her boots to press her ankles together, and the cold combined with the restricting rope made Samantha's feet numb.

At least it helped keep the pain at bay as she struggled against the frayed restraint cutting into her skin.

Samantha dug her nails into the tight knot. Her nails bent from the pressure, but she couldn't stop. Having her hands free would be useless if she couldn't run. She wiggled her feet back and forth and used her good hand to attack the stupid knot that wouldn't budge.

She choked down a scream of frustration. Margo would be back any minute. She needed to get her feet free.

Using her palm, she pulled the rope backward and tried to slip it down her heel.

It didn't budge.

My socks. She pulled at the only protection she had on her cold feet and the thick material snagged on the tight rope.

Samantha pulled harder.

The soft material slid under the rope and off her foot. She repeated the process with her other foot. A small gap opened up against her ankles and she yanked the rope over her ankle. This time, it slid over the skin... only to stop on the center of her heel.

If she could just get it over her heel, the rest of her foot would follow suit. The rope scraped against her skin, burning her flesh and causing needle pricks of pain to erupt over her dead-like limbs. Gritting her teeth, she pushed past the pain and pulled first one foot, and then the other through the small loop of rope.

Adrenaline pumped through her and she fell against the side of the van, her breath coming out in short, excited bursts. She did it. She could do this. She could get away. She lunged for the door to push it open, but it wouldn't budge. Hurrying, she turned toward the front of the van and gripped the door handle. Nothing. How the hell did Margo lock all the doors from the outside?

A stifled scream of frustration rang in her mouth.

Taking a deep breath of stale air, she calmed her shaking nerves and swallowed down her disappointment. All she had to do was wait for Margo to open the door and take her by surprise.

She glanced around the van and searched for a weapon. Anything to slam against Margo's head or gouge into her eye. It didn't have to be big, just sharp or heavy enough to leave her stunned. She leaned over onto her hands and knees and searched the ground.

Nothing.

Keeping her head low, she made her way back to the front of the van. Margo had said she wanted to grab stuff from the house, but maybe she'd left something inside. Samantha gripped the torn leather of the armrest and peeked around the passenger chair. Crumpled paper littered the floor and dried blood stained the tan seat. Leaning forward, she reached for the glove box.

The sound of footsteps competed with the nasty drizzle hitting the windshield.

Margo.

Samantha's heart sank. She hadn't found a damn thing to use against her attacker. She stumbled to the back of the van, pulled her socks onto her bare feet and crouched on the tips of her toes. She gave one last glance around the van as the footsteps grew louder, and her gaze landed on the hard chunk of plaster on her hand. Her annoying cast might prove useful after all.

Every muscle in her body tightened like a coiled cobra ready to strike as she waited for the door to open. The rapid beat of her heart pulsed against every inch of her body. The click of the handle from outside the van vibrated through the metal inside and Samantha leaned forward, prepared to pounce.

The door swung open and a gust of wind blew icy rain at her face. Margo's eyes widened and a growl purred from her throat. She lifted the gun, pointed it at Samantha's head and placed her finger on the trigger.

Indecision tore through Samantha and her heart threatened to pound through her chest. She had to act. She lunged at Margo, swung her cast back and brought it around as fast as she could against Margo's temple. Pain shot up her arm, but the crunch of plaster against

Margo's face was almost as satisfying as watching Margo drop to the ground with a hand cradling her cheek.

Samantha leaped out of the van and over Margo's temporarily stunned body. The gun lay on the ground, and Samantha cried with relief as her fingers curled around the grip. Not like she knew how to use it. Hell, she didn't even know if the safety was on. But at least it was in her hands now, not Margo's.

Margo climbed to her feet and growled before lunging toward her.

Samantha had to get away, and Margo blocked her access to the house. The forest was her only option. She took off at a dead sprint toward the eerie oasis of bare branches and couldn't hold her tears back any longer. Snow covered the ground, her throbbing feet crunching through the layers, and she zigzagged between the tall towers of trees. No sunlight penetrated the gloomy clouds; no shafts of light led her to the right path. Frozen slush pelted her face, each hit like an icy pellet meeting its mark. They melted on impact and mingled with the tears streaming down her cheeks.

Her teeth chattered and she searched for any indication she was heading in the right direction. She needed to find a person, a house, anything but the absolute silence surrounding her.

A twig snapped behind her and she stopped, straining her ears to listen for the sound. Footsteps pounded toward her. She turned in a wide circle. No hiding places lurked for her to rest her weary feet and stay out of Margo's sight. She had to keep moving.

Filling her lungs with the frigid air, she took off again. This time, trying to run as straight as possible.

The most direct path would be the quickest, even if she didn't know where the hell she was going. She could just be running deeper into the woods where hypothermia would kill her if Margo didn't.

More crunching snow, more snapping twigs alerted her to Margo's quickening pace. Samantha willed her legs to move faster. Her toe caught the underside of an upturned root and she crashed onto her hands and knees. Moisture seeped into the thin material of her pants and loose rocks scraped against her palms. She grabbed the dropped gun, scrambled to her feet and took off running.

A loud *thud* sounded behind and something latched on to her ankle and she fell forward once again.

She glanced behind her and fear stole her breath. Margo's long body stretched out on the ground, her arms reaching toward her. Margo tightened her death grip on her ankle. Her ponytail had come loose and her blond hair billowed in the gusting wind. Mascara trailed down her face, making her look like a deranged clown.

Lifting the gun toward Margo's head, Samantha pressed her teeth together and pulled the trigger.

Nothing.

Margo's hysterical laughter echoed around in the quiet night. "Looks like I was all out of bullets."

Samantha swiveled back around and clawed her broken nails into the snow. Cold bursts of pain shot up her arms, but she kept clawing, kept pulling herself forward. She had to get away.

"There's nowhere for you to run," Margo screamed through the howling branches. "You can die now or die later. It'd be easier to just give up."

Samantha lifted the leg Margo hadn't latched on to and kicked back, connecting her foot with Margo's nose.

Margo yelled and released her grip on Samantha's ankle.

Samantha jumped to her feet and took off. Ragged breaths ripped through her lungs and her side burned. Numbness settled into her face, but the tips of her ears stung from the cold. A loud grunt sounded behind her and lifted the hairs on the back of her neck. A hard shove pushed against her spine and she fell to the ground. Rough hands grabbed her arms and turned her onto her back. Margo straddled Samantha's stomach.

Samantha bucked and squirmed beneath her. Margo pulled back a fist and slammed it into Samantha's mouth. Blood trickled from her lips, but it didn't knock the fight from her. She reached up and shoved Margo back, but Margo tightened her legs around Samantha's hips.

"Help! Somebody help me!" Samantha's ragged breath strangled her screams.

Margo reached behind her back and pulled a large butcher knife from under her coat. She traced the edge of the silver blade along Samantha's jawline and down her neck, stopping when the point pressed against her jugular.

"No one's going to help you, sweetheart. Your time's up."

Max's tires slipped and slid on the treacherous roads. His white-knuckled grip tightened, but he couldn't slow down. He had to get to Samantha. Teddy pointed out the turn to Margo's house and Max yanked the wheel. Gravel flew in the air and the car skidded to the edge of the driveway. Max righted the spinning tires and pushed the gas pedal to the floor, flying down the straight lane that led to the main house.

A large white van sat at the end of the driveway, the back door wide open. The muscles in Max's stomach tightened. He slammed on the brake and the car spun on an icy patch on the smooth concrete. His elbows locked and he tried to straighten the car. It screeched to a stop inches from the van and he threw the car in Park.

"I can't believe you were right. I can't believe she'd do this." Teddy stared through the windshield at the van. He covered his open mouth and his hand shook.

Max didn't have time to deal with his shock over discovering his wife was a murderer. "Stay here. Backup should be here any minute."

He pushed out of the car and hurried to the back of the van. Bile shot up his esophagus as he approached the open door. If he found Samantha's dead body in there, he'd lose it.

I never even told her that I was falling in love with her.

Pushing from his mind the terrifying image of Samantha with a knife in her heart, he pulled the gun from his holster, lifted it in front of him and rounded the corner of the vehicle.

Empty.

A whoosh of air squeezed from his lungs and he bent at the waist to stop the nausea from boiling in his gut. Samantha wasn't in there. He straightened and scanned the inside of the van. Newspaper clippings and printed-out dating profiles covered the ceiling. If he wasn't certain Margo was the killer before, he sure as hell was now.

A pile of ropes on the dirty floor caught his attention. He hoisted himself inside and picked them up. One rope was long and unknotted, but the other was still rounded in a small loop with a tight knot connecting the frayed ends.

She got out of the ropes.

A sliver of hope sliced through the despair clinging to his soul. If she had gotten out of the ropes, she would have run. Jumping out of the van, he searched into the dark woods surrounding him. He wiped a flurry of sleet from his brow and strained to listen to any noise clueing him in to which way Samantha had gone.

"What the hell?" Shock and horror dripped from Teddy's words.

Max whipped around to face him. "I told you to stay in the car. Margo's dangerous and I can't worry about you getting hurt."

"Unless you plan on handcuffing me to the steering wheel, it's not going to happen. I need to help try to stop her. And you're going to need another set of eyes to look for them if you're going into the woods."

Max ground his teeth together. "I don't need—"

"Help! Somebody help me!"

The panicked words floated to Max's ears on a gust of wind. His heart leaped into his throat. She was out there. He turned in the direction of the footprints marring the snow and took off into the woods. Branches slapped against his face and the hurling ice rained down on him with the force of a hurricane. Sticks snapped under his feet and he fought to keep his balance over the uneven terrain.

Teddy's labored breath and faltering steps sounded behind him. If the guy wanted to walk into a life-and-death situation, so be it. His priority rested solely on finding Samantha and keeping her safe.

Footsteps in the snow dotted a path through the trees, weaving among them like a drunk asked to walk a straight line. Max stopped to catch his breath and crouched down to study the prints.

With renewed energy, he inhaled deeply and took off in a sprint toward the sporadic trail in front of them.

A gap opened up in the claustrophobic cluster of trees and Max sucked in a sharp breath. He slowed his footsteps and maneuvered himself so his gun was pointed at the back of Margo's head. "Drop the knife and let her go."

Margo's shoulder blades bunched together and her head whipped around. Blood trickled down her nose and she used the back of her knifeless hand to wipe it away. She kept the blade pressed to Samantha's throat. "Not going to happen. You can shoot me if you want, but I'll make sure she's dead before the bullet hits me."

Max fought every urge in his body to take his focus off Margo's wild eyes and glance at Samantha. He wanted to reassure her. Give her a look that told her how much she meant to him, and that he'd make sure this woman paid for trying to take her away from him.

But he didn't. He couldn't risk taking his attention away from Margo, even for a second. His presence would have to be enough, at least until he had Samantha safely in his arms. And once she was there, he'd never let her go.

"Do you really want me to shoot you? Trust me—it hurts. Just lay the knife on the ground, put your hands in the air and let Samantha go."

A twisted smile curled on Margo's lips and a soft whimper came from beneath her.

Margo gripped the black end of the knife and lifted it in the air above Samantha's heart. Max's heart stopped beating. Margo's hands came down.

"Margo! Stop!" Teddy's frantic plea came moments before his shuffled footsteps.

Margo hesitated and twisted to find Teddy. Fisting a hand, Samantha rammed her knuckles into Margo's stomach and her spine bowed back. She rolled to the side, sending Margo to the ground. Samantha grabbed for the knife, but Margo's hands never slipped from the handle. Both women lay on their sides, Margo's back to him and Samantha's fierce face poking over the side of Margo's shoulder. Grunts and screams mingled with the retreating sound of birds fleeing into the safety of the trees.

"Shoot her!" Samantha yelled.

He charged her but a sliver of light broke through the canopy above them and reflected off the metal blade of the knife. Margo yanked it from Samantha's bloody hands and raised the weapon once again. The knife came down, slicing through the gray air.

He planted his feet in a wide stance, pointed his gun and tried to line up a shot that wouldn't put Samantha at risk.

Bam!

Chapter 27

Both women collapsed and blood seeped into the pure snow. Max dropped his arm and kept the gun pointed toward the frozen ground as he ran to Samantha's side. Neither woman moved; neither woman made a sound.

Time stood still as Max fell to his knees beside Samantha's head. At some point during their wrestling match, Samantha had ended up on her back with Margo now draped across her chest. Samantha's pale face blended with the snow; only her halo of dark hair separated her from the white floor of the forest. Her eyes were closed and thick crimson oozed from the tangle of bodies, but he couldn't tell where it came from.

If Samantha died, it'd be his fault. He was supposed to keep her safe, not steal her life with a bullet from his own gun. His heart shattered as he brushed the tips of his icy fingers against her cheek. He couldn't live without her.

Samantha's eyelids fluttered open and a wave of relief stole his breath. A rush of love so strong slammed into him, it knocked him back on his heels. "Get her off me," she said, the words hard to hear from her strangled breath.

Max pressed his fingers to Margo's neck to check her pulse. Thready and weak, but there. Sliding one hand under Margo's armpit and placing the other on the nape of her neck, he rolled her off Samantha and onto her back. Blood gushed from a bullet wound on her shoulder. The pain and loss of blood must have combined to knock Margo unconscious. He ripped his coat off and tied the thick leather in a knot above the entry wound. If they didn't slow the flow of blood, Margo would never make it out of the woods alive.

Samantha scurried away from the motionless body and crawled into Max's lap. He wrapped his arms around her and buried his face in her neck. He inhaled her unique scent of lilac and lavender that was now mixed with dirt and blood. He fought the surge of emotion climbing up his throat. Frozen rain fell down on him, but he barely registered the cold. He had Samantha back in his arms and that was the only thing that mattered.

"Is she dead?" Teddy asked, and his voice broke.

"No, but she needs medical attention. She's losing a lot of blood."

Max glanced up into Teddy's horror-filled face. Teddy took a few tentative steps toward Margo and crouched down on the balls of his feet. He reached out and brushed a piece of hair from her forehead and then fell backward. "There's blood all over her face."

"I kicked her when she tackled me to the ground,"

Samantha said and shivered in Max's arms. He wrapped her tighter into him. "If I'd had the chance, I would have done a whole lot more."

The sound of frantic footsteps and crunching snow stole their attention. Max tore his gaze from Samantha to search for whatever was barreling toward them. Two men in police uniforms jogged through an opening in the trees.

"Over here," Max shouted and waved his arms in the air.

The men slowed their approach, each with a hand on the weapon at their side and gaze assessing the situation.

"Detective Caspano out of the Nineteenth Precinct in NYC put in a call for backup," the younger of the two men called out.

Max reached for his badge and held it in the air. "I'm Detective Green, NYPD. I have an injured woman who needs medical attention. Now. Bullet wound in the shoulder. She's currently unconscious, but the suspect is extremely dangerous."

The older officer clicked the transmitter attached to his shoulder. "We need a stretcher out here immediately. Suspect needs to be taken to the hospital for treatment."

"I need to go with her. I'm her husband." Teddy stood and lines of determination rippled across his face.

The officers looked at Max, and he nodded his consent. Teddy and Margo wouldn't have much time together. Margo would spend the rest of her life in jail if she made it through surgery. He had no doubt they'd find more than enough evidence in the van to connect Margo to the murder victims, not to mention everything that had happened today. And the FBI would be hauling Teddy in for his own charges depending on what they found on his computers.

Snow soaked into his pants and the splats of frozen rain morphed into thick snowflakes. He needed to get Samantha out of here. He glanced down at her. "What about you? Do you need to go to the hospital?" He ran his hands over her body and searched for any sign of injury.

She shook her head. "No. My hand needs to be cleaned up, but it's nothing we can't do at home."

Home. The idea of sharing a home with her buoyed his heart and chased the chill from his body.

He lifted her hand and turned her palm to face him. Blood mixed with pebbles and dirt, all embedded into cuts running from the tips of her fingers to her wrist. His gaze lifted to her face and a patch of dried blood marred her temple, the faint lines of a bruise hidden underneath.

Max brought his lips down to touch her forehead and then kissed down the side of her face and over to her mouth. Pulling away, he cupped her cheek in his hand and smoothed his thumb over her skin. "You need to let someone look at you. I'll drive you, but we're going to the hospital. I don't want to assume your injuries are all superficial and miss something. I can't lose you again."

Samantha's mouth turned up at the corners and tears glimmered in her dark brown eyes. "You didn't lose me. You saved me."

He snorted out a rough laugh. "You were doing a damn good job of saving yourself—I just showed up at the end to make myself look useful. You're one hell of a woman. If something would have happened to you…" Tears clogged his throat and he didn't care about the unexpected moisture that clung to his lashes. This was a woman he could give his heart to, one he could trust.

Samantha placed her injured hand on top of his. "I'm fine because you showed up in time. I'm not going anywhere."

His heart soared higher than the birds flying overhead. "Damn straight you're not. I love you, Sam. I would have died inside if I'd never gotten a chance to tell you. I love you so damn much."

Samantha's small smile transformed into a wide grin and tears streaked through the dirt on her face. "I love you, too. Now get me the hell out of this place. Let's go back to the city where we both belong. I've had enough nature to last the rest of my life."

Max laughed and stood with her in his arms. She snuggled against him as he walked, taking her away from the nightmare that had finally come to an end and to a future that he would make sure was filled with nothing but happiness and love.

Sunlight streamed through the window, the beams of light landing directly on Samantha's face. She opened her eyes and only a tiny *thud* of pain whacked against her head. Her palms tingled and a small itch tickled her skin inside her cast.

But for once she didn't care. If it hadn't been for her cast, she might not have gotten away from Margo. A shudder shimmied through her and she reached out to touch the hard, warm body beside her.

"Good morning," Max said with a groan and pulled her against his bare chest. "How do you feel?"

Samantha wrapped her arms around his neck and pressed her forehead to his. His eyes never opened, so she took her time studying the planes of his face. "Like the luckiest woman in the world."

He laughed and the rich sound vibrated against her. "Not many women would say that the morning after someone tried to kill them."

"The key word is *tried*. Did you get any word on how Margo did with surgery?" she asked and all humor left her voice.

Max opened his eyes and placed a light kiss on the tip of her nose. "I got a call last night after you fell asleep. She made it through surgery. They have a guard posted outside her room just in case she gets any ideas. Chances are slim since she's in a lot of pain and has a tough recovery ahead of her."

"And Teddy? I can't stand the guy, but I still feel sorry for him. No man should have to find out his wife planned on killing him, and then pinning multiple murders on him once he was dead." Samantha had told Max all about Margo's grand plan, after he had made sure she was all right. The ride back into the city had been plenty of time to get the whole story out.

"Teddy's still at his house in the Berkshires, but probably not for long. The guy's got his own crimes he'll need to own up to. It doesn't matter if Margo fixed him up with the mob to fit into her scheme. He's a grown man who made a bad decision. He'll need to pay for it."

Samantha ran her fingers through the small area of hair on Max's chest. "How can two people who seemed to have it all just throw everything away?"

"They obviously didn't have it as good as they wanted people to believe. They are angry, selfish people who didn't know how to deal with not getting what they wanted. That doesn't give them an excuse to act like criminals."

"I'm just glad it's over." She twisted on her side and laid her head in the crook of his shoulder.

Max smoothed his palm against the small of her back and rubbed slowly back and forth, soothing any frayed nerves left in her body. "Me, too. I never got a chance to ask how you're feeling about seeing Jose?"

Hearing Jose's name made her heart lurch. Seeing him was something she didn't know she needed. "I feel a bit of closure I never thought I'd gain. Sitting in that apartment with him and his mom was hard, but I'm glad I did."

His hand molded against her skin. "I'm glad to wake up with you beside me."

"Hmm," she moaned. She liked waking up beside him too, but his declaration of love the day before played on repeat in her head. He hadn't said it again, and she'd been too scared to bring it up. The day had been full of high emotions. Hell, the last week had been full of emotion. Max could have gotten swept up in all of it and said things he hadn't really meant.

Reality crashed down on her. She'd only known this man for a week. How could he possibly be in love with her?

But it was possible. She had no doubt in her mind that she was in love with him. She'd started falling for him almost from the beginning, but when faced with the possibility of never seeing him again, the depth of her emotion had smacked her in the face harder than the barrel of Margo's gun.

Taking a deep breath and gathering more courage than it had taken to fight back against an irrational woman who'd pressed a knife to her throat, she propped herself on her elbow and gazed down at him. Her hand cradled her head and she devoured him with her eyes. Lust darkened his crystal-blue irises and the dark stubble on his chin had grown to a scratchy beard.

She bit into her top lip and met his gaze, fighting not to let her own desire shine through. If it did, they'd never get around to talking. "Did you mean what you said yesterday?"

His black eyebrows drew together and the motion of his hand halted on her back. "A lot happened yesterday. I need you to be a little more specific."

Her heart dropped to her stomach. If he didn't even remember saying it, there was no way he'd meant it. But that didn't mean she shouldn't confess her own feelings to him. Life was too short to keep something so important locked inside. It was past time she started living the life she was blessed to have and stopped keeping people at arm's length. He needed to know she meant what she'd told him.

Dropping her gaze to her fingers on his chest, she whispered, "I love you, Max. I know it's impulsive and fast, but I don't care. I know what I feel for you is real, and if you're not there yet I—"

Max locked his arms around her and covered her mouth with his. His tongue pressed into her mouth and she savored the taste of him. He pulled back and stared down at her. "I meant what I said. I love you. I love you like I've never loved anyone before. I wasted so much time being angry about how my ex walked out of my life without a second glance, that I never opened my eyes to what my future could hold. You are my future, and I have the rest of my life to show you how much you mean to me."

Samantha's pulse thundered in her veins and she swallowed past the lump in her throat. "The rest of your life?"

"I know we haven't known each other that long and there are a lot of logistics to work out. Your mom might have a hard time understanding, but we'll figure it out together. I want to be with you, Sam. For as long as you'll have me."

Tears clouded her eyes and she fought to keep them from spilling over. How could something so horrible bring her something so wonderful? Bring her a man who not only loved her, but also worried about the well-being of her mother, a woman he'd only met once?

This was a man who understood not only her heart, but her soul.

A sly smile curved on her lips. "I might want to keep you around for a while."

"A while, huh?" he asked; a smile matching hers tipped up his full lips.

"We'll see how it goes, but don't plan on going any-where soon. I like having you around."

Max cupped the back of her neck and crushed her to him; their lips met again. But this time, Samantha didn't pull away. She sank into him, meeting his need for her with enthusiasm.

An enthusiasm she didn't see leaving for a very long time.

* * * * *

#2163 COLTON 911: UNDER SUSPICION
Colton 911: Chicago • by Bonnie Vanak
Widowed cop Harry Cartwright is investigating the death of a Colton patriarch, and all signs point to Sara Sandoval—the man's long-lost daughter. But Harry isn't sure if his feelings are clouding his judgment—until the real killer makes Sara a target...

#2164 PROVING COLTON'S INNOCENCE
The Coltons of Grave Gulch • by Lara Lacombe
Baldwin Bowe is a ghost bounty hunter who is determined to bring his brother to justice. But his professional resolve is tested when he falls for Jillian Colton, the woman his brother is bent on hurting.

#2165 TEXAS RANCHER'S HIDDEN DANGER
by Karen Whiddon
On the run from a serial killer client, therapist Amelia Ferguson tries to disappear in Getaway, Texas, going to work on single dad Ted Sanders's ranch. Something about the town and the handsome rancher appeal to her, but can their developing relationship survive a serial killer set on revenge?

#2166 HIS TO DEFEND
by Sharon C. Cooper
Amina Kelly may be divorced, but she wouldn't want her ex dead. When her ex is killed on duty, Maxwell Layton comes back into her life—and the passion between them is just as strong as ever. Now they have to fix their past mistakes—while dodging someone intent on making sure Amina doesn't get out alive...

HRSCNM1221

"All of that's true and I hate this has happened to you,"
Maxwell said. "But you've forgotten one important fact.
You weren't harmed. At least not physically. Everything
in that house can be replaced."

"That might be true, but—"

"But you—" he kissed the side of her forehead
"—sweetheart, you're irreplaceable, and I'm glad you
weren't hurt. Now, *that*? That would've made the evening
a helluva lot worse. Because if that had happened, I
would be out for blood. We wouldn't be sitting here
together because I'd be out hunting that bastard. Instead,
we have others looking into the situation while you and I
are getting ready to try to salvage our date. So how about
we start by enjoying an excellent meal?"

After a long beat of silence, Amina sighed dramatically and leaned back to look up at him. A slow smile tugged the corners of her lips. "Well, when you put it that way, I guess I should pick a restaurant, huh?"

He grinned and handed her the menus. "Yes, and I'll take the bags upstairs, then change clothes. When I come back down, we can order." He stood and headed for the stairs again but stopped when she called him. "Yeah?"

"Thanks for coming to the house. It meant a lot to have you there with me even though I know it was the last place you wanted to be."

He studied her for a moment. "That might've been the case at first, but I want to be wherever you are, Amina. And I'll always be here, there or wherever for you. Remember that."

Don't miss
His to Defend *by Sharon C. Cooper,*
available January 2022 wherever
Harlequin Romantic Suspense
books and ebooks are sold.

Harlequin.com